# THE MATTER OF A MARQUESS

## THE DUKE'S BY-BLOWS, BOOK 3

## JESS MICHAELS

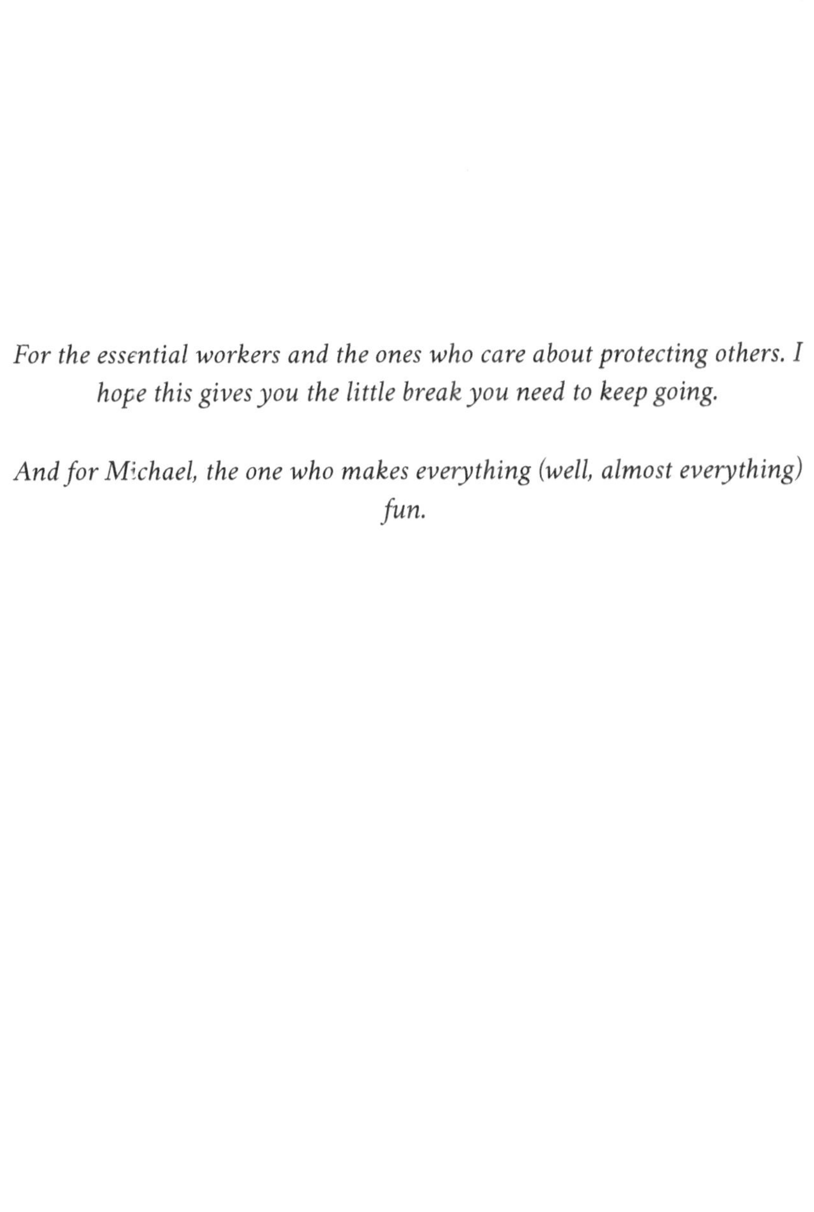

*For the essential workers and the ones who care about protecting others. I hope this gives you the little break you need to keep going.*

*And for Michael, the one who makes everything (well, almost everything) fun.*

# PROLOGUE

*1807*

The Earl of Bramwell didn't even bother to look up from his papers as Nicholas Gillingham entered his office for their appointment. Nicholas shifted in the doorway, uncomfortable, just as he was always uncomfortable, in the earl's company. The man reminded him of his father.

Not the man who'd raised him. No…his real father.

Cold, calculating, all too aware of his power and willing to wield it in the cruelest of manners. That's what men of title could do. What many *did* do. Those beneath them were often powerless.

"Gillingham."

The earl sounded out every syllable of the name and Nicholas shook from his thoughts to take a long step into the room. "My lord."

Bramwell sniffed as he looked Nicholas up and down, taking in the slightly ill-fitting jacket, the nervous way he clenched his fingers before him. Nicholas forced himself to separate his hands and smoothed his jacket, but he still felt out of place.

"You asked for this meeting, Gillingham," Bramwell snapped.

"Most irregular for the son of a servant, but out of respect for your *father*, I agreed. What do you want?"

This wasn't going to go well. Nicholas felt it in the air, crackling like a whip every time Bramwell spoke. A part of him wanted to simply apologize and walk away. His plans, after all, didn't have to include this man. He could do as he wished and deal with the consequences later. And there would be consequences.

Only he wasn't in this plan alone, was he? For her...for *her* he would face any demon, any lion, any earl with a cruel twist to his smirk.

"I wanted to speak with you about Aurora," Nicholas burst out, the words falling from his lips in a crushed-together jumble.

Despite that, Bramwell understood them. He leaned back in his chair and drummed his fingertips along his desktop. "The day has come at last," he murmured. Nicholas thought it was more to himself than to him.

"Being raised in this household, I've had the privilege to be a friend to your children—" Nicholas began, clinging to the way he'd planned to say these words.

Bramwell jumped to his feet, his cheeks darkening red and spittle flying from his mouth as he shouted, "You aren't a *friend* to my children, boy! Your father is my man of affairs—you are a servant's child! If my wife and I were too kind and let you pretend to be the equal of my son and daughter, that was clearly our error. And now you want to speak to me about Aurora, do you? Confession on your mind, is it? Fancy yourself in love with her after all those mooning stares and stolen brushes of the hand?"

Nicholas drew back, his heart throbbing hard and loud in his ears. "You...you..."

"Knew about your *tendre* toward my daughter?" The earl rolled his eyes. "Yes. Of course I knew. She may not be the spare I required, but she *is* an asset. I watch my assets."

Nicholas's mind flew to Aurora. The earl's daughter was three years younger than he was, and he'd only considered her a friend until about a year ago. He'd been standing with his father in a parlor, upset about…it didn't matter what. It had felt like the world was falling apart, and then Aurora entered the room and everything had screeched to a halt. Everything had focused in on her. Aurora with her dark blonde hair, Aurora with her chocolate eyes that were so easy to lose oneself in. She was all soft, lush curves and bright smiles and easy laughter. A light in the darkness.

The most shocking thing was that she seemed to return his feelings. Shy smiles across the room had turned to secret conversations that could last for hours. The first time he'd dared to take her hand…he would remember the feel of her fingers folding across his until the day he took his last breath. And when he'd gotten up the nerve to finally kiss her?

It was like every romantic poem and story finally made sense to him. It was like he was complete and whole.

"She is not an asset, my lord," he ground out. "I may not have a title, but I *do* have a future. For her, I will make sure of it. And I *will* protect your daughter with my life. I want to marry her."

"Yes, I know what you *want*," Bramwell snarled with a shake of his head. "Even if I didn't have two perfectly good eyes, I have ears all over this house. I know you two have been sneaking around, whispering in corners. It hasn't gone too far—that is the only reason I haven't stopped it before today."

"Sir!" Nicholas gasped as he realized the earl was talking about sex. A subject he pondered a great deal every time he was around Aurora, but certainly he would not disrespect her by ruining her! "I would never—"

"If you wanted to secure her and her fortune, perhaps you should have," Bramwell interrupted. "If it were any girl but my daughter, I might even congratulate you. You are reaching above your station and trying to make something of yourself through marrying a better."

"No," Nicholas said, taking a long step forward. "It isn't for a mercenary purpose. I *love* Aurora!"

"*Love.*" Bramwell pursed his lips and sniffed. "Love is for fools and the poor. Men of my ilk cannot afford such silly notions. My daughter will marry someone who will further my desires, that is the end of it. In fact, the marriage contracts have been signed just today. She will be Viscountess Lovell within a month."

Nicholas stared. If his blood had rushed like a roaring river in his ears before, now everything in the room had gone curiously silent. Like he'd been shoved under the water and now he had to fight to swim to the surface. Difficult with this man's boot on his neck.

"Marry...marry Lord Lovell," he repeated. "No. N-No."

"Oh yes," Bramwell said with a tiny smile. "Indeed, it is true."

Nicholas glared at the man. He'd always feared Bramwell. His entire life he'd known this man held his family's fortunes on the blade of a knife. One mercurial decision and they would be ruined. But in that moment, he hated the earl more than he feared him.

"She loves me. I *will* stop this marriage."

Nicholas expected an outburst at his words. Bramwell was well known for those. His father had been at the receiving end of them many a time. But to his surprise, Bramwell only nodded. "She told you she wanted you, did she? The girl is more like me than I ever thought. She lied, boy. Understand that. She has known about the arrangement with Lovell for months. And she is looking forward to the life she was always meant to have. You were *never* good enough for her."

"No," Nicholas said, but there was a kernel of doubt in the back of his mind that he hated.

How many times had he pondered himself that their positions were so disparate? How many times had he wondered if he would be able to keep Aurora happy when she was without her pin money and her gowns and jewels and parties?

Now Bramwell was drawing those doubts to the surface, picking them open and exposing them to the light.

"You still believe she loves you?" Bramwell said with a sniff. "Then I suppose I must be cruel to be kind. Who wrote that?"

"The Bard," Nicholas choked. "*Hamlet*. Act three."

"You're educated, at least." Bramwell shrugged. "Come along."

He crooked his finger, and Nicholas followed because he felt he had no choice. He was too numb to fight against a man with such power. They wound through the halls of this home he knew so well and out a parlor onto the wide terrace that stretched across the expanse of the back of the manor. It overlooked the garden. The place he'd first dared to kiss Aurora. In the orange and pink colors of sunset, he looked down over the green and found a woman not so far down the path from the house.

Aurora. Even from a distance, he could make her out. He knew her gait, he knew her posture, her knew the way she tilted her head as she paused at what she always called her favorite rosebush. She was the kind of woman with a favorite rosebush and he loved her for it.

Only today, she wasn't with *him* as she strolled those lovely paths. But she wasn't alone, either. No, in the romantic glow of the sunset, she was with a gentleman. Nicholas's heart sank.

"Lovell," Bramwell said, with a pleasure to his voice that said he enjoyed being cruel. "They look well together, don't they?"

Nicholas couldn't respond to the jab. He was too busy staring at the couple. Aurora's hand was in the crook of this man's elbow. He was speaking to her and she turned her face toward him. Even from the distance, Nicholas recognized she was smiling. When she smiled, she did so with her entire body. He'd made a study of how her shoulders lifted and her hands fluttered in those moments.

She looked…happy now. The kernel of doubt became far more.

"Now, you might wish to go confront her," Bramwell said softly. "Or exact some kind of revenge and break up this engagement."

Nicholas set his jaw. "I would never hurt her," he whispered.

Bramwell appeared confused at the concept, but he continued,

"If you do so, if you attempt to talk to her or convince her to back out of this, I will destroy you. Do you understand that?"

"I am already destroyed," Nicholas said, unable to keep his eyes from the couple. His voice no longer sounded like his own.

Bramwell chuckled. "Ah, the romance of youth. Well, if you don't care about yourself, then think of your family. I could sack the man who raised you, give him no reference."

At that, Nicholas pivoted away from the image of Aurora and her future husband. "My father has served you well for many years, my lord."

"Your *father* is the Duke of Roseford and you're nothing but a bastard he abandoned, along with all the others," Bramwell hissed. "My man of affairs lowered himself to marry your mother and legitimize you in the eyes of the law, but you know what you are. Do you want to make him regret helping you?"

Nicholas set his jaw. His father—the man who'd raised him—had always treated him as his own. Bertrand Gillingham had never been anything but an honorable man. A man Nicholas desperately wanted to be like, not the awful duke who had taken advantage of his mother when she was a servant in his home.

"I've heard the Duke of Roseford has taken an interest in you," Bramwell said when Nicholas didn't answer. "That the army is being bandied about as a future. I would consider taking that option, young man."

Nicholas had rebuffed that idea when he had thought himself about to marry Aurora, but now it didn't seem so very outlandish. She would marry someone else. At least if he was gone, he wouldn't have to see that. Wouldn't have to hear rumor of her happiness. Wouldn't have to see her increase with that other man's children, pass her in the park on Lord Lovell's arm and have her look at him like he was a pathetic stranger.

"It doesn't really matter what I do, does it?" Nicholas said as he turned on his heel and walked away. "I have no leverage over a man like you. It's over. I understand that."

"Gillingham?" Bramwell called out when Nicholas had reached the doors leading back into the house.

Nicholas froze there and slowly turned. Bramwell was smiling at him. Smiling as if stripping Nicholas of all his hopes and dreams was some kind of jolly pastime for him. "Yes?"

"Say thank you to your betters, boy," Bramwell said.

Nicholas fisted his hands at his sides. He wanted nothing more than to walk back across the long terrace and punch the earl. An action his birth father would certainly approve of. But he had to think of more than himself and his worst impulses now.

"Thank you, my lord," he said through clenched teeth.

"You're welcome. You are dismissed."

Nicholas left then without another word. He staggered through this house he would never return to, blind to all its familiar halls and out into the drive where his horse awaited him. He rode away just as blindly, tears stinging his eyes and broken heart throbbing madly. And in those horrible, pain-tinged moments, he made a promise to himself.

He would make a life that never left him beholden to men like the Earl of Bramwell again. Nor would he ever let something so foolish as love leave him open to pain.

# CHAPTER 1

*Nine Years Later*

Nicholas walked alongside his half-brother Robert through Hyde Park. It was slow going. In the cool of the morning, his leg hurt all the more. He limped while Robert strolled and Nicholas's bullmastiff, Fortescue, trotted at his side, always watchful of anyone who came near his master. Thanks to Fortescue's large and rather fearsome demeanor, very few did.

"I appreciate you coming out with me this morning," Robert said.

Nicholas thought it was to fill the silence between them. It had never been a comfortable one. After all, Robert was the Duke of Roseford's only legitimate son. He'd taken on their father's title years before and run it just as ragged and wrong as the man who'd sired them both.

That he had recently come to heel was something Nicholas didn't wholly trust.

He shrugged. "I needed the exercise, as did Fortescue."

Hearing his name, the dog tilted his head up toward Nicholas, watching. Nicholas fought the urge to smile like a fool at the animal and kept his attention on Robert.

"I suppose being seen with a duke also doesn't hurt your current plans," Robert drawled.

His brother was baiting him and Nicholas took a long breath so he wouldn't automatically take that bait. "Depends on the duke," he said.

If he had been trying to insult Robert, his brother didn't get angry. Instead, he laughed. "Truer words have never been spoken. There are definitely levels of respectability, even amongst those with titles. I suppose my marriage to Katherine has raised me in the ranks, but certainly I am not at the best advantage to help you in your quest to earn a title."

"Is that why you asked me to walk with you, to talk to me about the title?" Nicholas asked softly.

"It is a rare thing for titles to be bestowed for bravery and sacri-fice, though I suppose more common as of late for war heroes like yourself and Wellington."

Nicholas sighed. This was a topic he didn't really like to discuss. He didn't want anyone to know how much it meant to him. Most especially Robert. His brother hardly respected his own title—he would certainly tease Nicholas about desiring his own.

"I'm no Wellington," Nicholas said. "I have never claimed to be."

Robert's brow wrinkled. "In my estimation you are more valu-able than Wellington. He won a war—that means something. But you saved men's lives, at great cost to yourself." Robert glanced at his leg and Nicholas winced. "Including Selina's husband. Our sister would not be happy now were it not for your bravery. I think you are owed more than a mere title."

"A *mere* title. Easy for you to say," Nicholas said, casting his glance off into the park, watching the milling crowds that had gathered on this fine summer day. How separate he felt from them all. "You've been titled all your life, so you've never appreciated its power."

Robert was quiet for a moment, then cast a glance at Nicholas. Nicholas flinched, because they were his own eyes, their father's eyes, looking back at him on his brother's face. Dark brown, guarded, unreadable.

"I wouldn't have pegged you for being power hungry, brother," Robert said.

Nicholas shrugged again. "There are different kinds of power, you know. Both to destroy and to protect. But all of it requires the command a title can bring."

And now he'd said too much. Revealed too much to this man he didn't fully trust, even if their other half siblings, Morgan and Selina, said he was decent. Said he was better. Nicholas wasn't certain he trusted either of them, even though he was closer to them.

"You really want this," Robert said softly. "You really *want* to be named Marquess of Songstrum."

And there it was, his hope, his dream said out loud. After his injury, everyone had thought he would die. He had few memories of that bleary time except for pain and the worry on the faces of those in his life. But as he healed and grew stronger, whispers had begun. One of the men he'd saved that horrible day in the midst of battle and death was the youngest son of Viscount Ludlow. The viscount was a personal friend of the Prince Regent, himself, and apparently a campaign had been launched to gift Nicholas with a title. The Songstrum line had died out ten years before, returning to the Crown with little fanfare.

But now it could belong to Nicholas, just as Robert said in an incredulous tone. So Nicholas fought for a way to ignore it. To put up a barrier between them.

"Fortescue!" he snapped out.

The dog immediately sat at attention, locking his amber gaze with Nicholas's. He bent with a wince of faint pain and swept up a stick from alongside the path. He tossed it, not quite as far as he might once have been able to, and the dog's ears went higher at attention.

"Fetch," Nicholas said, pointing out at the expanse of grass where the stick had fallen.

The dog barreled off, onlookers gawking at his sleek focus.

"Do you really want this?" Robert pressed.

Nicholas shifted. So much for putting up a barrier. "Yes," he admitted at last. "I do. I was injured—I'll never be the same. I've come to accept that. But perhaps this will make it all worthwhile."

Robert stopped in the path and turned to him. His gaze was lit up, his cheeks flushed slightly. "No, it won't," he snapped. "Nothing in the world will make the fact that we almost lost you worthwhile. Or the suffering your family has watched you endure in the last two years. A bloody title won't pay that debt. And I will tell you that I would trade my own fucking title if that meant none of it had happened."

Nicholas caught his breath at the passion with which his brother said those words. "You wouldn't trade being duke," he said softly.

"Yes I would," Robert insisted. "It's not worth that much, I assure you."

"You've never been without it," Nicholas said.

"So you've said." Robert gave a wan smile. "Twice, in fact. And perhaps you're right. I can't truly judge what you desire because I've always known it was my… I suppose some foolish fops would say my right. Which is ridiculous. I just happened to be the one son my father sired in the confines of a marriage. That makes me no better than you or Morgan or Selina or any of the vast number of others out there in the world."

"Perhaps not," Nicholas agreed. "But you are certainly viewed differently by those around you. People like me, people like Morgan and Selina, we have all…"

He trailed off and shook his head because his mind was trying to take him back to a place he refused to revisit. Even after nearly a decade, this topic always took him to that place, that afternoon at sunset when the consequences of his position in the world had been made perfectly clear.

Robert tilted his head. "Nicholas?" He looked like he would press more, but then he glanced past Nicholas and his eyes widened. "Bloody hell, has your dog brought back an entire tree?"

Nicholas pivoted and let out a long, heavy sigh. Fortescue had, indeed, found a different stick to return with than the one that had been thrown. A log, if one wanted to be more specific about it. As thick around as a strong man's arm and probably the same height as Nicholas, himself, if stood up vertically.

"Fortescue!" he said, hoping to sound like he was admonishing the dog.

Robert laughed at his side and Nicholas joined in as the bullmastiff plunked the log down beside the path and looked up in pride and expectation that somehow Nicholas would casually toss this former tree for him.

Robert wiped tears of mirth from his eyes and straightened up with a sigh. "I won't pretend that I know all of your life," he said. "You are the most closed book of all my siblings."

"No, that distinction goes to Fitzhugh, I think," Nicholas said softly.

Robert flinched. "You may be right at that, since Fitzhugh doesn't speak to me at all. Perhaps it is a judgment on me that I haven't made more of an effort to read your book…or his. But my job as your older brother is to try to give you what you want, isn't it? So if it is this title, I will do anything in my power to assist."

Nicholas couldn't help but be taken aback at the earnestness with which Robert said those words. He actually seemed like he meant them. But could that be trusted? Trust was not a commodity Nicholas doled out easily, nor came by naturally. Once upon a time, perhaps, but bitter experience had hardened him. Made him more jaded.

And so to avoid the intimacy of the fact that Robert wanted so much to give him this, Nicholas snorted in derision.

The remaining humor on Robert's face faded and Nicholas thought he saw a flicker of hurt there in its place. But then it was gone. Wiped away by their family's ability to hide emotion when it was not useful or safe.

"I know you judge my life," Robert said. "Or what it once was. You think me too much like our father."

Nicholas set his jaw. "That monster was never my father."

Robert inclined his head. "Of course. But just because you think so low of me, you shouldn't think I can't help you. Being near me is, whether you like it or not, proximity to power, and that matters in these political situations. And if you don't think *I* have the influence you desire, then you must know I have a great many friends with far more of it. And far more of the honor you value so highly."

That gave Nicholas pause. Roseford was talking about his club of dukes, the 1797 Club they were called, though Nicholas wasn't entirely sure why. Robert and nine of his friends. They were certainly a most powerful force to be reckoned with, filled with some of the most honorable men in the land.

"You think they would help your bastard brother," Nicholas asked softly. "These men with such honor."

Robert's shoulders came back and a protectiveness flitted over his face. "You judge yourself far more harshly then they would do, for they are the best of men. They would help you of your own merit, but more so if I were to ask. Which I would do."

Nicholas let out a long sigh and reached down to scratch Fortescue's ears as he said, "Well, what do you have in mind?"

Roseford gave a flash of a wicked smile, the only indication that he felt he'd won in this exchange. "A week-long country party at my estate. With some of my most influential friends attending. And there will be others who have the ear of those deciding who gets a title and who doesn't. I'll invite Selina and Derrick, as well. Morgan and Lizzie were already going to attend."

Nicholas worried his lip. As much as he liked the idea of seeing his siblings and making the best impression he could, Robert wasn't just asking him to his estate. He was asking Nicholas to their *father's* estate. Nicholas had never been there. Never seen the place where his father had lorded over the world. The place where he'd take advantage of and later abandoned Nicholas's mother all those years ago.

Did he *want* to see it?

"I don't know," he said.

Robert clapped his hand around Nicholas's bicep and squeezed gently. "It's only a week, brother. You can endure anything for a week, I know you're more than strong enough. And you could come out of it with what you desire secured." He hesitated. "Please. I have never been able to do much for you. Let me do this."

Nicholas shifted. "May I bring the dog?"

Robert glanced down at Fortescue, who was glowering at him because he'd touched Nicholas. It was only good training that was keeping him from bearing those terrible teeth.

"Your dog hates everyone," Robert pointed out. "But certainly. He would be welcome. I'm sure he'll enjoy running free all over the grounds at Roseford."

"Then..." Nicholas let out a long sigh. "Yes. Yes, I'll do it."

Robert clapped his hands together with a laugh. "Excellent. Give me a few days to make the arrangements and I'll send word with all the particulars and a few names of those who'll be in attendance so you may strategize."

Nicholas motioned toward the path and they began to walk again. Fortescue trailed behind, dragging his tree with him. "Thank you."

Roseford cast him a side glance. "No thanks necessary. You may not like it, but we *are* brothers. And I'll do anything for my family."

Nicholas didn't know how to respond to that statement that felt too intimate and close, so he said nothing. And prayed he wouldn't regret taking Roseford's offer of help...and family.

~

Aurora gripped her hands at her sides and prayed that she looked cooler and more collected than she felt as she walked up the cracked staircase to the worn-down building above. A faded sign hung from rusty chains above the door. *The Cat's Companion.* She shuddered at the smells from the docks nearby and the glances she was receiving from the men gathered by the door, waiting for entry.

A big man with only half his teeth and a cruel glint to his eyes seemed to be managing who entered and who was refused. He noted her approach and licked his lips as he looked her up and down. She touched her hair to be certain her wig, worn to conceal her true identity, was still in place, and tugged her shawl closer, but that only elicited a burst of laughter from the men.

"Might as well not try to cover it up, sweet. It won't take long to get it off!" called out one faceless voice from the crowd.

She ignored it and girded herself for talking her way into the house of ill repute. "Sir," she said.

"New girls go 'round the back," the doorman said, his gaze flitting over her. "Maggie will like you. You look…fresh."

She swallowed hard, but ignored the bile rising in her throat. So he thought she was a new girl, come here to make her way on her back. That was fine. It would help her gain entry. She could only pray she'd find what she came for.

She nodded and slipped past the men in the line, around toward the alleyway that led to the back entrance. It was dimly lit, entirely unsafe. She knew the risk she was taking coming here at all. But it didn't matter. What mattered was Imogen. She had to find Imogen.

There was a door open around the back and a bored-looking woman stood there, smoking a foul-smelling cigar. As Aurora approached, she pulled it from her lips and puffed smoke in Aurora's face. "Come to work?"

Aurora coughed, waving at the smoke that seemed to stick in her nose and throat. Her heart was all but pounding out of her chest and her eyes stung with fearful tears as she nodded, playing out the lie that would get her inside. She didn't belong here. Of course, she hadn't belonged in many of the places she had been in the past few weeks. But she still went to them because her best friend had gone missing weeks before and Aurora had heard she was in one of these...places. Her desperation turned to action that would surely change her forever.

"Go inside then," the woman said with a shake of her head. "Maggie'll deal with you."

Aurora stepped through the door. Inside the place was far too hot and there was a faint stink of sweat and sex in the air. She shifted, looking for the twice-mentioned Maggie. She had no idea what she'd say to the woman who ran this house of sin, at least not without causing herself a great deal of trouble.

There was no one waiting for her in the small foyer inside the back entrance. No one was there at all. She looked around at the scuffed wooden plank walls, the stained furniture where a guest might wait to be received. She certainly hoped Imogen wasn't here.

How had things come so far? Just shy of a year ago, she and Imogen had both been somewhat unhappily married but sheltered in their homes, able to turn to each other for comforting conversation when their husbands humiliated them at places just like this one. It hadn't been much of a life, perhaps. Aurora had many regrets, ones that kept her up at night, haunted by a face she hadn't seen in almost a decade.

But it had been safe. It had been comfortable. And then in a span of just a few weeks, both her own husband, Viscount Martin Lovell, and Imogen's husband, the Honorable Mr. Warren Huxley, had died. Lovell of a sudden apoplexy in a place very much like this one, Huxley in a carriage accident, racing his phaeton like the fool he had always been.

They'd never spoken it out loud, but Aurora knew they'd each felt a sense of...relief? Amidst the sadness and shock, it had been there. The end of their marriages should have meant the beginning of new lives with freedom, for both men had been well off.

Except Lovell had left Aurora with very little. Her family had its own struggles since her father's death, so she'd kept most of her plight from them. Huxley had left Imogen with nothing at all. Desperation had set in. Despair. A constant fight to stay afloat had led to conversations about other options. Even unthinkable ones. When Imogen turned to this life, it hadn't been a total shock to Aurora. But when she disappeared into it?

That was another story.

And so Aurora searched for her, praying she'd find her and convince her to come home. They would figure it out. They *had* to figure it out, together. Only she kept coming to these places and never finding Imogen.

She drew in a shaky breath. If the woman who ran this place wasn't here to greet and assess her, that actually helped her cause.

Aurora stepped forward and slipped into the darker hallway off the foyer. It was nothing but a long series of doors. Thin doors, behind which she could hear various sounds of pleasure. She swallowed hard and crept along the hall, listening for Imogen's voice.

She stopped at a room that was quiet. No moans, no voices. There was some restless shuffling, though. Could it be Imogen inside? She had to take a risk and find out.

Her hands shaking, Aurora opened the door and eased her way inside the room. There was only a man there. His jacket was draped on a chair, his cravat on top of it, and his shirt was undone. She gasped as she realized it was her late husband's best friend, the Earl of Roddenbury.

She backed up, preparing to scramble out of the room, but her heel bumped the door and the thump made the man look up. His eyes met hers and he smiled.

"You kept me waiting, you naughty minx," he purred as he moved toward her. "But you'll make it worth the wait."

Aurora's heart leapt. It didn't seem that Roddenbury had recognized her, probably thanks to the dark wig that hid her blonde hair. But if she stayed too long with him, that would change swiftly. So she pivoted, turning her face away.

"I'm sorry, sir," she said, making her voice lower. "I've come to the wrong room."

She had never known Roddenbury to be anything but civil in the years she'd been in his acquaintance. He looked at her a little too long, of course, but he'd never been untoward. So she was utterly unprepared for him to lunge forward, catching her wrist in a cruel grip as he yanked her toward him.

"Now wait a moment. I've been standing in this room for at least ten minutes, and you're not going to tease and leave. You're here and you will do your job, girl."

Her lips parted at the cruelty of his tone and his touch. She yanked back. "I'm not meant for you, let me go!"

He refused, tugging her even harder. She snaked out a hand and, without thinking, slapped his cheek. His dark eyes grew even darker and his mouth set in a thin line. She could see she'd made a terrible mistake and her fear flew higher than ever. His grip loosened and she took the opportunity, pivoting away from him toward the door.

She wrenched it open, but he grabbed for her. In the struggle, he managed to grip her bun. Of course, she was wearing the wig, so as she pulled away, the pins came loose and her own blonde hair cascaded down around her shoulders as he pulled the false hair away.

"Aurora Lovell?" he gasped.

She froze, her name echoing in the hallway, which was now filling up with half-naked people who were wondering what the fuss was about. She recognized a great many of the men, just as they recognized her.

She pivoted back toward Roddenbury. "How dare you?" she whispered, wishing she sounded stronger.

He looked anything but chagrined as his gaze flitted over her from head to toe. "I always wondered what it would be like to fuck you."

She gasped at his crude words and equally crude expression. He reached for her again and she reacted out of pure instinct, lifting her knee hard into his groin.

He immediately dropped to his knees with a cry, clutching his manhood as he glared up at her. "You bitch!"

She ignored the slur and ran into the hallway, back out the door she'd come in. She ignored the sound of her name, echoing from the rooms, echoing from Roddenbury screaming it out into the night where the world could hear.

She hurtled herself into the carriage she had paid to wait for her and huddled in the dark as the driver turned the rig into the street, back toward the sad little home her husband's family had deigned to bestow upon her.

She had only made everything worse by coming here. She hadn't found Imogen, and now the foulest elements of her world knew what she'd done. They would assume even worse. And they would spread this tale far and wide. She covered her hands, shaking as she wept into her fingers.

What little she had left was gone. And she had no idea what to do next.

## CHAPTER 2

Aurora paced the parlor in her small home, trying to ignore the worn, lumpy furniture and the low fire that didn't warm the room. Once she had resided in a fine home just off Hyde Park, but now…

Well, her late husband's family hadn't allowed her to be settled with much. And she feared things would only get more dire now. It had been two days since she was caught at the Cat's Companion, and since then her greatest fears had come true.

The word of her appearance there had spread through the *ton* like wildfire. Friends had stopped speaking to her, invitations had dried up and it had even been a barely blind item in the weekly *Scandal Sheet* newspaper.

She sank onto the uncomfortable settee and covered her eyes. Everything was falling apart. While she was normally an optimistic person, one who sought to make the best in numerous bad situations she had found herself in over the years, she could not find that positivity today. Nothing could be done to fix the awful place where she found herself perched.

And beyond that, her horrible fall from grace hadn't even helped her find what she needed. Imogen was still gone. There was no word of where she might be. All that sacrifice had been for nothing.

There was a light knock at her door and she looked up to see her housemaid, Jeanette, standing there, her cheeks flushed. There was limited staff for her here, thanks to her lack of funds. Just Jeanette, Mrs. Swan to cook for her, and a footman.

"Yes?" Aurora whispered, girding herself to hear which party she had been uninvited from this time.

"You have a visitor, Lady Lovell," Jeanette said, looking over her shoulder with an expression of concern. "And I wasn't sure if you were in residence."

"I can only imagine who would come here to gawk at me in my current state," Aurora said.

"It is…" The maid's voice dropped lower. "It's the Duchess of Roseford, my lady."

Aurora pushed to her feet and stared in shocked silence at Jeanette. "What?"

Jeanette stepped into the room and handed over a beautiful calling card, one swirled with gold filigree, the Roseford crest on the back. Aurora didn't know the woman well. They had spoken a few times many years ago, but hadn't maintained the acquaintance. She knew about the path the duchess had taken, of course. Society had whispered loud and long when her first husband died in their bed in an indelicate way. Louder still when she returned to Society and landed herself the biggest rake in the kingdom.

Aurora could admit, if only to herself, that she had made a quiet study of that situation. After all, the Duke of Roseford was the brother of…

She cut off those thoughts. Thinking of *him* during these troubled times only made everything harder. She would not do it.

"I…I do not think of the duchess as one to refuse," Aurora whispered. "And I admit my curiosity about her reason for being here outweighs almost all my hesitance."

She looked around the room, and humiliation made her cheeks

hot. "I…you know, send her in. My shame can hardly be any higher than it already is. At least this offers some kind of entertainment."

Jeanette gave a small curtsey and stepped into the foyer. Aurora heard her speaking softly and another voice answering, though she couldn't make out the words. And in less than a moment, the door to her parlor opened again and Jeanette said, "The Duchess of Roseford, Lady Lovell."

The woman who entered the room could not have looked more out of place in the shabby parlor. She was tall and beautiful, dark hair done in an elaborate style. Her gown was impeccable, flowing over her like some kind of pink waterfall. Her presence made Aurora catch her breath. This was not the same uncertain young woman she had been acquaintances with a lifetime ago. Before the duchess lost her first husband. Before she married the duke.

"Your Grace," she said, wishing her voice didn't tremble. "Welcome to my home. Such that it is."

The duchess smiled at her, and in that moment Aurora was struck by something else in her. Kindness. For all her power and beauty and confidence, the duchess looked kind. When she didn't so much as look around at the horrible parlor, Aurora nearly wept at the gentleness that had been missing from her life for what felt like forever.

"I should have sent word around first, rather than so rudely appear on your doorstep. But I felt compelled to come and I…" She smiled again, still so gentle. "I thought it might be easier for you to refuse me if I wrote you. An unfair act, I suppose, but I did *so* wish to speak to you."

The kindness still existed in the other woman's eyes, but Aurora's chest tightened with anxiety nonetheless. There was no reason for the duchess to wish to see her so desperately. At least, no good reason that came to mind.

"Please sit," she said, and moved to the sideboard to pour tea into the mismatched cups there. She gave herself the chipped one and handed over the other before she took a place on the settee across from the duchess. She cleared her throat. "Was there some reason you wanted to see me so badly?"

The duchess pushed her shoulders back and nodded once. "Will you call me Katherine?"

Aurora blinked at the question. "You—you came all the way here to ask if I would call you Katherine?"

The duchess laughed, and it was a musical, light sound that warmed Aurora's heart despite the circumstances and her continued confusion. "I'm sorry, I'm a little nervous," she said.

Aurora blinked. "You are? You don't show it."

"I'm surprised," the duchess said. "My heart is beating out of my chest right now. Let me start over. You and I were once part of a rather awful little club. Women in loveless marriages."

Aurora nodded slowly. "I'm surprised you even recall it. If rumor is true, you are not in that club anymore."

The duchess's face lit up. "Indeed, I am not. I could not be happier. But I remember those terrible days, that feeling that life would never be bright again. And then my husband died and things got even worse." She shifted. "I don't mean to be indelicate, my dear, but I believe you know what I am saying better than most."

Aurora set her jaw. The kindness in this woman felt true, but her words still put Aurora on edge. She folded her arms. "Are you speaking of my financial fall from grace or the rumors that have burned through Society the past few days and destroyed all hope of a future? Have you come to gawk at one or both?"

"Not gawk," the duchess said, reaching out to cover her hand. Aurora gasped at the touch. Since Imogen had disappeared into the underground, Aurora hadn't had a kind or friendly touch. This one felt like sinking into a warm blanket.

But she had to keep her head. She pulled away. "Then what?"

Katherine pursed her lips. "I'm going to be blunt. It's the best way. When my first husband died, it was in bed, with me astride him. And everyone knew it. Everyone talked about it. When I returned to Society, there was even a dreadful wager going around of who would take as a mistress the woman who could kill a man with her body. I came here not to crow over your misfortune, but to offer support during what I know is a difficult time. I'm here to help you, Aurora, if you would like it."

Aurora blinked. "Help me?" she repeated, wishing her eyes weren't swelling with tears. Wishing her voice didn't sound so broken.

The duchess nodded as she dug into her pocket and drew out a handkerchief. Aurora took it and dabbed her eyes. "How could you help me...Katherine?"

Katherine smiled at the capitulation and then leaned forward. This time she took both of Aurora's hands. "Any way I can. So why don't you start by telling me what the real truth is of how you ended up in one of the worst brothels in London?"

Aurora blushed. "How do you know it's one of the worst?"

Katherine laughed. "I'm married to the Duke of Roseford, my dear. Before me, the worst brothels in any city were a bit of his specialty. But they can't possibly be yours. So tell me."

Aurora hesitated. She hardly knew this woman. They'd barely been passing acquaintances a lifetime ago. But Aurora didn't have many friends and the closest of those was the reason she had ruined herself. Telling someone else, especially someone she immediately felt she could trust like Katherine…

Well, it was tempting, indeed.

"I-I wasn't there for me," she whispered.

Katherine's eyes widened, and Aurora took a deep breath and then told her everything. From the bad marriages she and Imogen had both been in, to the ruin that had come after the death of both their husbands. To the moment where Imogen's desperation had led her down a dark path.

When it was over, Aurora realized tears were streaming down her face. She wiped them away with Katherine's handkerchief and sighed. "And that is the whole story. I am ruined, Imogen is still missing and I have no idea what to do next. I have no resources, no connections unless I want to drag my poor brother and mother into this, and they have their own problems at present. I have no way to save her or myself."

Katherine shook her head slowly. "The way of this world is infuriating," she muttered, Aurora thought more to herself than to her. Then she met Aurora's eyes. "You are wrong, though. You *aren't* unconnected. You and I might have lost contact over the years, never fully developed our friendship, but I'd like to remedy that. You have me. And I'm going to help you."

Aurora wrinkled her brow. "How? Why?"

"Because I know the cruelty of misunderstanding, and I won't stand by and let someone else be destroyed if I can stop it. As for the how…" Katherine pushed to her feet and paced the small room for a moment. "My husband and I are hosting a small gathering at our country estate next week. Invitations to Robert's events are always a premium. If we invite you, it will show you are not alone in this world."

Aurora blinked. "You cannot mean that. To bring me into your home would be to bring scandal."

Katherine arched a brow. "Are you pretending you don't know that my husband's life before me was a crowning achievement of scandal? I don't give a damn about that. It will help you, and it will let you escape the whispers for a while. It's settled, you are invited and you are saying yes."

Aurora could hardly draw breath at the suggestion. "It is a kindness I never could have expected and I want you to know how much I appreciate it, but…I can't."

"Why?" Katherine asked.

"My friend…she's still out there. Still missing. I can't run off to the country and engage in frivolity while I know she's in danger. That place, Katherine…that horrible place."

Katherine moved toward her. "Don't let your thoughts overwhelm you. Of course you won't want to abandon your friend. But may I suggest an alternative to you wandering into dangerous places where you might be hurt or killed?"

Aurora swallowed. "What's that?"

"I have friends in the War Department," Katherine said with another smile. "Ones with a very specific set of skills when it comes to finding people who don't want to or cannot be found."

"*Spies?*" Aurora gasped. "I cannot imagine."

"It's the most shocking and thrilling thing, I assure you." Katherine said. "Let me get in contact with them. Put them on the case. They'll have a much easier time finding someone with their resources than you will. And if there's trouble, far more ability to manage it."

"Will I be…kept informed?" Aurora whispered.

"Of course. I'll have them send reports daily if you'd like." Katherine stepped closer. "Please, Aurora. I already had a sense that you were being mistreated with these rumors and now that I know they were started because you so selflessly tried to save a friend, I cannot in good conscience abandon you to rumor and ruin. Come with us to Roseford. Enjoy yourself. Make new friends. Please."

Aurora bent her head. There was but one final reason why she would say no to this remarkable woman. That was the Duke of Roseford's half-brother: Nicholas.

Just thinking his name shot a shiver of awareness through her. A man with whom she shared a past, a broken heart. A man she thought of every day, despite everything that had happened between them. He was the remaining hesitation to going with this woman.

But everyone knew that Nicholas and Roseford didn't get along. They were opposites, after all. Nicholas filled with honor, Roseford once the biggest libertine in London. He'd never had a relationship with his brother. So there was very little chance that she'd have to encounter him. Talk about him. Think of him.

She worried her lip. "It's a kind offer and I'd be a fool to refuse. Yes, I'll join you."

Katherine clapped her hands together with a squeal. "Excellent. I cannot wait to renew our friendship and have you meet the others who will be in attendance. A few of them have also experienced scandals in their own right, and you wouldn't find women better equipped to save the day for a fellow survivor."

"I look forward to it," Aurora said, and realized it was true.

Knowing that someone with more resources was trying to find Imogen left her able to look forward to what sounded like a very pleasant gathering, indeed. One where she could clear her thoughts, perhaps even make decisions about the future that had been so foggy in the year since her late husband's death.

# CHAPTER 3

Nicholas sat in the parlor at Robert and Katherine's home, a book perched in his fingers, but too distracted to pay attention to the story. Instead, he stared at the crackling fire, his thoughts rolling in circles.

Did he belong here? Here in his brother's home? In the few days since his arrival, he'd found himself looking from place to place, thinking of his late mother and what she must have endured here. Where her place had been. How it had been used against her.

He blinked and pushed those hard thoughts away. They were replaced by others. Because it wasn't just the house that made him question himself. He wasn't sure he belonged in the family Roseford was starting to build with their half-brother Morgan and half-sister Selina and their spouses. They were all so similar. He was so different.

And Roseford had friends here, too. A member of his found family. The Duke of Northfield and his wife. He seemed a good man, honorable and welcoming.

But the discomfort Nicholas felt continued. Because he'd always been lost between two worlds.

"You look very pensive."

He slowly pushed to his feet, a lingering whisper of pain jolting through him as he did so, and forced a smile for his sister as she entered the room. Selina was lovely, as she had always been lovely, with her dark hair and bright blue eyes. But it was different now. She was different. She had married an old friend of Nicholas's from the army, Derrick Huntington, and the new couple's passion for each other was palpable.

"Did I look pensive?" Nicholas asked as she crossed to him and bussed his cheek. "I must have been caught up in my reading."

She arched a brow at him as she went to the sideboard and poured them both tea. She winked before she added a splash of whisky to the cups and then handed it over. He took the brew, shaking his head at her as they sat together. When he sipped it, he coughed and her laughter filled the room.

"Now is the point where I call you a liar," Selina said, drinking her tea without so much as clearing her throat. "You weren't reading. You were brooding. It doesn't suit those of our ilk, Nicholas. Roseford sons and daughters do not brood."

He knew she was trying to lighten the mood, but his frown pulled deeper. "I've never been the typical Roseford offspring, though, have I? I *was* brooding. I'll admit it since I know you well enough to recognize you won't let this go until I've given you my heart and soul."

Selina's brow wrinkled. "I hope I can be trusted with your words, if not the rest."

He met her stare. It had come out the previous summer that his sister was a master thief. He'd been horrified as well as impressed, but had watched her rebuild herself ever since, with the help of Derrick.

"You can be, I know that," he said evenly, and she smiled in thanks. "It's not about that… I just…in the day that I've been here, I've already felt outside looking in."

Selina pursed her lips. "Because of the duke connection? All those dukes our brother calls friends? You want to be one of them, don't you? Marquess of Songstrum, and I'll have to 'my lord' you all over town."

He shook his head. "You've never 'my lorded' anyone and I doubt you'll start with me. Yes, I...I want this. I *want* the title, Selina. I know you don't understand, neither does Morgan. But I want the respect that goes along with the title. I want...I want the knowledge that certain things can't be taken from me."

"Taken from you?" Selina repeated. "What do you mean? What was taken from you, Nicholas, that you think you can get back with a title?"

He flinched as his mind flashed to dark blonde hair, warm brown eyes, soft lips brushing his, a honeyed tone saying his name like it was the only thing that mattered.

"Nothing specific," he lied, pushing back to his feet and slowly making his way to the window. "I don't know, I'm just being maudlin, ignore me."

"I won't ignore you, but since the subject seems a painful one I will change it. Do you think some of your feeling out of place is because all these people around you are part of couples? And not just any couples, but in love?"

He faced her, his lips tight. She was watching him closely, one fine eyebrow arched as if she already knew the answer. "Are you matchmaking, sister?"

Her smile was instant, wide and catching. "Can you imagine me as a matchmaker? I'd be rubbish! No, I'm just making the observation that you might be feeling excluded because you haven't found someone to match with." She stepped closer. "Is there anyone in your life who makes your heart beat faster? Have you ever wanted someone and only that someone?"

Before he could find an answer to that troubling question, there was a racket from the hallway. Servants rushing and voices calling out. Nicholas wrinkled his brow. "What's that about?"

Selina shrugged. "I think Katherine invited a friend to join our party. She was saying something about it during our walk yesterday. Lady…Lady something or another. What was it?"

Nicholas laughed. "No one is less interested in the upper class than you are."

"Probably because not so long ago, I was very interested in them for what my husband says are the wrong reasons." She shook her head.

"Well, why don't we go see who this person is?" Nicholas said. "I won't even mention it if you are taking a quiet inventory of the lady's jewels."

"Old habits," Selina said, and took his arm. They made their way up the hall slowly and were met near the foyer by Selina's husband.

Derrick was tall and held himself like the military man he'd once been. He nodded to Nicholas, his gaze flitting to his leg before he said, "I heard the commotion. This must be our final guest."

Selina slipped from Nicholas's side and took her husband's arm instead. As she stared up at him, Nicholas couldn't help but flinch. He'd tried to ignore his sister's observation that some of his troubles might be because he was alone in a house full of people in love. Now he watched his sister and her husband walk in front of him, her fingers all but vibrating on Derrick's bicep, and the twinge of jealousy ripped through him.

But there was no way to explain that to his family. No way to change it. His life was what it was, and a grand romance like the ones his siblings had lived out, continued to live out, was not in the future for him.

They walked out into the warm summer breeze together, joining Robert and Katherine and their brother Morgan and his wife Lizzie on the top stair. Down below, the carriage door had already been opened, so the crest that might have revealed the identity of their guest was obscured. But it wasn't a moment before the footman reached inside and an elegantly slippered foot appeared from the darkness. The woman stepped out, her head bent as she paid attention to her footing. Her bonnet obscured her face and Selina laughed back at Nicholas. "I swear, it's like a game...who is the mystery woman?"

At that moment, before Nicholas could laugh or Katherine could say the name they'd been waiting to hear, the woman tilted her head back to look up the stairs, and everything in Nicholas's world came to a halt.

"Aurora," he breathed out loud, because he couldn't help it.

Derrick pivoted to face him. "What? *The* Aurora?"

Nicholas couldn't answer. He couldn't acknowledge or respond to his family's questions as they asked him who Aurora was. As Katherine stared at him in shock and dawning horror.

No, all he could do was look down that long set of stairs at the woman who had molded and changed and guided his life since he was hardly more than a boy. The woman who had haunted him every day and every night for almost a decade.

She stared up at him, all the color gone from those cheeks, her full lips parted in just as much as shock as he felt, her hands shaking at her sides. And by God, she was more beautiful than she'd ever been. Tendrils of blonde hair curled from the edge of her bonnet, framing her oval face, drawing attention to those high cheekbones. Her gown was spring green, fresh as the new leaves, and it flowed over her supple curves, hinting at gorgeous breasts and the swell of her hips.

*Nicholas* she mouthed, silent, and that broke him.

He slowly made his way down the stairs, the pain that usually accompanied that action dulled by the pain of seeing her. The thrill of seeing her.

"What are you doing here?" he asked as he stopped a few feet in front of her. He couldn't go closer. If he went closer, his itching palms might force him to reach for her. If he touched her, all was lost. All had always been lost.

She blinked at him. "Nicholas," she repeated, this time in a shaky voice.

"What is going on?" Roseford called from above, concern plain in his voice.

They were all coming down now to join them. Nicholas felt it rather than saw it, because he couldn't tear his gaze away from this woman. This woman he had almost convinced himself couldn't be real. How could such perfection be real?

She ducked her head, breaking their stare at last, and somehow that broke the spell, too. He was still captivated, yes, but now other emotions made their way to the surface. He hadn't seen this woman since that horrible evening when he realized she'd never planned to marry him, no matter what promises they made in secret. She'd lied to him and sent him on a spiral that had nearly killed him.

Looking at her, the emotion that rose in his chest, long-ignored and pretended away, was anger. He was angry that she was still so irresistible. Angry that she was here at his brother's house when she had to know their connection. Angry that she could look away from him, turn away just as she always had, when he couldn't stop staring.

"What's going on is a very good question," he said, still looking at her even though he was answering Robert. "And only Lady *Lovell* can answer it."

"Nicholas?" Katherine whispered, touching his arm and drawing him back to the part of the world that wasn't Aurora. Such a small world now. Such a dull one. "Please, what is going on?"

"Lady Lovell and I knew each other as children, Katherine. Or didn't she share that fact with you?" He noted how Aurora flinched, high color re-entering her cheeks. "Or did we know each other, my lady? Did we ever *actually* know each other?"

Aurora's gaze jerked back toward him. Tears glistened in her eyes, and for a brief, horrible, wonderful moment all Nicholas wanted to do was step toward her, gather her close, soothe her. Even after everything that had come to pass, he was still such a weak fool.

But he couldn't be. Not anymore. Not with a future to plan and a life to build. No, he had to walk away, just as she had done all those years ago. Until he could control himself, he had to walk away.

He pivoted on his heel and did so, limping back up the stairs and into the house. But even though he'd cut off the contact between himself and Aurora, the attraction, the thrill of seeing her was still there. He hated himself for it. Hated that years and sorrows and near-death hadn't cured him of this desire.

But he didn't hate her. He might have been harsh with her on the stairs, but he hadn't been able to hate her. And as he entered a parlor and all but collapsed on the nearest settee, he realized that had to change. He had to find a way to hate Aurora. Otherwise, he wouldn't survive her.

Aurora couldn't breathe. She stood before her carriage, knees shaking, as Nicholas walked away from her, and she couldn't breathe. Even when he was gone, she gasped for air.

How could he be here? And how could he be even more handsome than he had been all those years ago? Then he'd been a boy, his face still youthful. Now he was all angles, all soft ruddy beard, all piercing gaze of a man who had seen the world. He was everything she'd dreamed of, everything she'd longed for in those never-ending, empty years…and more.

And now he was here. In a house where she'd sworn to herself he would not be. And he looked at her with utter contempt before he limped away, reminding her of all he'd nearly lost when he bravely saved others. He had suffered enormously in the last few years since his injury. Seeing her obviously increased that.

"I…should…leave," she managed to say to no one and everyone. God, their eyes as the entire family stared at her. She'd left London to avoid judgment. She would have rather faced off with people who thought her fallen than this.

"No!" Katherine said, racing forward to support her elbow. "I don't understand what is going on, but you aren't going. Robert…" She turned toward the duke, who seemed to loom above Aurora on the step, his dark gaze focused far too intently on her. "Go speak to your brother. Selina, Derrick and Morgan, go with him. He seems to need all of you. And Aurora, you come with me and Lizzie."

The groups broke apart, and Aurora felt she had no choice but to do as Katherine had suggested. Plus, she had no interest in getting back into the bumpy carriage and taking a three-day ride back to London. She'd depleted her monthly funds already with the trip over.

So she was trapped.

Her head bent, she followed Katherine and the other woman into the house. They walked in front of her, whispering, and her stomach jolted. It seemed humiliation was bound to be her constant companion now. A punishment for some undefined crime, no doubt.

"Please sit," Katherine said, and she motioned to the other woman to close the parlor door. She did so and then moved to pour them each tea. Katherine flicked her hand toward the third in their group. "This is my sister-in-law, Elizabeth Banfield."

"Lizzie," Mrs. Banfield said softly.

Aurora lifted her gaze. The young woman was petite and blonde, and her expression was a little guarded but very kind as she turned over the teacup. Aurora set it aside. She could drink or eat nothing now—she would surely cast it all back up again.

"Married to Nicholas's brother, too?" she whispered.

Lizzie nodded. "Yes. Morgan."

Aurora covered her eyes. "I knew I shouldn't have come. I knew it was wrong to pretend that I didn't know the connections, that they didn't matter. I so wanted the escape you offered, Katherine. No, *Your Grace*, for surely you won't want to be friends anymore after I took advantage of your kindness so selfishly. You must hate me as much as he does. I should go, I should go, no matter the cost."

"Calm yourself," Katherine said, sitting beside her on the settee and taking her hands. "You and Nicholas have a history. Will you explain it?"

Aurora nodded. "You are owed that, of course. After what I did, you are owed so much more." She shuddered and tried to find words to a past that was so steeped in emotion. "His father...his adoptive father...served mine as man of affairs. We grew up together and were..." She fought the tears. "We were friends."

"More than friends, I think, based on that reaction a moment ago," Lizzie encouraged.

"Yes. Eventually more than friends. But it all ended..." Aurora shook her head. "I couldn't explain why. We haven't spoken in almost ten years. A lifetime. I married someone else, Lord Lovell. Nicholas entered the army and acted with bravery and honor."

"But you knew his affiliation to Robert," Katherine pushed gently. "You must have. It's very public, especially now that Nicholas is being considered for a title."

Aurora rubbed her eyes. "Yes, I did. Of course I did. But I understood that Nicholas...no, that isn't right either, not anymore. Not after the time apart and his coldness toward me. Mr. Gillingham is not close to the Duke of Roseford. I assumed there was no risk that he would be here. But I should have told you the connection. I should have told you so that you could decide if you wanted me in your home."

"I'm not sure I would have understood even if you had told me," Katherine said with a sigh. "You're right that Nicholas and Robert have been...I suppose *estranged* is the best descriptor. They have always been very different. In truth, there is little we know about his past beyond what is public."

"So he never spoke to any of you about me?" Aurora whispered. She tried to be happy about that fact, not hurt. She hadn't mattered enough to him to follow through on their plans, why would she believe he cared enough to talk about her to his family or friends?

"You said it didn't work out," Lizzie said with a blush. "And I hate to pry, but as Katherine already told you, Nicholas is a man who holds his emotions close to his chest. That outburst on the drive is far out of character. Do you have any idea what might have sparked it?"

Aurora drew in a long breath, thinking back to those wonderful stolen moments so very long ago. To the promises whispered and broken. Then she shut her eyes, wishing she could block it all out. Knowing it would only play in her mind just as it had been doing for years. It had never softened, never improved. Just haunted her, as he haunted her. Still haunted her. Forever in her heart and soul.

"*That* is complicated," she said softly. "So very complicated."

\# CHAPTER 4

"Nicholas," Robert said as Nicholas entered the duke's study. He'd known someone would follow. How could they not after his uncharacteristic outburst? And here was Robert, trailing just a few steps behind him, his gaze filled with concern and confusion.

Nicholas ignored his brother and went to the window, looking out over the drive. Aurora's carriage was moving away now, toward the stable. Which meant she was staying, if only for a short time while this drama was resolved.

He didn't know whether to crow or curse at that fact. She was still here. A heartbeat away instead of a continent or a city length or a title. All things that had stood between them for so long. All things he had come to resent with as much power as he resented her and her abandonment of their future.

"Nicholas."

He turned now, because it was his brother Morgan who said his name this time. Morgan, Selina and Derrick had all entered the room. He blinked in stunned silence. He'd been alone for such a long time, by design, that he wasn't sure what to do with a gaggle of siblings with similar expressions of deep concern. While his brothers and sister all spoke at once, Derrick just held his gaze, silent and understanding as he shut the door by leaning back against it.

Perhaps because Derrick was the only one with any inkling of what the hell was going on here. Now Nicholas felt a frisson of regret that he'd ever spoken Aurora's name even to his friend.

"What did she do to you?" Selina asked, and the flash in her gaze was perfectly readable. His sister was ready to go to war. It was heartening, really, to see her fierce loyalty turned toward him.

"My love," Derrick said, softly but firmly as he stepped forward and caught her elbow.

She glanced up at him and some of the rage in her stare was muted a fraction. "*Fine.* I'll listen before I plot." She glanced back at Nicholas. "What did she do to you?" she repeated, this time softer.

He flinched as he recalled his behavior on the drive. It wasn't like him to be so…rude. Confrontational. It was ungentlemanly, too much like the duke whose blood ran through his veins. Nicholas had fought long and hard to never be like the last man who'd held the title of Roseford.

"Nicholas," Morgan repeated, his dark stare finding Nicholas's. "Please. Let us help you if we can."

They were all so alike each other, Robert, Selina and Morgan. It was all the more noticeable when they stood as a group. All wild and untethered and driven by emotion and desire. Nicholas had always been on the outside when it came to them.

Right now he felt like he was in the thick of things with them, because all he had left in him was emotion. He didn't like how it burned in his chest, making him want to tear at his skin, making him want to scream and swear and run wild. He had to stop that. Now.

"As I said on the drive," he managed to choke out, "Lady Lovell and I grew up together. I once thought we…we meant something to each other."

Derrick bent his head and Nicholas blushed. How could he not?

He'd once told Derrick the story, or at least part of the story, of him and Aurora, during a drunken night when they'd all thought they might die in battle the next day.

"But she disabused me of that notion a long, long time ago," he finished with a frown.

"I see." Robert shook his head. "I hope you know Katherine wasn't aware of any of that when she invited this woman to our home."

"I'm sure she didn't," Nicholas said, and meant it. Katherine had not a cruel bone in her body. But it still begged a question. "But why *did* she ask her? Selina said they were friends."

"Not friends, just old acquaintances from long before Katherine and I were married," Robert said with a deepening frown. "And she invited Lady Lovell because she has a big heart."

"Don't dance around it, Roseford," Selina snapped. "Not anymore. Katherine invited her because she fixes broken wings. And this scandal about Lady Lovell has broken both of hers. She'll *never* fly again. And to think I was actually feeling sorry for her. Now I admit I'm *happy* she's suffering if she gave you even an ounce of pain."

Warmth flooded Nicholas at such loyal adoration. But Selina's words confused him. "Scandal? What scandal?"

"You didn't hear? The story has been circulating all over Society for more than a week," Derrick said.

"Yes," Robert said. "I assumed you were paying attention to those rumors and innuendos with the matter of the title hanging over you. Those in that sphere must know at least a little about their equals and the messes they make."

"It's not a habit I've yet formed," Nicholas admitted, and pulled a face. "I cannot abide gossip and I try to avoid it whenever possible."

"Then let me explain," Derrick said, moving toward him at last. "It's rumored Lady Lovell was frequenting the Cat's Companion. She was seen there by a gentleman."

"I wouldn't call the Earl of Roddenbury a gentleman, no matter what bloody title he's dragging behind him," Robert growled. "He's a drunk and a cad, and that's coming from me."

Nicholas staggered slightly at that shocking statement. "The Cat's Companion. You mean the brothel?"

"The worst brothel in London," Robert corrected with a grimace. "And that has stiff competition. There are places for fun, but that hellhole is certainly not one of them. The women are treated badly, the men are less than savory. It's…dangerous."

"Then Aurora would never go to such a place," Nicholas said, somehow desperate to defend her honor.

"She did, though," Selina insisted. "And as you said on the drive, perhaps you never really knew her at all."

His own words repeated back to him found their mark, and Nicholas bent his head. "Perhaps not. If it were Donville Masquerade or Vivien Manning's place, I would say her visiting there was about pleasure. As a widow, I suppose one might…understand her seeking it out."

He hesitated because those words made him think such wicked thoughts. All those years ago, they had only kissed. Yes, there had been passion, a desire that bubbled beneath the surface, but it had never gone too far. He'd denied himself because he wanted to do the right thing. He'd wanted to wait to call her lover until he could also call her wife.

That hadn't stopped wicked, heated, desperate thoughts from haunting him all these years, of course. Imaginings of all those soft curves naked beneath him, above him, all around him.

He pushed the thoughts aside and refocused on matters at hand. "But the Cat's Companion?"

"I tend to agree," Robert said. "But the rumors are rampant. And considering Katherine's own history with those kinds of cruel whispers, my wife felt compelled to offer her assistance."

"Didn't Lady Lovell give her some kind of story?" Morgan said. "About a missing friend or some such thing?"

Nicholas's head was spinning with all this new information and he held up a hand. "It isn't right for us to stand around talking about her."

Selina cocked her head. "You are too good, Nicholas. Are we certain he is our father's son?"

He smiled despite the fraught topic. "More often than I wish to be. Today on the drive is a good example. I behaved…badly. Perhaps I should just leave. It sounds like Aurora…Lady Lovell…needs to be here more than I do if she is indeed being dragged through the mud. A connection with Katherine and the friends you have in attendance could buffer Aurora from the worst of it."

"No," Robert said, stepping forward. "That isn't fair to you. Please don't go."

It was the *please* that hit him, curling into him. Making him stare at his older brother for what felt like a lifetime and see…well, a connection he'd long tried to avoid. Did he really want to walk away? From Robert and his siblings? From the potential support he could find here amongst them and Robert's friends?

Away from Aurora after he had just found her?

He didn't even try to push the thought away this time. It was undeniable, after all. No matter his other thoughts on the drive, when he'd seen her, he wanted her. He understood that a great deal more now that he'd had more experience in the world. He had a far more vivid imagination about what he could do about it. So if he stayed, if she stayed, he would have to find a way to manage those ever-present desires. A way that didn't involve burying his cock in her like a libertine.

The cock that twitched with that thought.

"I should…speak to her," he said softly, and tried not to groan at how difficult that would be. "It's been a very long time, and despite my outburst made in surprise, perhaps there's a way for us to be at peace with each other so neither of us has to walk away from the opportunities this party offers us."

Selina worried her lip, and Morgan and Derrick exchanged a look, but Robert stepped forward and clapped a hand on his upper arm. "It's a good idea. At least if you speak to her, you'll know better where you stand. You can decide what to do based on fact, not some emotional reaction because of an unexpected reunion.

Nicholas shot him a look. "Are you being...*wise?*"

Robert pulled a face as the others laughed. "God help me if I am."

"God help us all," Nicholas said, and was shocked by how much it warmed his heart to tease with his siblings like this. It felt so... comfortable. He sighed. "I'll speak to her now. Assume we'll both be staying."

He moved to exit the room, but Robert clenched his arm a little tighter. Their eyes met, so similar, and his brother said, "Whatever you decide, I support you fully. I hope you know that."

Nicholas froze. He'd created an environment where he was alone, never depending on anyone else for a very long time. Even in his injury and recovery, he'd fought for autonomy. What his brother offered was...bewitching. Still, could he trust it?

He forced a smile. "Thank you, Roseford. I appreciate that."

He drew a deep breath, saluted the room and walked out. But with every step that would take him to the parlor, his heart began to beat louder. He was going to finally confront the woman who had haunted him for a decade.

And he had no idea how to approach her and save himself from sinking into everything that once might have been.

Aurora clenched her hands at her sides as she paced the room restlessly. She felt Katherine and Lizzie's eyes on her, watching...judging, even if they did so kindly.

She had been asked a question a moment before. She didn't have an answer. How could she explain what had happened between her and Nicholas when she wasn't entirely certain of that, herself? One moment they'd been planning a madcap elopement, all consequences be damned. The next he was gone and she'd been rushed into an arranged marriage with Lord Lovell. Everything had changed, everything she'd wanted had been lost and she'd never been the same.

And yet Nicholas seemed angry with her for their past. Accusatory of *her*. As the shock of seeing him wore off, she pondered that.

"Aurora?" Katherine said. "You don't need to tell us any secrets. I think all of us are just confused by this turn of events. All of us are trying to find a footing."

"So am I," Aurora admitted. "It isn't that I don't want to answer your question. I just can't. I don't know the answer. Only Nicholas knows why things turned from a dream to a nightmare all those years ago."

Before she could say anything more, a shadow appeared in the doorway. She tensed as Nicholas, himself, entered the parlor, his gaze sliding to her immediately and holding there. The shock of seeing him should have worn off by now, but it hadn't. In this moment, there was no breath. No words. Nothing but this man standing so close and yet leagues away, watching her just as he'd watched her so many times in another lifetime.

Even though she knew his gaze was one of contempt now, it still rolled over her like water, like a memory that had come to life. His eyes were the same as the eyes of that boy she had loved so desperately. The rest of him was so much more beautiful than the boy she had been obsessed with as a young woman. All his angles and edges were sharper and she wanted to…God help her, but she wanted to touch him.

He cleared his throat and the silent spell was broken. "Ladies, I'd like a moment with Lady Lovell." He held her gaze and his tone softened. "Please."

She nodded without breaking the gaze, almost completely unaware as Lizzie and Katherine got up and slipped from the room. Katherine stood in the doorway for a moment, and then she shut it behind her, regardless of the propriety of that action. Aurora had never wanted to hug another person so much in her life. She needed the privacy of that closed door more than she needed breath.

He was silent for what felt like forever. She had no idea if that was because, like her, he was struggling to find purchase or if he just had no words to say in the quiet. He looked at her, though. His dark brown gaze never left hers, and it was like all the time in the world hung between them…and no time at all.

"Aurora," he said at last.

Her knees trembled when her name came from his lips in that deep voice that was the same and different. No one else had ever said it and made her feel so many things with those three little syllables. No one else ever could.

"Nicholas," she whispered back. A prayer. A benediction. A faint sliver of hope that she had long ago released into the world. Now that little bird had returned and she feared it would roost in her heart and break her.

He swallowed. She followed the working of his Adam's apple. How she wanted to touch him, press her lips there. She wanted to count the beat of his pulse and see if it matched the wild rhythm of her own.

"We—" he began. His voice cracked. He shook his head. "We obviously need to talk, Aurora. There is so much that needs to be said."

# CHAPTER 5

Aurora was shaking. She didn't want to tremble, to reveal her weakness to this man whose intentions were unclear, but she couldn't stop. She couldn't think. She couldn't do anything but look at him and wonder if this were just a dream.

If so, it was one she'd had many times during the time they were apart. Dreams of him walking into her home, her life, of him in her bed and her arms. Every dream in nine years, both waking and sleeping, had been of him. That had colored every aspect of her life and her marriage until this moment.

Only this moment was real.

"Yes," she gasped out because it was clear he was waiting for a response to his statement. "Talk. You're right, of course."

He bent his head, and that broke the intense eye contact they'd been sharing since he entered the room. She was able to find breath again when he did and slow her racing heart. She was glad of both those things. A lack of control wouldn't serve her in this situation. Not when Nicholas held himself like he had complete sovereignty over his faculties.

He cleared his throat. "I wanted to start by saying I'm...sorry, Aurora."

She had pictured a dozen scenarios of what they would say to each other since he came down the drive toward her less than an hour before. Rows and accusations she had expected. This?

Well, this was entirely unforeseen, and she blinked up at him in shock. "For…for what?"

His lips pinched. "I'm sorry for my outburst on the drive. It was ungentlemanly to confront you like I did, but especially in front of others. The fact is that I didn't expect to see you, certainly not here of all places. I wasn't prepared for what that would…would do to me."

"I wasn't either," she admitted, because his vulnerability stoked a tiny bit of her own.

She moved a step closer and watched his dark brown eyes dilate with desire. She recognized the desire now, in a way she hadn't been capable of doing as a virginal young woman. Her hands shook from the recognition of it. If he wanted her, that meant he didn't fully hate her. And that was something small she could cling to with all her might.

"You look beautiful," he breathed, his gaze flitting over her from head to toe. More of that desire flowed from him, heat that pulsed over her and merged with her own.

"So do you," she said with a smile.

She expected him to return the expression, but to her surprise, his gaze went flat and he turned away. "No, I don't. I just look broken."

Her breath caught and she moved to him without hesitation. "You're speaking about your injuries?"

He nodded without looking at her. "I'm certainly not the same man I was when you last saw me."

"You are better." She didn't dare say that in full voice. Even as a whisper, she was revealing too much of her heart. She did it anyway. "Your bravery was revered, as it should have been, and those acts have only made you stronger and more…"

She stopped herself because his gaze had swung back toward her. "You followed my actions, did you?"

"Of—of course," she stammered. "When I heard you'd been injured in the war, I—" She caught herself. If she said too much now she might never stop. But she still needed to say *something*. "I was devastated. I'm so glad you lived, Nicholas. And that you will likely be rewarded for your bravery and selflessness."

His gaze narrowed and flitted over her, like he was reading her. She couldn't tell what decision he'd made about whatever he thought he knew now.

"The title isn't guaranteed, Aurora," he said, his tone suddenly tense. "Just as *nothing* in life is guaranteed."

The sharpness in his voice was back now. The judgment of her and her actions. She found herself turning away from it and from him, unable to bear his harshness when she wanted something softer and sweeter that she'd never have again. If she'd been bewitched by a flash of longing, she couldn't ignore that more of him was wary and unyielding when it came to her.

"I have offered to leave this house," she said. "And your sister-in-law has said that I should stay. But in the end, it isn't about what she wants. It's you, Nicholas. This is your family and I've obviously intruded into a space where I'm not just unexpected, but unwelcome. I should go."

She pivoted away, moving toward the door before she did something foolish like touched him. Kissed him. Fell to her knees and confessed all her heart to him.

But to her surprise, he reached out and caught her hand, dragging her back toward him a fraction. Lightning crackled up her arm at the touch of his hand on her body, even in this relatively benign way. It had been so long since he last touched her, but she'd been dreaming of it ever since. And now his lean fingers had strength, but didn't punish or hurt.

His dark stare bore down into hers, unreadable but for one

thing...heat. He was looking at her with heat, and her stomach fluttered in needy response.

"Stay."

Nicholas could barely breathe. Aurora wasn't wearing gloves and neither was he, so his skin was on her skin, and it was everything he'd fantasized about since the horrible moment he lost her. Now this was sweet torture to hold her, and he wanted nothing more than to drag it out until he burned alive in her heat.

Which was exactly why he could not, should not, do that. He released her with a shudder and forced himself to take a step away.

She was staring up at him in confusion, and he couldn't blame her. He'd been so cold on the drive. He'd hoped to come into this room and continue to be cold toward her. There were so many questions that loomed between them, about the past, about this scandal she was apparently dragging behind her.

But when he looked down into those warm brown eyes that had always been so kind, so gentle, it wasn't so easy. She looked... exhausted. Being here would help her, as much as it would help him.

Could he truly rip that away from her? This woman he had loved for all of his adult life?

"You can't mean that," she whispered.

He shrugged, hoping it seemed that he didn't care. He needed that barrier, at least, between them. "Whatever happened between us, it's in the distant past. Isn't it?"

Her gaze darted away, pink filled her cheeks. She almost looked...*disappointed,* but that couldn't be. After all, she had walked away from him, married someone else, lived a life that had nothing to do with him. Why should *she* be disappointed?

"Yes," she said at last, her breath hitching.

"Neither of us is the same person we were all those years ago," he continued. And that was true. He hadn't been that green, hopeful boy for a very long time. War had changed him, injury had changed him…*she* had changed him. "And I think we both *need* to be here for various reasons."

Her face jerked toward his, and the pink on her cheeks immediately transformed to bright red. "You—you are referring to the scandal, I suppose."

He shifted. God, how he would like to ask her about that. Press her, demand to understand what had driven her to such a thing. But it wasn't his place. They weren't friends, not anymore. They weren't lovers, they never had been. He was owed no answers. And perhaps if he ignored that urge to demand them, it would create a required distance that would make the next week and a half more bearable.

"It is none of my affair," he said, and turned away from her. "I'm not asking you about it, nor judging you for whatever happened back in London."

"I see." Her voice was very small.

He forced himself to look at her, gripping his hands behind his back so he wouldn't try to touch her again. "Can we put our past aside for the sake of our futures? Pretend to be strangers who just met? And proceed as we both intended when we each agreed to come here, not knowing the other would be in attendance?"

She was quiet for so long, he started to wonder if she'd heard him. But finally she gave a shaky nod. "I-I can do that. If you can."

"I can," he said immediately.

It was a lie. He couldn't do that. Couldn't pretend she'd never meant something…everything…to him. But he would. He'd *make* himself do it, use that military discipline that had guided his life since almost the very day she left him.

He shook his head to push that thought away and extended a hand as if they were meeting for the first time. "Nicholas Gillingham, my lady."

She stared at the outstretched fingers, and her hand shook as she took them. "Lady Lovell."

He pulled his hand away after a perfunctory shake that sent the same electricity up his spine that taking her hand had done a moment before. "A pleasure. And now if you'll excuse me, I will allow you to go settle in to your room. I'm sure you're tired after the long journey from London. Good day, my lady."

The fact that this distance and dismissal hurt Aurora was plain by the hurt that flickered across her face. But she forced a smile and nodded. "Good day, Mr. Gillingham."

He pivoted and walked away. As he exited the room, he was finally able to draw a full breath, and he did so as he made his way down the hall toward any parlor that would allow his escape onto the back terrace. He needed air desperately. He needed to be free of the soft scent of Aurora's skin, the warmth of her breath, the shiny beauty of her hair. All the things he'd tried to forget and failed at miserably and totally.

"This is a test," he muttered to himself as he burst out into the sunshine of the afternoon. "You've had many of those over the years. And this is one you have to pass, that is all there is to it."

Aurora stared at her plate of uneaten food, though she hardly saw what was before her. She was too distracted. The party staying at the Duke and Duchess of Roseford's home was a large one, so the long table was filled with people all talking and laughing at once. And yet her attention continued to be drawn, always and forever, to one man, even though he had been obviously placed as far away from her as humanly possible.

Nicholas. He was situated between his two half-brothers on the opposite end of the table from her. He talked to them, though it didn't appear easily. And he never looked her way. Not once. Not even from the corner of his eye. It seemed he would have an easier time with their promise to pretend they shared no common history than she would.

"I have heard you are an accomplished horsewoman, Lady Lovell."

Aurora blinked and turned her attention to the lady who had been seated beside her, the Duchess of Northfield, a beautiful blonde woman with dark blue eyes that seemed to take in everything around her. She had also insisted that Aurora refer to her by her first name, Adelaide, almost immediately upon meeting her. And how could one refuse a lady of such charm and grace?

Adelaide's husband was at the other end of the table closer to Roseford and Nicholas and was equally as handsome as his wife. She'd seen the two of them whispering close together in the hallway earlier. They were obviously in love.

She forced her attention back to what the lady had just said. "Er, yes. I have always enjoyed riding," she said. "I suppose one becomes accomplished at those things they enjoy enough to repeat."

Adelaide's eyes lit up with mirth and she cast them toward her husband briefly. "I would say that is very true. But I heard you went so far as to break and train the animals?"

Aurora bent her head. This subject was not meant to be a painful one, she was certain. But it still was. "On my late husband's estate, I was allowed to house several mares and fillies. I did break the horses and breed them." She cleared her throat and wished her voice were not so thick as she said, "But since his death, I have not been able to see the animals. I heard most were sold off by the new viscount."

Adelaide's face lit up with pity. "That must be painful. I'm so sorry. Animals can be such a comfort. I didn't mean to bring up a difficult subject."

"Don't worry yourself," Aurora assured her, for she didn't want Adelaide to feel bad about the painful topic. And she also didn't want to be known as the woman who could only talk about her pain. That didn't endear her to anyone, she was certain.

"You mentioned your late husband," Adelaide said with a

gracious smile toward her. "You just came out of mourning, I know. Do you have any plans?"

Aurora almost laughed. Out of one painful conversation and into another. But she forced her tone to be light. "I'm not certain. I suppose expectation will normally be for me to come back into Society and even find a new mate. Whether or not that will be possible remains to be seen."

Adelaide arched a fine brow. "The right friends will get you far, my dear. And our Katherine seems determined you will have those. Don't fear. Anything can be overcome."

Aurora found her gaze sliding back toward Nicholas. Was that true? If it was, what did that mean for the two of them?

If her anxious mood was obvious, Adelaide swiftly put it at ease. She changed the subject to books and soon they were happily chatting about a topic far less full of fraught emotions. Supper flew by far faster then, and Aurora felt herself relaxing. She hadn't been able to have many friendships as of late. And Imogen's disappearance had put even more pressure on her. Just this moment of normalcy did help.

Finally the last plates were cleared away and Roseford got to his feet. "We'll retire to the west parlor, where there will be music and some games."

Aurora got to her feet. "The gentlemen won't separate from the ladies for their port?" she asked softly.

Adelaide chuckled. "In this group? Sometimes they will, but often everyone stays together. The marriages are all so happy and the friendships so close."

They walked out together and Adelaide continued to chatter on at her side, but now Aurora was distracted. She hadn't realized how close the group was, but now it became clearer. All these established friendships and all these couples in her midst.

In fact, the only uncoupled attendees staying at the house were… she caught her breath…her and Nicholas.

She and Adelaide reached the parlor. Her new friend squeezed her arm and murmured something about talking later, but then she was off across the room to step into the circle of her husband's arms. All the couples, none of whom had been seated with each other at supper, did the same. And now the mood in the room changed.

Aurora stared. Her own marriage had been unemotional. Lovell was not affectionate. He could have been parted from her for a month and he would have done nothing more than shake her hand when he returned. These people had spent no more than a few hours without being next to each other and they all looked like they were relieved to be reunited.

She sighed and crossed to the sideboard where she poured herself a glass of madeira. At least it gave her something to do with her hands, some distraction so her discomfort wasn't clear to the room at large. But as she set the bottle down and turned toward the room again, her breath hitched.

Nicholas had all but ignored her all night. But now he was staring at her across the room, his dark gaze boring into her, through her, reading her, judging her. She was captive under the spell of it and him.

Worse when he began to move and she realized that against all odds, he was coming across the room to speak to her. And she had to prepare herself for what in the world she would say to him.

# CHAPTER 6

Nicholas shouldn't have made his way across the room toward Aurora, but that's what he found his legs doing. Even after all their fine talk of forgetting the past, of pretending to be strangers at this party, he was drawn to her just as he always had been.

But if he *were* a stranger, if they didn't share whatever the past was between them, and this beautiful woman was the only unattached person in the room besides himself, wouldn't he approach her? Not to flirt. No, that would be a bad idea. Only out of politeness, since she seemed just as uncomfortable with the couples pairing off as he did.

That gave him an excuse, at any rate, as he stepped up beside her and poured himself a glass of whatever she had just taken. He didn't even look to see what it was.

"Is it just me or did the temperature of the room just go up a few degrees?" he asked, tilting his glass toward her in mock toast.

The others had circulated away from their pairings, mingling into the room again, talking to their friends and family members, but still...the love they each shared had been seen. It couldn't be ignored now that it hung in the air, bright and beautiful and...and accusatory.

"They do all seem…enamored of each other," Aurora admitted, not looking at him as she took a long sip of wine. "It seems an unusual thing, so many couples at such a high level of Society being obviously in love with each other."

He arched a brow at her. "I suppose it is rare. Are you saying you did not share such a connection to your late husband?"

She stiffened at the question he never should have asked. Her lips tightened. Her shoulders pushed back. A posture of defense. She glanced at him from the corner of her eye, and he saw a flicker of desperation and pain in her gaze. "I thought you and I weren't going to discuss the past."

"Fair," he said. "Then what should we talk about?"

She cleared her throat and her smile was false as she looked up at him. "I would happily discuss the future. It seems a less dangerous topic, at any rate."

"I wouldn't say that," he murmured.

"Marquess of Songstrum," she said, and the smile turned more real. "What a thing, Nicholas…er, Mr. Gillingham, to be considered to take over that title."

"A dead title," he said with a shake of his head. "It doesn't bode well."

"It's a strange idea, but of course a title has to be dead in order to be bestowed rather than inherited. If it helps, I think Songstrum has been dead a very long time. At least two generations."

"You know a lot about the title," he said softly.

She blushed. "Er…I suppose. It's difficult not to hear about it when the world is discussing your potential move to possess it."

"I suppose there's no getting around the talk." He frowned. "And yes. It is an honor to be considered for such a thing."

"Your bravery has earned you many accolades," she said as she looked out over the group before them. "You're celebrated in many circles."

"And yet *they* still question if a common man like me, the kind with bastard blood, the kind raised by a servant …should *he* truly be gifted with such a title? Every move I make is being watched now, as much for reasons to strip the opportunity away as to grant it."

She worried her lip and he tracked the action. Such a lovely, full bottom lip. He remembered the taste of it and wondered if it would be the same now, even after all this time. Honey-sweet, soft as satin. "Is that why you're here? You mentioned you needed this party as much as you assumed I did."

He nodded, for there seemed no vulnerability in telling her that. Anyone with sense could have guessed his reasons. "Yes. My brother and his club of dukes are some of the most influential men in Society. He invited Northfield here as a buffer. Seems a decent bloke. He hasn't judged my lack of credentials, at any rate."

"His wife was lovely, as well," Aurora said. "I sat with her at supper and she was friendly and open. They would make good friends to you, I'm sure."

"The kind that open doors," he said, and frowned. How he hated to count relationships on such terms. That reminded him of the last Duke of Roseford. And of Aurora's father, too. "I suppose it is the way of the world when one is dealing in something that comes with so much money and land."

She frowned and her gaze flitted over his face. "It's so odd to hear you speak in such terms, even if they are practical. You were never one to be interested or impressed by those kinds of things."

He drew back. Was she judging him for looking at the world through this lens? Especially after she'd thrown him over for a title?

"Well, things change," he snapped, a little sharper than he intended. "People change. A man with a title has power. You should know that better than most."

Aurora caught her breath and turned closer toward him. He could scent her now, something floral. Despite the undercurrents of this conversation, he found himself wanting to glide his fingers into her hair, bring it down around her shoulders and drag in a deeper breath of that scent.

"What do you mean, I more than most?" Now it was her tone

that was sharp. "Why would I have a deeper connection to such mercenary desires?"

"It's the world you grew up in," he said. "Your father was a man with a title. Your husband. Surely you must have seen what they could do with such power. Power to help others or destroy them. Power to protect themselves."

She blinked and her lips parted. "Protect?" she repeated. "And that is what you want, is it? To protect yourself?"

He narrowed his gaze. What had started off as a conversation of generalities was now too intimate. She would see into the heart of him and he already knew that wasn't a good idea. Let her in and she could cut him open with just a flick of her wrist. He couldn't risk that.

"Everyone wants to protect themselves," he snapped. "It is our nature. Now I see that Huntington has managed to extract himself from my sister. I needed to discuss something with my old friend. Excuse me."

He left, not waiting for her to respond, and headed across the room toward Derrick. He didn't necessarily wish to talk to his friend, but he also didn't think he was capable of standing with Aurora for one more moment. Not when what had begun as a benign enough conversation had pivoted to something with more meaning. Would it always be that way? Would their past and the feelings he hated himself for still sheltering keep him from being able to be casual with this woman?

If that was the case, perhaps he *should* leave.

Derrick arched a brow as Nicholas reached him, and for a moment they just stood together, unspeaking. A little of the tension in Nicholas's shoulders eased. He had always liked that about military friendships. Those men didn't feel the need to fill a room with idle chatter.

"Do you want to talk about her?" Derrick asked at last, and the comfort of the silence was immediately shattered.

"Bloody hell," Nicholas muttered, and downed the remainder of his wine in one glug. "No."

Derrick pivoted toward him more fully. "Do you *need* to talk about her?"

Nicholas's first instinct was to answer in the negative to that question, as well. Only he stared into his old friend's eyes and found it far more difficult to do so.

"I'm assuming because you always keep everything so close to the chest, no one else here understands what she truly meant to you. What happened between you," Derrick pressed. "And perhaps you regret that I know the truth, or some version of it. But since I do… won't you let me be of service to you?"

Nicholas shifted. "A drunken confession isn't in my nature."

"I hope you know I can be trusted with what you told me all those years ago. If it helps, I haven't even told Selina about that night." Derrick gave a half-smile. "Not that she doesn't keep trying to wheedle out anything interesting I might know, especially about you. She's very persuasive."

Considering how Derrick and Selina could scarcely keep their hands off each other, Nicholas could only imagine the tactics his sister employed to obtain information. If Derrick could hold up against that kind of torture, he could certainly be trusted. Especially since everything Nicholas felt boiled up inside of him, generating pressure that made him feel like he would burst.

"I have avoided any situation that could have forced this kind of encounter," he admitted softly. "When I exited the sickbed and started being paraded around as a hero with a potential title, I scoured guestlists, made inquiries, all to avoid Aurora. Not because I didn't want to see her, but because despite all the time between us, despite the fact that she threw me over for a man with better prospects than she thought I'd ever have…I *do*. I have wanted to see her every day since the last. A weakness, I suppose."

"Some might call that love," Derrick said softly.

Nicholas flinched. If he called it that, even in his head, he would be fully lost. Loving her had been the greatest experience of his life.

Losing her the worst, even something he held above the physical pain he'd endured after the war. The physical pain faded, but this? This was always just below the surface, making every part of his life a little duller.

"Though there may be an argument to be made about whether or not she deserves devotion from a man such as you."

"A man such as me?" Nicholas repeated. "What does that mean?"

"We served in the army together many years," Derrick said. "You saved my life."

"You saved mine," Nicholas responded, meeting his friend's eyes. "You were injured that day, as well, but you kept me from bleeding out on the battlefield."

"Either way, no braver or more honorable man have I ever met in my life," Derrick said. "And seeing you struggle over this young woman…a person I know hurt you deeply, I worry. And I hope that you'll be careful."

"I will be," Nicholas said. "I am determined to pretend as though I've never met the woman before. We're nothing but strangers, so the danger is less."

Derrick said nothing, but the expression that came over his face said volumes about how incredulous he was.

"What is that look?" Nicholas asked. "You don't believe me?"

Derrick shrugged. "I was watching you with her just now. You didn't look like a man being polite with a stranger. Like it or not, the tension between you two is palpable."

Nicholas pursed his lips. That wasn't good, not at all. He was accustomed to being able to control himself. He had honed that skill during his time in the army, practiced it until it was second nature. Now it seemed he wasn't doing a decent job at it at all.

"Then perhaps the best thing I can do is avoid her entirely," he said, and hated how his hands shook at the very idea of such a thing. "I could…I could pretend she isn't here. The party is small, but large enough that complete evasion isn't out of the question."

Derrick shook his head. "I wasn't implying—"

But Nicholas raised a hand to stop him. "Perhaps you weren't. And perhaps it's an extreme measure. But given the past, perhaps it's also for the best." He swallowed hard and pushed his shoulders back. "It *is* for the best."

Derrick was looking at him with shock and concern. Both were thick in his voice when he said, "And will you tell the lady this? That you will not speak or interact with her again? Is that your plan?"

Nicholas looked across the room. Aurora had joined Lizzie, Katherine and Adelaide by the fire. She was smiling as the four women chatted. She looked...happy. Relieved. And he knew if he told her he didn't want anything to do with her, more of that hurt and concern would cross her face. He couldn't do it tonight.

"I will," he said. "Tomorrow. I'll tell her tomorrow."

His brother-in-law didn't look convinced of that, and for a moment Nicholas thought his friend might say something more. But then Derrick shook his head slightly and changed the subject. "Barber sent his regards before I left London," he said. "He would have come—Roseford invited him—but he was working on a case."

Nicholas smiled in relief at the topic. Edward Barber was their mutual friend, a man who had served with them. After the incident that had nearly killed Nicholas and injured several others, including Derrick and Barber, everything had changed. Derrick and Barber were partners in an investigative business, something that catered to the needs of the Upper Ten Thousand when they didn't want to go to the guard, when their silver was pilfered, or a swindler relieved them of an investment. Sometimes they were even called upon when there was a murder.

The topic was a fascinating one, and Nicholas relaxed as he discussed the finer points of the trade with his old friend. But every so often, he couldn't help but dart his gaze to Aurora. And when he did, when he looked at her with her bright smile and her full curves and her dark eyes...the idea of pushing her away was almost impossible to fathom. So he had to figure out a way to do just that, and quickly.

# CHAPTER 7

Aurora lifted her face toward the bright sunshine of the summer morning. It kissed her face and she sighed as she drank it in. Then she removed her bonnet and let out a long sigh. There was nothing like a long walk alone to clear one's head.

She had always been an early riser. While others of her class lounged until midday, Aurora did her best thinking and planning early in the morning. An added bonus was that she didn't have to see anyone while she did it. That had been the perfect escape during her marriage. Not that Lovell had truly cared what she did or where she did it, as long as she stayed out of his way.

She pushed those thoughts aside, but was left with a cacophony of others. There was so much all crowded into her mind and it made her feel like she'd been spun around a dozen times and been set free into the world to stagger helplessly. Even sleep hadn't given her respite. She had tossed and turned all night. Every time she'd fallen into even the slightest state of sleep, Nicholas's face had ripped her awake.

Back to a reality where he was just a few chambers down from her. Practically arm's length. Being this close to him was like going back in time. And talking to him? That was even more intense.

When he stood near her, she could smell that pine-and-leather scent of him that made her body tingle in all the most outrageous places. And when she could feel the body heat of his long, lanky frame? She had such thoughts. Such wicked, passionate thoughts.

She huffed out a breath and fisted her hands at her sides. That was more than enough. She was about to start walking again when she heard a sound from behind her. She turned back toward the house far above on the hill and was surprised to see an animal racing toward her. A dog, though he was so large he could have been mistaken for a small pony. He didn't bark as he barreled over a slight rise in the field, but he was focused intently on her as he ran.

As he got closer, she recognized him as a fine bullmastiff, ruddy tan in color, with thick, muscular lines. He was a dog meant to intimidate, but she didn't feel intimidated as he skidded to a stop in front of her and just…stared.

"Well, good morning, fine sir," she said, smiling at the animal.

The dog titled its massive head quizzically and let out a little whine of confusion.

"What is a good boy like you doing out here by himself?" She crouched down. "Hmmm? Tell me, good boy?"

The dog lolled his tongue out of one side of his mouth and let out a playful bark. She reached out, allowed him to smell her hand and then began to scratch behind his ear. The dog immediately flopped down, back leg flexing as she scratched.

"You must belong to someone," she continued, unable to help herself from using the same tone she would with an adorable baby. "A pretty boy like you has to be so loved."

The bark-whine combination was the only response, and she laughed as the dog rolled on his back and offered his belly for pets. There was no refusing him, so she sank to her knees in the grass and went to work at rubbing the fine, broad chest and belly.

"You are a vicious dog, aren't you? A guard dog, no doubt. So frightening. Who do you belong to, eh boy? Who is your master?"

"That would be me."

She jolted at the sound of Nicholas's voice and looked up to find him coming slowly toward her, cane in one hand. Her breath caught, for from her angle on the ground, he looked impossibly tall and lean and strong. And stern, as the sunlight caught off his expression as he stared down at her and the animal that was apparently his.

"Oh," she squeaked, and shook her head. God, could she be any more obvious in her attraction to him? That wasn't good for either of them. "Good day," she managed, and shoved back to her feet.

He arched a brow at the dog still lolling on the ground at her feet, whining for her to come back and finish what she'd started. "My guard dog seems not to be much on guard."

She laughed, for at the moment the dog wiggled and his tongue flopped from one side of his mouth to the other. "He's very sweet."

"Sweet?" Nicholas repeated, and then he laughed. All the air was sucked from her lungs at that sound she had once loved, craved. How many times had she found amusing things for him just to make him chuckle in that low, husky tone? "Not many would say that about him."

She struggled to find breath enough to respond. "What is his name?"

"Fortescue," he said, and at that the dog stopped playing and jerked to his feet. Nicholas smiled as he flicked his hand to his side. The dog trotted over and sat down at full attention. He continued to send Aurora side glances, but now he looked every inch the guard dog Nicholas had said he was.

"Oh," she said. "So a proud, Norman warrior."

His smile widened. "Indeed. Despite his drooling over female affection."

"I'm sure that same desire must have afflicted soldiers of old," she reassured him. "You cannot blame Fortescue for that."

Nicholas shifted and his gaze slid over her face, settling on her lips. "No. I suppose not."

The sun suddenly felt warmer, and she lifted a hand to her

throat in the hopes she would cover the flush she felt spreading on her skin. "When did you get him?"

Nicholas held his stare on her a beat too long and then cleared his throat. "Since my dog interrupted your walk, why don't we join you so that you may continue?"

She hesitated. They had agreed to pretend as if their shared past didn't exist, and there was no harm in two strangers sharing a walk if they bumped into each other. But it still felt...dangerous. And alluring. And something she wanted more than anything.

So she pushed aside her hesitations and nodded. "As long as it isn't too taxing on your injuries."

He glanced at his cane. "I've been told to exercise the leg. In order to keep it mobile. So this is my morning constitutional. Perhaps a bit taxing, but essential."

She blinked up at him anew. His life had changed so much in nine years, but he was never anything but calm about it. Steady. Then again, he always had been. It was something she'd always admired about him.

"Then away we go," she said with a smile. They fell into step together, she slowing her gait so that he wouldn't have to push too hard past whatever remained of his injury.

"You asked when Fortescue came into my life," he said, and reached down to pat the dog's head as they walked. "After the war."

She nodded slowly, but in truth he had broached a subject she didn't know if she could leave be. The war and his time in it had been in her thoughts since well before they met again. "Was he a war dog?"

He gave the dog a playfully stern look and laughed. "I would have said so before I found him offering surrender to an unarmed enemy this morning."

She knew he meant to be funny, but the statement hit home regardless. "I hope I'm not your enemy," she said softly. "Or his."

He didn't reply but looked off toward the horizon. "Fortescue was trained for patrol, yes," he said. "And took to me, as I did to him.

When I was injured, he wouldn't leave my side and so was gifted to me."

She smiled. "Good boy," she said, and Fortescue's thick, curved tail thumped as he wagged it. "I'm glad he was with you, I'm sure those must have been difficult days." She glanced at Nicholas's leg, memorizing the way his gait had changed with his injury. The limp wasn't pronounced, but it certainly changed the man she'd once known. "How did it happen?"

He cleared his throat. "I thought we weren't discussing the past."

She glanced at him from the corner of her eye. He looked uncomfortable. "I thought that included a moratorium only on our shared past. But if you don't wish to discuss the subject with me, it's none of my business."

They were silent for a moment, walking together. Then he sighed. "The battle was at its height and the mortar shells started falling."

She cocked her head. "Shells?"

"A big…blast from a cannon," he explained. "My men had been holed up near our munitions, and I went against orders and forced them to move. Just after I did, a shell hit the powder kegs. There was a massive explosion."

"They would have been killed if you hadn't disobeyed orders," she gasped, and tears filled her eyes.

"Some of them were," he said, and his tone was so faraway. Like he was back there, in that horrible place that had nearly snatched him from her world. "And others were injured. I was blown off my feet by the blast. Metal in my leg, burned."

She covered her mouth with one hand and came to a stop on the path. "Oh, Nicholas."

He shook his head. "Please don't pity me."

She stepped toward him and caught his hand, lifting it to her heart. "Pity you? Who could pity you? You acted with forethought and bravery, and saved the lives of those you served with. I only picture the pain you must have endured and I hate it. I hate that you had to suffer. That you still do."

He stared down at her, those dark brown eyes locked with hers. Suddenly she was very aware of how close they were. How warm he was. How strong his arm was beneath her clenching fingers. The last time she'd been so close to him, they'd been young and, she'd thought, in love. He'd kissed her.

Right now she would have done anything if he'd do that again. She thought he might. His gaze slipped to her lips, he leaned in just a fraction. She tilted her head back out of instinct, offering her mouth without thinking about it.

But then he stepped away. "It wasn't the first time I suffered, my lady," he said, his form of address putting up an invisible but no less insurmountable barrier. "I'm sure it won't be the last."

She blinked as he turned his face away from hers, looking back toward the house. "Nicholas," she began.

He ignored her. "I think it might be best if I went back. Too far a walk is hard on the injury and I have something to discuss with Huntington at any rate. But I'm glad you got to meet Fortescue. Enjoy the rest of your walk."

She opened her mouth, seeking some way to bring him back to her side. But it was evident he wanted to be away from her. So she stepped back and nodded. "I'll see you at supper, I suppose. Good day."

"Good day," he said, and turned, snapping his fingers toward Fortescue in some silent command. The dog gave Aurora one last look and then the two walked back up toward the house.

She sighed as she watched them go before she forced herself to put her attention back on her own destination. If Nicholas had briefly wanted the same thing she did, it seemed he was more able to control that desire. But then, he'd always been more capable of walking away. She'd do well to remember that before she lost her faculties and her heart.

From experience she knew she would have a hard time getting them back once she did.

Nicholas pointed Fortescue toward the stairs with the order, "Bed!" The dog gave him a look, the same one he'd been giving since he made the animal walk away from Aurora, but he plodded up the staircase. It was a fifty-fifty chance Fortescue would take to Nicolas's bed rather than his own, but Nicholas didn't have the energy to argue with the eight-stone goliath.

Right now he had something else to do. He made his way through the hallways. Robert's butler, Jenner, had told him that Derrick was in the green parlor, and Nicholas found himself at its entrance. He stepped inside and came to a halt. His friend was not alone. Selina was with him, perched on his knee on the settee, whispering close to his ear. His usually serious friend chuckled low and then leaned up to kiss her.

Nicholas turned his face, and not just because he didn't want to see his sister seduced by her husband. It also made him think about that moment on the estate with Aurora. She'd been standing so close to him, her fingers wrapped around his arm, her face upturned and her gaze foggy with…desire. And despite all he knew, despite all he'd endured because of her…he'd wanted to take that sweet mouth. And then take more.

How he'd found the strength to walk away was not something he entirely understood. But now his mouth tingled with the mere memory.

"Bloody hell," he muttered.

Selina and Derrick started at those words, and both stood up and faced the door. Derrick, at least, had the decency to look a bit chagrined at being caught in such a public display. Selina just smiled at him, as if there was nothing abnormal about such behavior in a public parlor.

"Nicholas," she said.

"Forgive the intrusion," Nicholas said, ducking his head. "I can leave you."

"Nonsense," Selina said with a wink for Derrick. Then she moved around the settee to look more closely at him. Her playful expression fell. "Are you well? You look troubled."

Nicolas looked past her to Derrick. His old friend was also watching him through a hawkish gaze. He stifled a sigh. Why in the world must he always be surrounded by intelligent people who could see through any mask he wore? This was why he kept himself alone so often.

"I'm fine," he lied, and forced a smile for her. "But I did hope I could have a moment with your husband. I have something I need to discuss with him."

Selina wrinkled her brow and glanced back at Derrick. Nicholas could see she was troubled by being left out. There was a bit of fight in her eyes, like she would deny him.

Derrick must have seen it too, for he arched a brow at her and his voice was rougher as he said, "Selina."

Something in her shifted at the way he said her name. Nicholas watched the fight bleed out of her and her gaze light up with something much different. It made the exchange between them on the settee look tame. "Very well," she said. "Come find me after, Derrick."

"You know I will," he said, and smiled as she patted Nicholas's arm and slipped from the room, closing the door behind herself to give them privacy.

"I ruined your fun," Nicholas said, crossing to the sideboard and pouring himself a drink. "My apologies."

"We're married," Derrick said, his tone concerned. "I can have my fun whenever I want. It's a bit early for that, isn't it?"

Nicholas slugged back half the tumbler and shrugged. "Not in the world of the marquess. Don't they get to do anything they want? I'm just practicing. At any rate, I'm sorry if I upset my sister."

"Selina isn't very good with tact," Derrick said softly, but his gaze glittered with what was obviously love for her.

"No, she never has been," Nicholas agreed. "When I first met her, I hardly knew what to do with that free-spirited attitude. I tried to protect it out of her, I think, the first six months we knew each other. But eventually I came to accept it."

Derrick smiled. "She adores you, you know."

"And you adore her." Nicholas stared toward the door where she had departed. "You make her happy, which she deserves more than anyone I've ever known."

Derrick stepped closer. "And it is the great pleasure of my life to love and protect her." He tilted his head. "But that's not why you came to find me. So stop stalling."

"You'll be happy to know you were right," Nicholas said.

Derrick arched a brow. "I'm probably right about a great many things. What specifically are we talking about?"

"Aurora," Nicholas said. "You tried to talk to me last night about Aurora, and I told you some damned fool thing about distance and pretending she wasn't here. You knew I was a fool and I'm telling you that you were correct in that assessment."

Derrick's expression softened. "You saw her again?"

"On a walk with Fortescue. You know that dog tries to protect me against everyone. The first time you came to call, he growled at you from the corner for twenty minutes. And he *knew* you!"

"He's intimidating as hell, yes. I assume he was...not so vigilant when it comes to Aurora?"

"He rolled over on his back and gave her his belly to rub." Nicholas clenched his teeth. "And I understand why. When I was watching her rub his stomach and coo at him, I never wanted to be a dog more."

"It's understandable."

Nicholas grimaced. "Well, a dog's life is fairly charmed."

"Not because of that," Derrick said with a shake of his head. "Don't play games. Lady Lovell is beautiful."

Nicholas sighed. "She is that. Exquisite. Perhaps even more than she was nine years ago, and that is a feat."

Derrick was watching him far too closely. "You may have wanted to try to be strangers, but of course you aren't. It's natural that old feelings might come back to the fore."

"She was everything to me. She…still…is," he whispered, letting his mind ease back to all those years ago. Letting himself feel the love for her that he'd tried to pretend away and hide and crush down. When he let it free, it swelled up in his chest and pushed every other pain and heartbreak away.

It became as large and as powerful as it had ever been. And he knew then that it had never faded. He'd never forced himself to hate her enough to forget it. It was just there, waiting for a moment when she would step into the frame of his life and drag him back to the past.

Derrick let out his breath in a long stream. "I see. Then this goes deeper than desire."

Nicholas nodded slowly. "Yes."

"Obviously, as a friend, this concerns me. I know she hurt you. When she married for a title, when she walked away, all that ripped you to shreds. But you aren't the same boy you were then. You're a man who has endured loss and pain and heartbreak. You're stronger now."

"I don't feel stronger when I look at her," Nicholas scoffed.

"Well, there's only one way to deal with this, then, and that is to face it head on. Address it."

"Yes," Nicholas agreed. "Only I would say it's not the *only* way to deal with it."

Derrick's eyes went wide, and Nicholas could understand why. Others in their company had been braggarts about lovers, but Nicholas had never been one to share his exploits or bring bawdy talk to the table.

"You mean bed her to forget her," Derrick said softly. "Purge the want with action."

Nicholas shrugged. "Crude, I know. But it's all that goes through my head when I see her."

Derrick paced the room a moment before he faced him. "That is…it's a dangerous path, my friend. How many men have claimed this was how they'd forget a woman only to fall deeper in love?"

"Perhaps she wouldn't even have me," Nicholas said. "I have no idea if she feels the same way."

But was that true? After all, he'd thought he'd seen the flicker of desire in her stare that morning when they'd nearly kissed. But then again, he'd never been very good at seeing the truth of her. He'd believed the surface and never been able to scratch it.

Derrick shook his head. "You could have her, I'm certain. I saw the way she looked at you last night. She obviously wants the same thing you're talking about."

Nicholas's stomach clenched. That others could see Aurora's desire for him should have made him feel better. More certain. And yet it didn't. Because the fact that she wanted him made everything that boiled inside of him all the more powerful. After a lifetime spent reining in control over himself so he would never feel like he had when she walked out…he was instantly and powerfully back to the same spot.

Aching for her. Fearing for the future. Uncertain with what to do with all this.

"Fuck," Nicholas muttered. "What am I doing? What the hell am I thinking?"

Derrick crossed the room to him and rested a hand on his upper arm. "Think of this as an opportunity."

"An opportunity to be ripped to shreds all over again?" Nicholas said with a snort of derisive laughter. "Oh good."

"No." Derrick rolled his eyes. "You have unfinished business with this woman, don't you?"

"Yes."

"And this is an *opportunity* to conclude it." Derrick squeezed his arm before he released him. "If you don't manage it here and now, you'll have regrets. So do whatever is right for you. Whether it is face the past or…or the other option."

Nicholas bent his head and sighed, because he knew his friend was right. He also had no idea which option he would pick when it came to how he dealt with Aurora. "I'll think about it."

"Good." Derrick sank back into the settee. "Did your dog really submit to her?"

Nicholas laughed, this time something real as he swept up his abandoned drink and took a place on a chair across from his friend. "Like a spring pup. The woman is practicing witchcraft."

They laughed together and the subject changed, but even as Nicholas relaxed into casual conversation with Derrick, his mind whirled on what to do. Because the next time he found himself alone with Aurora, he had to have an answer to that question.

## CHAPTER 8

Aurora sat in the window seat of the blue parlor, a cup of tea in her hand, overlooking the garden below. She was pretending to take in the green lushness of the summer garden. Pretending to enjoy the loveliness. Except that wasn't what had her attention.

Standing amidst all that beauty was Nicholas. He was with his brothers and Selina's husband, Mr. Huntington, as well as the Duke of Northfield. Fortescue sat at full attention at his side, the dog's amber eyes flitting from one man to another with caution. From time to time, Nicholas would drop his hand and stroke the dog's head gently.

The group was standing close, talking and occasionally laughing. She could almost hear Nicholas's laugh. That rich, deep resonance that tugged at her heart and regions far lower.

It was nice to see him so at ease with the men. She'd been observing him for two days, since their encounter on her walk. He'd avoided her ever since. She hadn't bumped into him alone, nor had more than a polite greeting with him since.

But when she watched, she saw how complicated his relationship with his family was. She saw how much he wanted Northfield to like him. She saw him straddling the world he'd grown up in and the world he was so intent on inhabiting in the future, and the tension between the two was palpable.

Down below, he tensed a fraction and looked up toward the window where she sat. She started and leaned away, hoping he wouldn't see her spying on him. He certainly caught her at it often enough when they were standing across rooms from each other. And when he did look?

Well, he always had the strangest expression, as if he were trying to work out a particularly difficult cipher in the classroom he'd once shared with her and her brother, Thomas. Now looking at the window, he had that same troubled expression on his handsome face until his brother Morgan touched his arm and brought him back to their group.

She let out a breath she hadn't realized she was holding and shook her head. The distance Nicholas kept putting between them made her a fool for continuing to track him. To want him. To dream of him and picture him as she touched herself at night. And yet she kept doing it all.

"There you are."

She started at the voice behind her and turned to find that the Duchess of Roseford had entered the room. Katherine had a bright smile on her face, one of kindness and welcome.

"Were you looking for me?" Aurora asked as she shoved to her feet and nearly tipped her half-empty cup of tea onto the fine rug beneath her feet.

Katherine lunged to help right the cup, and her musical laughter filled the chamber and put Aurora at ease. It seemed in the duchess's nature to do that. It was much appreciated. "I was going to ask you to come have tea with the other ladies. Though it seems you got a head start."

Aurora shifted with a little discomfort. "I wasn't even thinking. But I'll always have room for more tea, I assure you, if you'll still have me."

Katherine took the cup and set it down on the sideboard, then linked arms with Aurora. "I'm pleased to have you. We're in my private drawing room today."

They strolled down the hall together, arm in arm, and Aurora let the worrisome thoughts of Nicholas fade to the background where they were just a light pulse, not a heavy drum. She was so enjoying her time here. She refused to let anything ruin it.

"Are you excited about the ball tonight?" Katherine asked.

Aurora staggered slightly and might have deposited herself on the floor had Katherine not steadied her. Heat flooded her cheeks and she sent a glance to her hostess. "I suppose that answers your question."

Katherine stopped walking and faced her, the kindest expression on her lovely face. "It is natural to be nervous. This is the first ball you'll be attending since…"

Aurora bent her head. "Since I was caught in that brothel, yes. And it's almost the first since the death of my husband just over a year ago. I had a few invitations just after my mourning period ended, but they obviously vanished after I went looking for Imogen." She shifted. "Have you heard anything from your friends in the War Department?"

Katherine's expression was troubled. "I had a letter today, but there are no substantive updates. They continue to search for Imogen and have a few leads."

Aurora fought back the tears that suddenly pricked her eyes. "And here I am getting nervous over a ball while she is enduring God knows what."

Katherine's brow wrinkled. "My dear, you are allowed to be worried or anxious about your own life even as you keep Imogen in your thoughts. We can contain multitudes, you know. And pain is not a competition where somehow none but the person suffering most is allowed."

"Th-thank you."

"You're worried about the ball," Katherine said.

"I'm looking forward to the ball," Aurora corrected. "I did always love to dance. But I'm more worried about the…the attendees."

"The strangers, I hope you mean. No one in our party has been unkind to you."

"Of course the strangers!" Aurora agreed. "I'm very comfortable here. The ladies are very kind, the gentlemen, as well. Even…"

She trailed off, for she didn't think it wise to open up the subject of Nicholas to this woman. Katherine had been very kindly dancing around it. The only attendee who seemed to acknowledge it at all was Nicholas's sister, Selina. She sometimes watched Aurora a bit too closely. Protectively, which he deserved.

"I assure you, my dear, you will be surrounded by friends who will make their full-throated support of you very clear," Katherine said.

"Thank you again." Some of the tension left Aurora's body and she sagged briefly. "I do appreciate your continued kindness, especially after the way my arrival to the party played out."

"Nicholas, you mean," Katherine said softly.

Aurora worried her lip. Well, there was that subject, dragged forward at last. She nodded. "I'm sure you must have many doubts about me, so your acceptance and help is even more appreciated."

"Not doubts," Katherine said. "Questions, perhaps, but never doubts." She sighed, and for a moment her gaze went faraway. "Life is complicated, my dear. Love is more so. And I watch you two at our little party, I see you navigating those complexities."

Aurora bent her head. Sometimes it felt like all she was doing was treading water when it came to Nicholas. "Those waters are… they're very deep, you know."

"But they're manageable, I think. If you work hard enough at it."

Aurora drew back. Was this woman encouraging her when it came to Nicholas? Even when he made it so clear he had mixed emotions about her at best? When their past was so muddy she could scarcely see a foot in front of her?

"I hope you'll find a way," Katherine finished.

"Wh-why?" Aurora whispered.

"Because when he looks at you, it's clear this is not finished," Katherine said. "I know a little about that. You both deserve a period at the end of the sentence of your past. And a new sentence going forward if you'd like it."

The very idea of such a thing was very bewitching, of course. That she and Nicholas could face the past, address whatever had happened between them and even find a way forward. But when she thought of his angry reaction when he first saw her, the way he pulled away if they got too close…she wondered if that was possible. If they had a next sentence, would it only be another goodbye?

"Aurora?" Katherine said.

She jerked as she realized her mind had wandered and she'd been staring off at nothing. "I appreciate your support," she said. "I don't know what will happen in the future, but if there is any hope for me, any hope for Imogen, it will all be because of *your* kindness."

Katherine blushed and shifted as if the comment made her uncomfortable. Then she laughed. "Enough of that. Let's join the others, shall we? And leave the future to the future and the past to the past."

Aurora nodded and followed her friend into the parlor, where they were greeted by the rest of the party. But she had a great deal to think about. And a great deal to hope for, even if she knew that hope could be a dangerous thing.

Nicholas stood in the parlor, a drink in his hand as he looked out over the drive below. It was a busy scene, with carriages arriving and guests of the ball pouring from them. His stomach fluttered a bit with nervousness he didn't often allow himself to feel.

This ball was for him. Robert and Katherine never said it out loud, but it was true. This was a way for him to connect with more of their powerful friends, to make an impression in his bid to be gifted the title. It was a kindness he appreciated more than he could have expressed to his brother, and he needed to hone his focus on taking full advantage of that opportunity.

"Oh, Nicholas!"

He jolted at the voice behind him and turned to find Aurora had just entered the room. His breath caught. She was wearing a green gown that clung to every voluptuous curve he'd ever worshipped from afar. Her breasts made his mouth water, he wanted to grip those hips and tug her against him. Her golden hair was pulled up in a high Greek-style bun with tendrils of curls teasing the line of her jaw. Her pink lips trembled as she took a step closer and her dark eyes swept over him in his formalwear.

"I-I didn't realize you were the only one in the parlor," she whispered, her voice trembling.

He cleared his throat. "I—er…you know me. If I'm on time, I'm late."

She tilted her head back and laughed, and for a moment the world stopped spinning and everything in his being swirled in to only see her. "That was always true," she said. "It must have served you well in the army."

He nodded. "If they'd given medals for it, I would have a chest full."

She smiled, mesmerizing him all over again. Making him think about only her and not the plans he'd been making for his night when she'd walked into the room. And making him think about what he'd talked to Derrick about a few days before.

Resolve the past. Or give in to the desire. He still didn't know the right answer, but he had a chance here and he had to take it.

"Aurora," he began, taking a long step across the room toward her.

Her gaze lit up, desire and fear and warmth all at once. "Yes?"

Before he could say anything more, though, Morgan and Lizzie came through the door together, laughing and talking, and were swiftly followed by the Duke and Duchess of Northfield. Nicholas pursed his lips at the interruption, even as he tried to force a polite greeting. Yet another opportunity stolen.

Aurora shrugged slightly in his direction, as if to tell him that they'd tried. Then she began to compliment Lizzie on her beautiful gown. The moment passed, and he wondered when the next would come. Could he manage it differently so he could actually have what he wanted, figure out what he needed, and move the hell on at last?

Within an hour of the ball starting, Nicholas was looking for a way out. He certainly wasn't in the mood to participate in frivolity and small talk, not when his gaze kept shifting across the room toward Aurora. It was difficult to tell how her night was going. She smiled and chatted with their friends, but in the moments when she was alone, she looked exhausted. A reflection of his own feelings, truth be told.

He'd always watched this world from a comfortable distance. As a child, a servant's son, he'd peeked in through the curtain. Later, when he was dragged to things by friends who had a higher place in the world, he'd stood on the edges. But tonight he was on full display, the center of attention thanks to Robert's actions. People approached him, talked to him. Ladies watched him. He had no idea if that was a positive or negative, but it was happening and it was very disconcerting.

"…don't you think, Mr. Gillingham?"

Nicholas blinked and forced his attention back to his companion. He was currently standing with a viscount whose name he had promptly forgotten the moment the man started droning on about his vast wealth and holdings. Was it Stephenson? Sweetington? Something with an S, at any rate.

"I…yes," Nicholas said. "I agree."

He found it was easier to play along than to try to figure out what the real topic was. And the answer seemed to make the man happy, for he grinned. "I had my hesitations about you, I admit. A title should be a birthright, I've always said."

Nicholas's jaw began to tighten and he gripped his cane until his knuckles went white. "I'm sure you're not the only one."

"But talking to you, I'm sure you'll make an excellent addition to the Upper Ten Thousand."

Nicholas forced a smile, but felt no joy. He supposed he should. Every time a man of title supported his cause, it created another voice to add to the chorus of those who said he should be marquess. It would all filter back to those in charge of those decisions. But in this moment, staring at the grinning face of the man at his side, Nicholas found himself questioning the future he'd wanted.

A lifetime making chitchat with people like this? Of agreeing to God knew what awful statement just to create a sense of camaraderie with a man who wasn't fit to shine the boots of those Nicholas had fought beside years ago?

Not that there weren't decent and good men in their upper ranks. Northfield had proven himself of great distinction and decency in the few days Nicholas had known him. And Morgan talked often about his employer, the Duke of Brighthollow, as a man one could have faith in. If Nicholas could call those kinds of men friends, he would be proud.

But this wasn't pride. This was...*bootlicking*. And his stomach turned at it.

"It was a great pleasure to meet you, my lord," Nicholas said with a deferential nod. "However, I think I ought to..."

"Check on that rascal of a brother of yours?" the viscount said with a chuckle. "Best do it or he might find himself on the outs with his duchess." He motioned to the dancefloor, and Nicholas turned.

Robert was dancing with Aurora. His brother guided her around the dancefloor and they were obviously having an animated and pleasant conversation.

"Why should Roseford not dance with one of his guests?" he asked, mesmerized by how right this image was.

He felt no jealousy that Aurora danced with Robert. His brother's reputation was an old one. He clearly loved Katherine. Nicholas was actually very pleased with the fact that Robert would give Aurora some of his shine when she needed it by sharing the floor with her. It made him soften toward his brother in a way he hadn't allowed before.

"*That* guest?" the viscount said with a shake of his head. "I mean, you must have heard the rumors about what Lady Lovell was doing and where not so long ago."

Nicholas jerked his head toward the man, but the viscount continued, apparently oblivious to the peril of those cold, cruel words. "It's positively scandalous. *Why* she would be invited here amongst good company does beg the question: is your brother as tame as he has pretended to be these last few years?"

Rage rolled up in Nicholas. The kind that made everything red and raw around him. The kind that made him dangerous, despite his injuries and the future he was trying to build. It took every bit of his control to stop himself from swinging on this man. Instead, he gritted his teeth together and said, "I would not disparage the lady, my lord. That isn't a good idea."

The viscount's gaze lit up in surprise and then he grinned. "Oh, I see. Were you one of the *lady's* friends at the bawdy house? Honestly, Gillingham, you ought to be careful about where you're seen. You will soon be able to afford far better brothels and hells than that sad place."

Nicholas edged up closer and now he towered above the man. "I will not say it again, my lord. Shut your mouth when it comes to Lady Lovell."

His companion's expression flickered with real fear and then his gaze narrowed. "Watch yourself, boy," he said softly. "You can threaten with all the base physical strength that you wish to, but I'm the one with real power."

He said nothing else, but turned on his heel and marched off into the crowd. Nicholas flexed his hands in and out of fists at his side as he tried to calm the raging beat of his heart. So much for making a good impression. He was certain Robert would be annoyed.

And yet, despite that, Nicholas found he didn't give a damn. He could have just made some dismissive remark regarding Aurora and pushed the subject off, implying agreement when he certainly didn't agree.

But he hadn't. Even if he didn't understand her reasons for going to the Cat's Companion, he would never disparage her for them. So he'd remained true to his own values. His own heart. He hadn't traded it for the title. "I think I can live with myself for that," he muttered.

He watched as Aurora gave a playful curtsey to Robert as the song ended. They were laughing as they left the floor and joined Katherine and the Duchess of Northfield.

At least Aurora didn't know that someone had spoken of her in such an ungentlemanly way. But then again, perhaps she did. She'd come to the countryside to be sheltered by the friendships Katherine offered her access to. The rumors were why she'd been driven away from London.

She'd always been such a sensitive person. She'd cried over broken wings and sentimental sonatas and letters from friends. He'd always loved that about her, that so much moved her so deeply. And he hated that right now she had to be in so much pain over what was being whispered about her.

As the next song began, Robert leaned close to say something to Katherine. She laughed and the two swept off to the dancefloor together. The Duchess of Northfield touched Aurora's arm, smiling before she, too, glided off to find her husband across the room.

Aurora's expression fell as she was left alone. Her head dipped slightly and he could almost hear the tiny sigh that was surely leaving her lips right now. He found himself moving, though he didn't remember deciding to do so. About halfway across the room, she looked up and saw him. Her chocolate eyes widened, her spine straightened and her hands shook as he reached her.

"Good evening, my lady," he said.

She swallowed, the action working her lovely throat. How he wanted to feel her do that beneath his lips. "Good evening again," she gasped out. They stood together for a moment, watching the couples bounce in a lively scotch reel. "Are you enjoying yourself tonight?"

His mind went to the viscount who now stood on the other side of the room, talking to some other titled fop. The two men cast their gazes toward him and Aurora, and he had the strongest urge to put himself in front of her as a barrier to their stares.

"It's tolerable," he said softly.

She smiled up at him. "*Tolerable?* Oh, do wax poetic, Mr. Gillingham."

He couldn't help but laugh at her teasing, and for a moment the tension of the night bled away a fraction. "I admit, I'm not accustomed to such gatherings," he said. "Obviously I attended assemblies and the like, but this is different. There are so many people who could be…I suppose they could be *important* to my future."

She nodded solemnly. "Yes. I assume that was the purpose of the ball, to introduce you to some of that Society."

"Yes." He sighed. "I've probably made a muck of it."

She pivoted and now all her focused attention was on him. "How so?"

He could scarcely breathe as he stared down at her, all earnest questions and sweet floral perfume. Good God, but time had been kind to her. And he longed for her just as he'd always longed for her.

"Nicholas?" she asked.

He shook his head, pushing aside the thoughts that kept intruding whenever she was too close. Or too far. Or too friendly. Or too reserved. Whenever she was…her.

"Small talk and agreeable conversation is what is required in these situations," he said with a shrug. "And I am not particularly good at either."

"This conversation is very agreeable," she said with another smile. "Perhaps you had the wrong companions." She leaned a little closer. "I saw you with Lord Sweeting a moment ago."

"Sweeting!" Nicholas gasped out. "That is his name. I forgot it immediately."

She giggled into her palm. "Lucky you. He's most disagreeable. He was once a friend to my—"

She cut herself off and he frowned. She was going to say *husband*. Another viscount. One Nicholas had hated almost as much as Sweeting.

"Well, I agree the viscount is not someone I'd want to count as a friend. I suppose I can't now. I offended him."

Her eyes went wide. "How so?"

He stared at her, unwilling to tell her what Sweeting had said about her and make her more uncomfortable. But she was waiting for an answer, waiting for him to fill the silence between them.

"Would you dance with me, Lady Lovell?"

She caught her breath at the question and her gaze flitted down his body. Toward his cane.

He shook his head. "I will balance myself by holding you, if that is your worry."

"That was never my worry, Nicholas."

# CHAPTER 9

As the swell of the waltz filled the air, Aurora stepped out onto the dancefloor with Nicholas. They'd only danced together once all those years ago, at a ball at her late father's house. She'd found Nicholas watching on the terrace and taken his hand. They'd danced together in the moonlight and everything in the world had seemed possible.

Now he placed a hand on her hip and she felt the pressure of every finger through her gown. He stared down at her, eyes locked with hers, as they turned into the first pivot. He was not as smooth as he had been that long ago night. His injury was evident. But none of it mattered.

When he touched her, when he held her, nothing mattered but him. That, if nothing else, hadn't changed.

They spun around the edge of the dancefloor once more, and Aurora caught a glimpse of Lord Sweeting. Nicholas said he'd offended the man, but had refused to say why. Now Sweeting smirked at her, and she caught her breath.

Could it have been *her* they were discussing so seriously a short time before? God, she hoped not. Nicholas already thought so low of her. The tales of her exploits at the Cat's Companion certainly wouldn't make that better. Unless…

She looked up at him.

Was *that* why he'd been so angry with her on the drive? Did he know about her being caught at the brothel all those weeks ago? Did he judge her as the rest judged her, for what they saw as a fall from grace?

Her heart sank at the thought.

"You know, you look very troubled for a woman dancing a waltz. Am I so unpracticed?" he asked, smiling at her.

The smile filtered her worries away for a moment, and she laughed. "Quite the contrary. You are still a fine dancer." She worried her lip. "Does it…hurt?"

The smile faded a fraction. "A bit here and there. I've become accustomed to the pain, in truth. It's far better than it was just after the injuries." He shook his head. "I'm not the same, but I'm still…whole."

"Of course you are," Aurora said, and meant it. "Anyone who thinks otherwise is a fool."

The music had begun to fade, and she realized soon he would release her. They wouldn't dance together again tonight—it would cause too many whispers if they did. So this was it. Her last moments of touching this man until the next accidental graze of fingertips or brush as they passed each other in hallway.

She tried to memorize it all as she stared up into that handsome face. The warmth of his presence against her, the smell of leather and pine that made her entire body feel tingly, the weight of his fingers and the sure way he guided her as they moved. She drew in a long breath and tried to paint a portrait of this moment in her mind.

His lips parted, his pupils dilated, and suddenly it was only them. Forever them.

"Aurora," he whispered, his voice rough.

"Yes," she answered, shocked she could find the word, the breath to say it.

"We need to talk, don't we?" he asked.

Her heart rate elevated. So here it was. The real conversation they'd both been trying to avoid. The one Katherine had urged her to have. The one that terrified her.

"Yes," she said. "I think we do, even if we tried to pretend we wouldn't be forced to do so."

The music ended, and Nicholas stepped back. He bowed slightly and took her hand, guiding her back to the edge of the dancefloor, where he took the cane a servant had been holding since the dance began. Once the footman had departed, Nicholas looked at her again.

"Meet me in the library?" he asked. "In half an hour? No one will be there with the party going on. It should be...private enough for this."

Her entire body felt shaky, like she might pitch over at any moment, but she managed to nod. "I will."

His mouth tightened and then he stepped away. "Until then."

She was left to watch him depart, crossing the room toward his brothers and sister, who were now gathered together. It was evident they had been watching her dance with Nicholas. They were all trying to look innocent, but couldn't hide their interest.

She had no idea what they would say to him. And if their warnings would change the tenor of the conversation she would have with him shortly.

She pivoted away from the seeking eyes, and staggered out of the ballroom and onto the terrace. She needed air and to collect herself before she saw Nicholas next, before she had her questions answered and heard his.

She rested her palms on the cool, rough stone wall of the parapet and stared up at the sparkling stars. She breathed in the night air and felt her anxiety ratchet down step by step. She was almost calm again when she heard the terrace door open. She peeked over her shoulder to find Lord Sweeting coming toward her.

She flinched. This was the last person she wanted to see right now.

"My lady," he said as he stepped up beside her and placed his hands too close to hers on the wall's edge. "A beautiful night, don't you think?"

She cleared her throat. "It is," she agreed. "I didn't expect to see you here, my lord. It's been a long time."

"Too long," Sweeting said, and turned to lean back on the wall's edge. He looked her up and down. "I think I last saw you at Lovell's funeral."

"Are you here to offer further condolences?" she asked, edging away.

He followed the movement, disregarding her need for extra space. "I could find ways to offer consolation, I'm sure. Is there a price?"

She pursed her lips. "Have you been drinking, my lord? You forget yourself."

He shrugged. "I drank a little," he admitted. "Watching you across the room, thinking about the fact that you were found in a brothel of the worst kind not two weeks ago. And yet you're here."

She tensed her jaw. "I will not discuss this with you, Sweeting. Good evening."

She moved to step away, but his hand came out and caught her wrist. She flashed briefly to Roddenbury and how he'd done the same at the Cat's Companion. And just like that night, she had no protector coming.

"If you're hunting for a lover, Aurora, I'm sure there will be many who'll oblige. Make you their mistress, pay for access to that voluptuous body of yours."

"Stop it," she whispered, and tugged at her arm. He refused to release her. "I'll scream."

"And cause more trouble for yourself? I don't think so." He

leaned in then, his wet mouth coming toward hers. She leaned back, tugging her arm helplessly.

"Let her go."

They both froze at the deep voice that came from the door. She looked toward her savior and flushed hot when she saw it was the Duke of Roseford, himself, staring at them. Nicholas's brother, a man who certainly must already judge her, despite his wife's kindness.

Sweeting let go of her arm and she backed away toward Roseford, putting as much distance between them as she could. When she reached Roseford's side, the duke subtly edged in front of her, blocking her from Sweeting even further.

"I have no idea why you'd invite such a harlot," Sweeting said, though his hands were shaking and he would not meet the duke's eyes.

Roseford's nostrils flared. "How dare you speak to my guest that way? Get out of my house."

"Your Grace," Aurora whispered. "I don't want to cause any trouble—"

"You didn't, my dear. He did."

"Want her for your own, do you?" Sweeting said with a nervous chuckle.

Roseford took a long step forward. "Watch yourself."

Now Sweeting shifted, his gaze darting toward the doors the led into the ballroom again. "You cannot take her side. You *need* me or you wouldn't have invited me here. Your brother's ambitions, his hopes of being gifted a title he hasn't earned through blood right…I can raise my voice against all that."

Roseford's gaze narrowed. "Threaten my brother again, Sweeting. See how that ends for you."

Sweeting shook his head. "You know I could go back inside and—"

Roseford cut him off by taking a long step forward. He caught Sweeting by the ear like he was a recalcitrant youth rather than a viscount well past his majority. He cast Aurora a quick glance. "Please return to the party and enjoy yourself, my lady. I'm just going to take care of this refuse and I'll be back in soon."

She blinked at the sting of humiliated tears as Roseford dragged the viscount away from her, toward another entrance back into the house that would not require a scene in the ballroom. She pivoted away, trying not to hear Sweeting's repeated slurs against her as he was hauled away.

She reentered the ballroom, hands shaking and heart throbbing. All around her, the voices were too loud, the smiles too wide, the gazes too focused. She might cry and she didn't want the world to see that and judge her. Just like Roddenbury had judged her at the brothel, like Sweeting had judged her tonight. Like Nicholas clearly judged her even if he hadn't the dangerous, cruel bent the other two men shared.

If anything, the encounter had proven to her one important fact: she would *never* recover from the rumors that had been spread about her. No matter how much friendship the duchesses offered her, no matter how she proved herself a lady in the eyes of those who apparently mattered, in the end, she was spoiled, ruined, and there was no going back.

She staggered through the room, trying to maintain a false smile with every step. She would go to the library. That was where she'd promised to meet Nicholas shortly. If she got there early, she could try to calm herself once again. Try to find a way to pretend that none of this mattered. That she was not affected by the lies and the past and the pain she'd endured in the years since she last touched her lips to his.

She had to. Because she didn't know that he would allow her anything else.

Nicholas trailed behind Aurora as she stumbled through the hallways toward the library. He'd watched her come in from the terrace, her smile false and her steps ragged. He'd watched her pretend to be fine as she escaped the room, even going so far as to smile and say good evening to those who acknowledged her. To anyone who didn't know her, she might have looked well.

But *he* knew her, even after all these years and all that had kept them apart. She still worried her lip the same way when she was afraid. She still stooped her shoulders slightly when she was carrying the weight of the world. He knew her pain and the sudden dread that haunted every step she took.

He shouldn't have followed her from the room. They'd intended to leave separately, not be too obvious to the eyes of his family and anyone else keeping track. But how could he not follow her when she looked so forlorn? He couldn't help himself. Or at least he *hadn't*.

Still, she hadn't noticed him following in her distraction. She turned the corner into the library, and he hesitated. After their agreement to meet here, he'd pondered all the questions he'd wanted to ask her. All the things he'd wanted to say. But now all he could think about was the broken expression on her face and he wanted so desperately to comfort her.

Which meant he should walk away. He was compromised, after all. Weak to whatever was happening between them, whatever remained of what they'd been to each other all those years ago. The very best thing he could do was retreat, not put himself in her path.

But he couldn't do that, either. Walking away now was impossible, so he drew in a ragged breath and entered the library behind her. She was standing at the fireplace, one hand gripping the mantel above her, the other pressed to her forehead. She was drawing in breath, short, rapid gasps, trying not to cry, and his heart broke to see her like this.

"Aurora," he whispered as he shut the door behind them.

She turned her attention toward him. She refused to meet his stare and wiped at the tears that sparkled in the corners of those warm, brown eyes.

"I—you weren't meant to come for a few more minutes," she said. "I was trying to gather myself so you wouldn't have to see. I don't want your pity, or for you to think I'm trying to manipulate you."

He shook his head. So *that* was what he'd created between them since her arrival here. Because of his outburst on the drive, because of their agreement to pretend they shared no past, because he pulled away from her whenever they edged too close. All those things made her feel she had to hide herself, hide her feelings, hide from him.

Perhaps he should have let that be. Perhaps it was for the best. But he couldn't help himself, not anymore. His hands shook as he reached behind himself and carefully locked the door. Her eyes went wide at that inappropriate act. Even wider as she tracked him when he moved toward her, slow step by slow step.

"Aurora," he whispered, his voice rough with the desire he felt and the emotions he couldn't control. "There are *many* things I feel when I look at you, but none of them are pity. And there are many things I want and need to say, but none of them is an accusation. I don't know what happened out on the terrace that made you so upset, but the only reason I followed you early was because I felt an uncontrollable desire to…to comfort you. Even if it isn't my place, even if it makes me a fool."

She was staring at him, eyes wide and filling with renewed tears. Her throat worked as she swallowed hard, and then she said, "The only person in the world that I would want comfort from is you, even though it's equally wrong."

He had almost reached her, and now he took the last step that separated them. He caught her hand, smoothing his thumb along the silky fabric of her gloves as he drew her even closer. A hair's breadth apart, and then less as he wrapped his arms around her.

"Do you know how long I've waited to do this?" he whispered.

He didn't allow her to answer. He dropped his mouth to hers, and nothing else mattered as he kissed her.

Aurora had warmed herself with memories of Nicholas's kiss for years, but now that he was doing it this…this was something far better.

His lips were firm and warm as he dropped them to hers. For a moment they just stood there, mouths touching lightly, his arms so strong around her, and time stopped. They might have stood there for a day or a week or a year—none of it mattered. This was happening and she wanted it more than she'd ever wanted anything in her life.

At last she shivered, he opened his mouth, and suddenly the gentle brushing of lips transformed into something else.

His tongue pushed into her and she welcomed him, lifting to get closer as they sank into each other at long last. They moaned together, the sound merging in the quiet of the library. She drank him in, marking how he tasted faintly of whisky and mint and his favorite chocolate and everything good in the world.

The world that was now spinning out of control around her. She gripped her hands into fists against his chest, clinging to the fabric of his jacket for purchase in the stormy seas of desire.

He grunted and one of his hands that had been cupping her back moved lower. He traced a path down her spine with the back of his fingers, and she shivered with the feather-light touch. His hand came around to cup her hip, heavy against the curve that had been made for him to grip. He did so and tugged her even closer.

"Please," she whispered against his mouth.

He groaned again, his fingers digging harder against her. They staggered together, hitting the bookshelf with a thud. He leaned there, caging her in and deepened the kiss even further.

Memory hadn't been enough. She recognized that in this moment. Memory had been sweet and gentle, an inexperienced boy with a shy girl all wrapped up in love and hope and plans that never came to fruition. It had been a desire of something they didn't yet fully understand.

Nine years had changed them both. Now he kissed her with purpose, with passion, with a decade of life that had made him a man. And she returned that kiss with the perfect knowledge of what could happen next. What she *wanted* to happen to next.

It was all inevitable, perhaps.

He leaned up closer, pressing her harder into the shelf. She felt the hardness of his cock against her belly and keened softly as she ground against him out of instinct. He swore into her mouth, a sound that resonated through her entire being. He broke their lips, but remained pressed to her, hard against soft as he looked down into her eyes, her soul, all the way through her.

"Aurora," he panted.

She managed to extract her hand from where it was wedged between them and lifted her fingers to his lips. "Please don't tell me you can't or you won't or we shouldn't," she whispered, far braver than she felt as she stripped herself down in front of him emotionally. She wanted to do it physically. She *needed* it.

"All those things are true, though," he said, but he leaned in, bypassing her hand as he brushed the tip of his nose along the side of hers, his warm breath tickling her lips.

"If all those things are true, then why aren't you stepping away?" she asked, dragging her fingers down his harsh jawline.

"Because I can't," he admitted with a sad smile. "I could *never* resist you."

She would argue that point, but not right now. Not in this moment when she was so close to getting what she needed.

"Then *don't* resist me." A blush turned her cheeks to fire. Just because she knew what she wanted didn't mean she was accustomed to the request she was about to make. It felt like lead in her throat. "I'm—I'm offering myself to you."

His eyes went wide. "You mean—"

"Yes!" she said. "And I see those protests back in your eyes. Some kind of gentlemanly refusal you think you should make, but I'm a widow, Nicholas. You can't ruin me. I don't have a guardian who will rush in and call you out. My father is dead, my brother doesn't treat me like a child. I know what I want. So take me upstairs to your bedchamber, and let's stop pretending that what we wanted all those years ago doesn't still hang between us, made worse by the fact that we can each imagine just how good it will be."

For a moment she thought he might refuse. There was a flicker of concern on his face, a cataloguing of all the reasons why this would be a very bad idea. So she decided to tip the scales in her favor, however unfair it might be. She lifted up on her tiptoes and brushed her lips to his once more.

"Please, Nicholas," she whispered. "Please give me what I've dreamt, imagined, fantasized about for so long."

His jaw flexed, his pupils dilated, and then, without a word, he caught her hand and tugged her toward the door, toward his room, toward the future that had been stolen from them so many years ago.

# CHAPTER 10

Nicholas opened the door to his chamber, and before he even guided her inside, his mouth was back on Aurora's. He couldn't help it. It was as he'd always feared, really. Once he started touching her, he was never going to stop, and everything that needed to be said and confronted was forgotten. Delayed? Forgiven like a fool?

Right now he didn't give a damn. She made a soft sound of pleasure against his lips as he kicked the door shut behind them. His cane hit the floor with a clatter and he gripped her hips to balance himself as they backed across the room toward his bed.

And nearly tripped over his dog. Fortescue was curled up at the foot of said bed, watching the two of them through a slightly annoyed and sleepy gaze.

"Christ, dog," Nicholas said, pointing toward the adjoining room. "Bed."

Fortescue grumbled as he got up, stretched his back languidly and then padded from the room with just one last look toward Aurora, as if to ask for her help managing Nicholas. He shot her an apologetic glance and then followed the dog, shutting the door behind him to give them privacy once more.

As he pivoted back, he couldn't help but smile at Aurora's sympathetic gaze toward the place where Fortescue had been lying. "I feel bad for him having to get up," she said.

He shook his head. "He has a very nice bed of his own in the dressing room," he explained. "And a giant bone the cook was kind enough to share after that roast yesterday."

That seemed to appease her, for she nodded. "Then he'll be happy. I feel a little better."

He eased back across the room to her, slowly, both to adjust to not having his cane and also because he needed to take his time before this exploded out of control. "Aurora, do you really want to talk about my dog right now?"

She shook her head. "No," she whispered, and reached for him, drawing him back to her arms, to her lips, where he drowned all over again, only this time slower. With less desperation.

He supposed he'd have to find the dog another, even better bone as thanks for that. He angled his head, deepening the kiss, slowing it, at least for a short time. He wanted to savor every moment of this.

He never wanted it to end.

But desire was an insistent mistress, and eventually the pulse of it drove him harder. Faster. And he wasn't alone in that, apparently. She pulled away after what seemed like forever, her breath short, her dark eyes almost black with desire. Her shaking fingers found his cravat and she struggled to loosen it. He dug his fingers into her hair, sending pins to dance across the floor. Blonde, perfumed silk fell around them, wrapping around his fingers, covering her shoulders. He breathed it in, breathed *her* in, and marveled at how much more beautiful she was with her hair down. He'd never seen her like this before, at least not since she was a very little girl. They'd never come this far.

She finally got the cravat loose and unwound it, then tossed it over her shoulder. She lifted into him, demanding another kiss as she shoved at his jacket, pulled at his buttons. She was desperate, she was hungry, and he loved it. But he still pulled away.

"Please don't rush this," he said.

That brought her up short and she lowered her hands. "I…it's just that we've waited so long. I've wanted nothing but this for so bloody long."

He drew a shaky breath. "You do test a man."

That elicited a smile from her lips. "I'm *trying* to test you."

"So I see." He caught her hands and gently tugged her glove away before he lifted her palm to his lips and kissed it. She shivered as he sucked gently, harder, licked as he turned her hand over and pressed another kiss to her knuckles. "But because I've waited so long, too, I don't want this to be some fast, hard fucking."

She didn't flinch at the crude word. "What do you want it to be?"

*Forever* was the word that flickered through his mind. Forever was the most dangerous word of all when it came to her. He pushed it away.

"I want it to be worth the wait. I want it to be everything."

She nodded slowly as she threaded the fingers of her bare hand into his. "It already will be."

He tended to believe her. He dug his fingers into her hair, tilting her head back, and kissed her again. This time he went slowly, tracing her lips, sucking her tongue, devouring her like he would his last meal. She gave a full-body shudder and he smiled against her. At least he knew how to make this night good.

He wanted it to be, just in case he never had another with her.

"Turn around," he said as he broke the kiss.

Her full lower lip pouted out, but she did as he directed, putting her back to him. He pushed her hair aside, forward over one shoulder, then leaned in to kiss the long expanse of neck he had exposed. As he sucked and licked, he unfastened the first button of her gown. She arched her backside against him, rubbing wickedly and making his vision blur for a moment from the pleasure that arced from his cock through his entire bloodstream.

He unfastened the second button, determined not to let her rush even though the driving pulse inside of him screamed *claim, fuck, mine!* over and over until it was like a drumbeat in his skull. But he was a man of discipline, and he called on every bit of that to keep himself from rending the delicate silk of her gown in two.

He unfastened the last two buttons and parted the dress. Her chemise was a creamy color, edged in lace, and he smoothed his fingers across the fine silk before he leaned in and kissed the place where her skin and the lace met.

"Please," she whimpered again, and her backside ground back again. "Please, please, please."

"You can't rush me," he declared with a laugh.

"I could," she said with a wicked chuckle of her own. "But I won't. No matter how much I want to."

He pushed the gown forward and she slid it away from her arms and pushed it to the floor before she turned around and faced him. He stopped moving, stopping breathing and just *stared* at her. She was glorious, just as he'd always imagined she would be. Her chemise was short, just skimming the top of her voluptuous thighs, and she wore no drawers. She was all curves and softness and so many places to touch and worship, he almost couldn't decide where to begin.

She swallowed hard as she reached up and slid one chemise strap down her arm, then the other. She tugged it away, wiggling it past the full swell of her hips and letting it crumple to the floor at her feet.

She was naked. Aurora was naked before him, trembling. Or was it he who was trembling to be standing before this goddess he'd never thought to see again? But here he was, standing before her with the opportunity to worship. He stepped forward and extended a hand, letting his fingers glide across her collarbone, down over one heavy breast. She tensed as he touched her there, her breath shortening. He let his hand move lower, over the soft swell of her stomach, the rounded curve of her hip, the soft flesh of her thigh.

"You are more beautiful than I ever allowed myself to imagine," he murmured. "And I imagined, Aurora. Every day, every night, for nine unbearable years."

She shifted, her gaze fluttering over his face. "I'm here now. You don't have to imagine anymore. And I'm yours, even if it ends up only being for tonight. You can have everything you ever dreamed of. Just give me what I dreamed of, too."

"I can do that," he whispered, then wrapped his arm around her waist and drew her against him. The feel of her full, naked curves pressed to his still-clothed body was amazing, and he dropped his mouth to hers. Their tongues warred, she lifted against him. The only sound in the room was the desperate panting breath as they gasped for air between kisses.

He pushed her back, back to his bed, and finally found the strength to part from her as he pointed to his pillows. "Please," he said softly.

She smiled and settled herself onto his pillows, met his eyes and opened her legs in invitation. His vision blurred a little with the power of what was happening. He felt dizzy with it, drugged, like this was all some amazing dream. Only it was real. When he pinched himself, it was real.

He crawled up on the bed, ignoring the twinges of pain that action always caused. Nothing mattered but her right now. Nothing but covering her with his body, settling in to the v of her thighs and grinding up so that his still-clothed cock bumped her sex.

She gasped and her hands gripped his shoulders tighter. He responded by grinding into her again, again, again. She dipped her head back and he nipped at her exposed throat, loving the soft sounds of pleasure he elicited.

But this wasn't enough. This was an appetizer and he was ready for a meal, so he slid down that lovely throat, tasting her skin as he eased his way lower and lower. She arched into him as he stroked his palm over one full breast, squeezing gently, strumming his thumb over the nipple.

She watched him touch her, her lips slightly parted, her tongue darted out to wet them. The action sent a jolt of heat sluicing through his balls, shocking through his system. Animal desires, the ones he could normally control when he did this, overwhelmed his senses, and he ducked his head and licked the nipple he'd been pinching.

Her fingers dug into his hair, her voice ragged as she called out his name. He continued to suck, lifting her breast, puckering her nipple with his tongue before he switched to the opposite side and repeated it all again. She was writhing beneath him then, her hips bumping him and her head lolled against the pillows.

It was remarkable to bring her pleasure, especially since she was so responsive to it. He grazed her skin and she jolted, he sucked her and she moaned. She was a glorious celebration of decadent pleasure and he wanted to feast on her forever.

He slid lower on the bed, kissing the softness of her belly, his fingers digging into the flesh of her hips. He loved all her curves, always had, and even more so now that they were spread out on display before him. He intended to worship them and her.

He placed a hand on each thigh and pushed, opening her wider as he settled between her legs. Her sex glistened and he breathed in the musky scent of her, memorizing every nuance of it as he spread her outer lips open and stroked a thumb along the slick pink entrance.

She was shaking as she stared down at him, and he lifted his gaze to hers, watching as he pressed his mouth to her trembling sex at last.

Aurora had read about such things. She and Imogen had discussed this act in detail, because her friend had experienced it and Aurora had not. But she'd never imagined the intense sensation of it, not perfectly.

Nicholas's whiskers kissed her thighs, her sex, as he licked her in one long, languid stroke. She jolted with pleasure, the kind that had been building and building since he first kissed her in the library. The kind that only burned hotter now that he'd moved that kiss decidedly southward.

He licked again, and this time he swirled his tongue around her clitoris. She gripped the coverlet in both hands, grinding against him helplessly and moaning in an incoherent plea for more. He did not disappoint. With a low, feral chuckle, he proceeded with gusto, holding her open as he licked and sucked the length of her sex over and over again. He painted her with pleasure, stimulated every sensitive nerve ending as she writhed in hopeless, helpless bliss beneath him.

Just as she thought it couldn't get better, that these endless ripples of sensation were everything, he got serious. He focused, putting all his attention on her clitoris. He sucked, pulsing endlessly, tapping her with the tip of his tongue.

Orgasm had always come with a great deal of effort for Aurora. She'd only found it a few times with her late husband, more often with her own hand. But it was something she had to reach for, strive for, work for.

This orgasm hit her like a wave crashing over the shore: effortless and unexpected. It went on and on, rising and rising as he continued to torment her with this mouth. She bucked against him, muffling her screams of pleasure against her palm so she wouldn't bring the house down around them.

Finally, he seemed to have had enough of riding the waves of her pleasure. He lifted his head, looking up at her, beard slick and lips tilted in a decidedly wicked smile.

"Just as delicious as I always imagined," he said. "Want to taste?"

Her body jolted with the question and she nodded, unable to form coherent words when she was still tingling from head to toe. He crawled up the length of her body, caging her in with his arms, then bent his head and kissed her gently, deeply.

She tasted herself on his lips, just as he'd offered. Sweet and earthy, and the knowledge that she was doing something so wicked made her want to do more and more and more with this man. He seemed to have the same thought, for he reached between them and began to wrestle with the placard on his trouser front.

She pulled away from his mouth and blinked up at him.

"You aren't going to take off the rest?" she whispered.

The wicked, lazy pleasure on his face faded at the question and his gaze darted from hers. "I'm not sure you'd like what you'd see."

"How could that be?" she asked. "I have waited so long to be with you like this. My fantasies never involved being naked while you only freed your…your cock—"

He rolled away from her and frowned. "Those fantasies…did they involve scars?"

She caught her breath. "Is that what you're worried about? That I'll see your scars?"

He didn't answer, but his gaze slid away from hers and said what he couldn't. She shifted to her side, propping herself up on one elbow as she placed her hand on his chest. Even through the layers of his jacket and linen shirt, she could feel his heart pounding.

"Has no one seen them since your injury?" she asked.

His jaw flexed. "None but my doctors," he said. "If you're asking about lovers, I have been with no one since the war."

Her eyes went wide. It had been over two years since his injuries. He had been celibate that long? That made his pleasure even more paramount to her. Almost like he was an innocent and she the one to pleasure him. Perhaps it wasn't for the first time, but the first time in a long time.

"I want to see you, Nicholas," she whispered as she slowly rolled, pushing him onto his back, straddling him. "I want to see *all* of you. Please."

She leaned down as she spoke, her hair coming around them like a curtain. She kissed him and he let out a ragged sigh against her lips as his fingers dug into her hair once more. The slide of them against her scalp made her already wet sex even slicker with need. And she knew if she just wrested his cock free, she could have what she wanted in an instant.

But that wasn't how this was going to end. If this could possibly be their only night together, and she knew full well that it could be…it was going to be everything. She was going to make sure of it.

He struggled to sit up, their mouths still merged, and tugged at his jacket. He freed himself and it fell back beneath them. His arms came around her, tucking her closer as their kiss deepened. She ground down on him, feeling the hard length of him under all those awful clothes. She wanted it, she wanted him, she wanted everything.

With effort, she broke the kiss and scooted from his arms. He said something under his breath as she did it, she thought a curse. She laughed as she pushed to her knees next to him.

"May I help you remove all this?" she asked.

He let out a low sigh. "Maybe with the boots."

"I can do that."

She slid downward and went to work on the boots. Above her, he pulled the shirt free and tugged it over his head. Her fingers fumbled at the sight of him, half naked.

He was…spectacular. A visual feast of hard muscle peppered with light chest hair. She pulled his first boot off and tossed it on to the floor, then the other. Now that he was free, she pivoted and licked her lips.

"I don't even know where to start," she whispered.

He didn't smile. He just pushed his hands behind himself so he could support his weight by leaning back. "It's worse below the waist," he said.

She wrinkled her brow, and then she realized he was talking about the scars. She'd been so mesmerized by the man as a whole, she hadn't noticed them. But there they were. A scar along the front of his shoulder, bright against his skin. Another on his ribcage, set amongst the most fascinating lines of muscle.

A third on his stomach. A burn scar this time, red and rough. She reached out and then hesitated as his mouth tightened.

"If you don't want to touch me, I understand," he said softly.

Her eyes went wide. "I want to touch you so much I can hardly breathe," she promised. "I just don't want to hurt you."

He was silent a moment, studying her face. Then he said, "There's pain, but not from the scars. If you touch me, you won't hurt me."

"Good," she whispered, and placed a hand flat on his shoulder. She pushed, urging him back to settle on the pillows. When he was propped back on them, watching her every move, she leaned in and kissed him. She felt him relax beneath her lips, felt his body shift from warning to wanting. She wanted to keep him there. She wanted him to never feel warning again, at least not with her.

And she wanted to see him, all of him, and show him that the damage to his skin made no difference in how she viewed him. She slid her lips down, his beard tickling her as she traced his throat, down across the wings of his collarbone, and then she rested her lips on the scar on his shoulder. She licked the length of it, this proof of what he'd gone through.

He shuddered beneath her lips and she could feel the tension in him. This desire to both have more and to stop her, to keep her from seeing what he thought made him weak. Or less.

The fact that she could never see him that way wasn't something he knew or trusted. Time had done that. Pain had done it. And she wanted so desperately to repair all that damage since she couldn't fix the physical. She edged her mouth lower, kissing the scar on his ribs. Lower to the one on his stomach, just above the waistline of his trousers.

She unbuttoned the placard there, loosened the buttons at the waist. She looked up at him. "Take them off?"

It was a question, not an order. If he didn't want to show her what had happened to him, she wouldn't press. He held her stare for a long moment, what felt like forever. Then he hooked his thumbs into the waist and pushed them away, kicking them from his feet.

He was naked then and she stared, first at the hard cock thrusting toward her. One that made her mouth water. But she shifted her gaze, and for a moment her ardor was not the most important thing.

The damage that had been done to him was undeniable. It was written in his skin. More burn scars crossed his right hip and down the same leg. Deeper scars crisscrossed along the flesh. They were the story of bravery, of pain, of Death coming so close that she realized now Nicholas must have felt the brush of the robes.

"Nicholas," she breathed, reaching to touch them and then pulling away. If she touched them, she'd have to feel how real it was. How close she'd been to losing him.

"I know," he said. "Hard to look at."

She shook her head. "Hard only because they tell a story of your pain." She blinked at the tears that stung her eyes. "This is worse than I imagined. How did you survive?"

He drew in a long breath. "Luck," he said, his voice rough. "And the bravery of the men who I'd saved, including Selina's husband, Derrick. They worked to staunch the deepest wounds. They got me to the field doctor. Some of them are butchers, but ours was a good man. He saved my leg, my life. A hundred men with the same injuries would have died."

She bent her head as emotions overwhelmed her. Pain on his behalf, fear at what had almost been, gratitude to the men who had kept this man in her world. But also a strong sense of how fragile life was. How short.

She didn't want to waste even a moment of it.

"I realize the scars are…disturbing," he said.

"They are not," she said. "And I don't know why you keep trying to convince me that I want you less after seeing the evidence of your bravery. Of the man you have always been, that I always knew you to be. If anything, I want you all the more."

His nostrils flared slightly, and in that moment she saw the truth. This man, this strong, powerful man who had endured so much, become so much, always *been* so much…was vulnerable now. To her. And that was a gift as much as anything else that would happen tonight or any night.

She wanted to return that gift. To show him how she could be trusted with what he had revealed of himself, physically and emotionally.

"I want to touch you now," she whispered. "May I?"

He swallowed hard and then nodded wordlessly. She kept her gaze on his, watching him track her as she placed a hand on the damaged skin of his hip. She felt him stiffen as she traced the web of rise and fall there.

"Pain?" she asked softly.

"Not physical," he answered.

Her eyebrows lifted. "Do you want me to stop?"

"No," he choked out. "I never want you to stop."

She caught her breath — that admission had to be as hard for him as showing his scars. Then she leaned down and brushed her cheek against the scar. Her hair fell against his cock, and he hissed out a sigh.

She turned her mouth against him. She kissed the scars, tracing along the length of them down the side of his leg, then back up along the front. Across his hip, tasting the flesh, soothing with her tongue.

And finally she reached what she really wanted. That cock. All her attention focused on that, on him as she reached out and traced her finger along the length of it.

His back arched and he sucked his breath through his teeth. "Aurora."

She smiled up at him, watching his face as she fisted him, squeezing gently, then stroked him from base to head. He was hard as steel, the skin soft as velvet. Bigger than what she was accustomed to, the flesh a shade darker than the rest of his skin, a subtle pulse throbbing through the vein she was now rubbing with her thumb.

She kept watching him as she nuzzled him with her cheek. "Do you know what I'm going to do now?" she whispered.

He shook his head. "No."

"I'm going to do exactly what you did to me a moment ago, Nicholas." She held his gaze. "I'm going to do what I've dreamed of doing for so very long."

Then she darted her tongue out and licked him.

# CHAPTER 11

When Nicholas had brought Aurora to his bedchamber, he had expected a great many things to transpire. A great many heated dreams fulfilled, a great many emotions revealed and passions explored.

What he had not expected, not even dared to think about, was for her to take him into her mouth and suck his cock as she swirled her tongue around him with the precision of an expert bawd. Pleasure shot through him, tightening his balls, making him throw his head back as he cried out her name into the quiet of the room.

She responded by stroking over him, withdrawing almost entirely, then taking him as far as she could go again. He lifted into her, giving her a fraction more, his fingers digging into the back of her scalp. She made a soft sound of pleasure that reverberated up his cock, and smiled around his girth as she glanced up at him.

She held his gaze as she sucked him, stroked him, brought him to the brink of coming, then backed away until the edge was out of sight. He knew he should stop her. After all, wasn't this meant to be *his* seduction? Only he couldn't. This gift of hers was too powerful, too pleasurable, for him to find the strength to refuse it.

So he sank into it, surrendering to her. Like his dog had days before, Nicholas offered her his vulnerable underbelly and hoped she would only scrape her teeth along it rather than cut him down to the bone. After all, she had already proven herself trustworthy. He hadn't shown his scars to anyone but the doctors for years. He hardly looked at them, himself, they were too much proof of what had been changed, torn away.

But Aurora had looked and touched and soothed and for the first time in a long time, he felt...whole.

She gripped his cock harder and he was torn from thought back into sensation. She was driving him hard now, pulling him always closer to release. He would spend and that would be the end of it, at least for a while. Would they repeat this night? Would they ever touch again?

He knew from bitter experience that they might not. He reached out, gliding his fingers through hair that was soft as the finest silk. She moaned and pumped harder over him, and for a moment he just held her there, his fingers flexing against her, lost in pleasure.

"Aurora," he managed to choke out at last, finding words somehow even though his mind was hardly functional anymore.

She glanced up at him, question in her eyes, but she didn't stop as she murmured, "Mmm?"

"I'm going to spend," he moaned, arching into her even though he was supposed to be stopping this.

"That's the idea," she said with a chuckle, then licked him again.

But she had broken contact to speak, and in that moment he was able to gather himself. He wrapped her hair around his hand and gently tugged so that she looked up at him.

And God, what a sight it was: her naked between his legs, all those Rubenesque curves so perfect and soft against him. She was a wicked angel with his wet cock in her hands, her lips red from sucking him, her eyes glazed with desire, her hair tangled around both of them like a net that had snared him.

"I have waited a lifetime to touch you, Aurora," he grunted as he tugged a little harder and brought her crawling up the length of his body like a seductive cat. "And I want to be inside of you."

There was a flash of another wicked smile that crossed her face just before her mouth collided with his. The kiss was passion and fire and flame. All things that could destroy…had destroyed him in the past. But this time it was worth it. Touching her was worth any price.

She straddled him, her breath short as she broke the kiss. Their eyes met as she reached between them and positioned herself over his cock.

"Ready?" she whispered.

"For almost ten years," he responded.

Her expression softened as she glided him inside of her. They moaned in unison as he filled her inch by inch. Her body stretched to accommodate him, flexed and massaged him with steamy heat as he claimed her at last. When he was fully seated inside of her, she rested her forehead against his. Their gazes were still locked as she flexed around him.

"It's everything I ever wanted," she murmured, her voice cracking a little.

He cupped the back of her neck, holding her where she was, forcing that eye contact to remain. "Ride me," he ordered.

There were no more words then, no more thoughts. Just sensation as she rocked over him as he'd demanded. She held his stare, never wavering as she took him and took him. He watched her pleasure turn to frantic need as she ground down harder and harder, reaching for her release. When she found it, he froze, mesmerized by the expression of pure pleasure on her face. Her body rippled around him, stoking his own fire and sending sensation arcing up his cock. He caught her hips as she cried out and lifted into her, harder and faster, drawing her release as long as he could before she collapsed over him, her hands gripping his shoulders.

They kissed, her mouth desperate as she keened against his lips. He whispered her name, drowning in her as the world spun down to the need to release. He wanted to fill her, overflow inside of her, let her milk every drop from his body until he was utterly spent and slept with her surrounding him.

But that was pure folly. If he created a child with this woman, they were bound for life. And he still didn't even know her intentions or her reasons or really anything at all about the last decade of her existence except that she had ensured he wasn't part of it.

He rolled her and she gasped as she was pinned beneath him. Still she writhed, gripping him with her slick heat as he pounded hard inside of her. He gave her everything, clinging as long as he could to control before he pulled away from her. She reached for him, and together they stroked his ultrasensitive cock as he came and came and came for what felt like forever.

At last he collapsed onto the bed, yanking her into his side as their legs and arms and lips tangled. It was done. He'd made love to her at last. He had no idea what it meant or what would happen next.

And in that moment, he didn't care because she was in his arms. She was in his bed. For a little while he wanted to pretend that nothing else mattered.

Aurora smoothed her hand against Nicholas's chest, her fingers tracing the little scars and hard muscles there. It was almost hypnotic to touch him—she could get lost forever in exploring his body and all the ways to give and receive pleasure from each other.

Even now, she had no idea how long they'd lain like this together since they made love. A few moments? A few hours? Time had no meaning when his strong arms were around her, his fingers tracing patterns on her skin that made her feel alive in a way she hadn't since...well, since he'd left all those years ago.

"This is heaven," he said softly, lacing his fingers with hers. She looked at the intertwined digits, she felt the love for him that she'd never lost, no matter the circumstances, and she nodded.

"It was everything I ever dreamed and more," she agreed. "And I needed you so much tonight. I-I've needed you so many nights."

He had been flexing his fingers in and out between hers, and now he stopped. She felt him stiffen a little beneath her, and she looked up to find him watching her intently. "You needed me tonight because you were upset."

She frowned as she thought about the horrible encounter with Lord Sweeting on the terrace. His cruelty and judgment, which mirrored all of Society at present.

"Yes, I was upset," she whispered, and wished her voice didn't break.

He slid a finger beneath her chin, searching her expression with a frown. "You are still upset. Despite everything, you're thrown right back there. What happened?"

She sighed. "That viscount you were talking to before we danced?"

His jaw set. "Yes. Sweeting, you said his name was, since I didn't care enough to recall it."

"Well, he came onto the terrace behind me after you and I parted," she admitted. "And he was...vulgar."

Nicholas's nostrils flared, rather like Roseford's had done on the terrace a few hours before. She saw their similarities then, the connection of their tenuous brotherhood. "That scoundrel. What did he say?"

"He essentially called me a whore and tried to kiss me," she said, summing up the encounter with as much efficiency as possible. She certainly didn't want to relive it.

"What?" Nicholas sat up a bit straighter and stared at her in shocked horror. "He said that, he *did* that, and after all his talk to me about—"

He cut himself off but it was too late. Her assumption about Sweeting's discussion with Nicholas had clearly been correct.

"Warning you off me, was he?" she said. "Telling you what a scandal I've become and how I will take the shine off your diamond if you're trying to be given the title of marquess?"

He frowned, but the truth was written all over that handsome face. Of course that was exactly what had been said. Worse, it was true. She knew the ways of that world, better than Nicholas did, even if he'd been raised on its edges. She knew how quickly a man could be cut down to size if he associated himself with the wrong company. A woman cut down even harder and faster.

"I'll have words with him, consequences be damned," Nicholas muttered.

She shook her head. "Don't, Nicholas. He could impact your future in ways you can't even imagine. His isn't a high title, no, but he has some influence in the inner circle of the prince. Besides, your brother handled it."

"Morgan?" Nicholas asked. "I'd wager that was an earful of swearing and threats."

"No, not Morgan. Roseford," she said softly. "The duke was incredibly kind. Incredibly protective. He tossed Sweeting out of the party."

Nicholas stared off away from her for the first time, his gaze moving to the fire across the room. "Then I suppose I owe Roseford…my brother…a debt of gratitude."

"No, I do."

His gaze returned to her and he sighed. There was frustration to the sound, though she didn't completely understand why. She wasn't his, no matter what they'd shared tonight.

"You seem resigned to the fact that men like Sweeting will do what they do," Nicholas said.

She shrugged. "Because that is the truth. I've known it all my life, it will only be worse now because of—"

She cut herself off abruptly. God, why had she brought that up? She didn't want to talk to Nicholas about what had happened at the

Cat's Companion. He didn't need to be brought into her personal drama, not now when he was so close to his dream.

"Worse now because you were spotted at a brothel," he said, drawing forward the very topic she didn't want to discuss.

She shifted and tucked the sheets higher around her breasts. As if covering her body could also cover something more, something deeper. Foolish. This man had already seen it all, touched it all. Covering it was just a game now.

His expression darkened. "If you want to hide from me, we both know you are expert at it. But I admit I'm curious about the truth. Do you want to tell me what brought you there?"

Despite the harshness when he'd begun, his voice turned gentle as he asked the question. It felt entirely lacking in judgment. She found herself wanting to tell him the truth. He had always been that way, though. Her friend who had made her feel safe. Her love who had made her feel cared for.

She drew in a long breath. At least if he understood, he wouldn't judge her. Not for this, at any rate. For other things, it seemed he would.

"Over the past ten years, my best friend was Imogen Huxley. Imogen was married to the third son of the Earl of Briarstone, Warren Huxley. We were both in arranged marriages…" She sucked in a breath and watched his reaction. "Not particularly happy ones."

He flinched but said nothing, so she didn't know if he recoiled because he felt guilty he'd left her to that fate or something else.

"Our husbands died within months of each other last year. I was so lucky to have her with me. Her help as I navigated what had happened and how I might find a future after my mourning period ended was all that kept me going during those dark months."

"He died of an apoplexy, yes?"

She tilted her head. "Yes. In a brothel, actually."

His mouth tightened. "That's why you went there, then? Because of his death?"

"Not because he died in a spot like that one, no. You see, one more thing Imogen and I ended up having in common was that we were left destitute by our husbands. Her because Huxley's family ripped her inheritance out from under her. Me because Lovell settled me with nothing."

"I'm sorry," Nicholas said, and she could tell he was being sincere. He *was* sorry, even though this wasn't his fault. Not truly.

"I was too," she said. "But I was luckier. I had my family that loves me."

"More than loves you, I hope," Nicholas said softly.

She tilted her head. "Do you pretend you don't know how poorly my father handled his estates? That Thomas has been overwhelmed by debt and shame since the last earl's death a few years ago? Your father must have mentioned it."

Nicholas glanced away. "It's come up in passing. My father is a professional, though. He would never give details. I wasn't aware it was so terrible."

She shrugged and hoped that covered some of the pain this conversation caused. She didn't want his pity. Or to have him believe this story was some kind of manipulation meant to make him help her. "Well, because it is so terrible, I have been loath to involve my brother overly much. He can barely manage things for himself. I keep most of the particulars of my situation quiet."

"You protect him," he said.

"And I wanted to protect Imogen, but her situation was something else entirely. She had no family left, no help of any kind. And she's such an independent spirit. She decided she would take a lover, as many women of our situation do."

Nicholas arched a brow and his gaze flitted over her. She blushed. She hadn't thought of tonight as taking a lover, not in that sense. But of course she had. The lover was just the love of her life. Still and always and forever, her foolish heart be damned.

She pushed that aside, for it would do her no good to feel it, and said, "Because of her husband's awful family, she couldn't hunt for a lover in more…elevated places. They threatened to take her home, to eliminate everything she had left. So she started going to worse places looking for a protector."

"The Cat's Companion isn't where you find a protector," he said. "Men go there for a night of pleasure, nothing more."

She shivered. "I told her that, but she was so desperate. She was convinced that if she just pleased the right man the right way, she could still convince him to take her on as his mistress. She had a frightening experience one night—" She cut herself off as she tried not to think of Imogen's story. Of how Imogen had barely escaped that horrible place with her life. "And I begged her not to go back there."

"But she did."

Aurora nodded. "She did, and I got word of it, and I…I tried to find her. But she has vanished. I've been searching far and wide for her. That night at the Cat's Companion was the culmination of my search, but…but *I* was found out instead, and now I'm no good to Imogen at all because the world is watching and judging me."

His expression softened and he nodded slowly. "I owe you an apology."

She drew back. "Why?"

"I assumed I understood the story of why you'd go to such a place." His brow wrinkled. "It makes me wonder what else I have misjudged."

"You thought I'd gone there for pleasure?" she asked.

He nodded.

"Some of the bawdy houses were…titillating, I admit," she whispered, feeling her cheeks warm. "But some were just frightening. That last one was very frightening."

His jaw set. "I'm gutted you had to go through that alone. I wish…I wish I could have been there."

She tilted her head, those words sinking into her skin and her heart and her soul. *There* was the man she'd known all those years ago. He'd been hiding from her, just peeking out now and then. But now he was truly there, looking into her eyes, his kindness and his compassion on full display.

"You and I have been estranged for so long, I wouldn't have thought to come to you," she said slowly. "But if I had, I know you would have helped me even if you…even if you hated me like it seemed you did when I first arrived here. Because you're you, Nicholas, and you have always been so good."

"I'm not as sure about that. But perhaps I can help you now. Derrick—er, Huntington—runs an investigative service, you know. He might be able to help you find your friend. He's very trustworthy. Your story and hers would be safe with him."

She hadn't expected this offer and leaned in to rest her hand on his chest. "I appreciate it and I may take you up on it later. But when Katherine came to me, she offered me help from their friend in the War Department. He's looking for Imogen now. I'm hoping when I return that he'll have more information on the matter and I can work with him to find her at last."

"Ah." He nodded, and she thought she saw a flash of something dark in his eyes as he bent his head. "Well, I'm glad of it. You'll be safe with someone who works for the Crown."

"I worry more about her than me," she admitted with a sigh.

"Of course you do," he said with a faint smile. "You are you."

She tilted her head because he was watching her so intently and there were so many emotions on his face. As if there could still be something between them. And though she had put those dreams away a long time ago, she couldn't help but feel them sparked by his expression. By the way his fingers flexed against her skin.

"Nicholas," she whispered, lifting her hand to his cheek to caress the soft whiskers along his hard jaw.

He turned his lips into her palm and kissed it gently. "Yes?"

She drew in a long breath, trying to settle and focus herself. Trying to keep all her hopes and dreams and feelings from her voice so she wouldn't complicate things between them. "What happens now?"

That question echoed through Nicholas's mind, and he sucked in a deep breath as he pondered it. A few hours ago he would have called this a surrender. Only to happen once. Not to make him forget what he wanted for his future and what had been done in the past.

But now, after hearing her story, he questioned everything he'd always believed and been told. There was no denying Aurora's bravery. He'd been to a few bawdy houses in his day. The kind she'd ended up in wasn't a good place. Frightening was an understatement, he thought meant to minimize how terrified she'd been.

There was also no arguing against her loyalty. She had been friends with this woman, Imogen, for a long time, it seemed, but not many would go as far as she had. Most would only cluck their tongues and shake their heads sadly and faintly wonder whatever had happened to a friend in such a situation. He could count on his hand the number who might swing into action and try to save a friend. Even fewer were those who would risk their own life and reputation in the process.

When Aurora spoke to him, it had made his mind turn back to all those years ago. To the night he'd been told she threw him over. He'd been so young then. So uncertain of himself and if he was worthy of a woman so high above his station. It had been easy to believe her father that he'd been wrong about her intentions and walk away to mitigate any further hurt.

Now years had given him far more confidence and experience in reading people. And he questioned everything he'd been told that long-ago night.

"Nicholas?" Her voice broke, and he shook away the thoughts and focused on her. Those brown eyes shimmered with tears and her fingers trembled against his jaw. "What do you want?"

She repeated the question and his gut clenched because the

answer was so perfectly clear. Just as it always had been. The question and the answer always the same.

And yet he didn't fully trust that answer with her. Not yet. So he met her gaze. "What do *you* want, Aurora?"

She lifted up on her knees and leaned in, then her mouth found his. "This," she whispered as he sprawled back on the bed and she moved across him, her soft body molding to his and bringing him back to attention with just the slightest of touch. "For as long as we can."

He slid his fingers into her hair and held her closer as he kissed her. Deeper. Deeper, until she moaned and wiggled against him. When at last they broke apart, her breath was short as she added, "Is that unfair?"

He nodded. "But it's unfair that it's what I want too. For as long as we can."

He pulled her back to him and kissed her again as she straddled his lap and aligned their bodies. And as she took him deep inside once more, starting over the dance from earlier in the night, he pushed away all his questions and worries and uncertainties. There would be plenty of time for those later.

# CHAPTER 12

Nicholas stood on the terrace, Fortescue at his side. He let a rare bright and sunny morning warm his face. Perhaps he would have also stood outside if it were rainy and cold in the hopes the shock would wake him. After all, he'd spent a long and very passionate night in Aurora's arms. She'd only slipped away just before dawn. Her whispered promises that this wasn't over still rang in his ears.

He opened his eyes and looked down over the garden with a sigh. He sipped his tea and drew in a long breath. As he let it out, he recognized that for the first time in a very long time he felt…lighter. Freer.

"Boy," he said, glancing down at the bullmastiff, who thumped his thick tail against the stone. "I think we're in trouble."

The dog huffed out a sigh, though Nicholas wasn't certain if it was a sound of agreement or derision.

"There is my handsome brother."

He looked over his shoulder to find Selina slipping from the house. She had a bright smile on her face, but in her eyes he saw concern, and shook his head. Selina was a bulldog and it was obvious she had something to say.

"Good morning," he replied, and his smile was genuine as she bussed his cheek and moved to the small table where the pot of tea and a few scones had been placed by the staff.

"This is a cozy little breakfast," she said as she popped a corner from one of his scones and ate it. "May I join you?"

He laughed at her cheek and motioned to the table. "It looks as though you already have. Please sit with me."

She did and poured herself tea. They shared the plate of scones, and for a little while it was very comfortable. They spoke of her husband, since he had always been a good friend to Nicholas. Both smiled as they noted how besotted their brother Morgan was with his bride, Lizzie. And she baby-talked Fortescue and gave him treats she'd hidden somewhere in the folds of her fine gown.

But all the while he saw Selina calculating. Trying to decide when to strike. Old habits, perhaps. She had, after all, been a thief until just a few months before. It was her nature to watch and ready herself.

Eventually she dabbed her mouth with the corner of her napkin and said, "Although I don't normally enjoy such things, last night's ball was quite nice, I must admit."

"Yes," Nicholas agreed. "Very nice. It was kind of Katherine to put on such a show for my benefit."

"Mmmm," Selina murmured noncommittally. "And yet you didn't stay to enjoy it. You slipped out to follow Lady Lovell, after all."

"And there it is." Nicholas grunted as he pushed to his feet and grabbed for the cane he'd leaned against the table edge. He moved back to the terrace wall and leaned there.

"There *what* is?" Selina asked, all innocence as she stared up at him from the table.

"Don't look at me like a little wounded doe, I know your tricks," Nicholas said with a laugh. "You wanted to talk to me about Aurora. It's probably the entire reason you dragged yourself out of bed so early and came out here. I assume you saw me from…" He looked up and counted along the wall of the house. "…that window. That's your room, isn't it? You saw me down here alone and thought this your opportunity to come pry into my life without Derrick or Robert or Morgan to tell you to stop."

If he thought she'd argue or pretend offense, he was wrong. Instead, she made a show of slow applause. "A fine deduction, inspector," she said. "You ought to go work for Derrick and Barber with this sharp mind of yours, rather than surrender yourself to the boring life of a useless marquess."

"Ah, so that topic is on the table, as well," Nicholas said with a roll of his eyes. "Christ, what else do you want to lecture me on?"

Selina pushed to her feet then. "Nothing. I know better than to lecture you on anything."

"What does that mean?"

She put her hands on her hips. "Please don't pretend that you actually listen to any of us. You are so blastedly independent, and I know you think all three of us are at least partially untrustworthy because of our wild pasts."

He blinked at the accusation. "I…no. I don't think any of you are untrustworthy, Selina." She arched an incredulous brow and he folded his arms at the unspoken challenge. "I am reserved, I know. I do hesitate when it comes to letting others in. But you and Morgan and Robert are my family. I do trust you all, and if I have left you with another impression then I am sorry."

"I'm glad." Her expression softened, but then she turned back to her usual playful, arch self. "We'll leave the topic of the title alone for now. I know you're set on it. But yes, I did see you, and *yes*, I thought it a good opportunity to speak to you about this situation with Lady Lovell. Because everyone else will dance around it and I think you had quite enough dancing last night."

Nicholas shook his head. "You will not be stopped, will you?"

"Indeed, I shall not," Selina agreed with a laugh. "So it serves you better to simply talk to me because you know I have your best interests at heart. I want to protect you, you great oaf."

His shoulders rolled forward. "Yes. I do know your heart is true."

Her nose wrinkled. "God, it is. How far the mighty fall."

He laughed at her quip and sat back down at the table. She joined him, and they stared at each other a long moment before he said, "What do you want to badger me about, then?"

"You followed her out of the ballroom," Selina said again, this time more quietly. "Everyone saw it."

He flinched. "*Everyone*, eh? Was there much comment on the subject?"

"Only in our family and friend circle," Selina admitted. "I don't think anyone else realizes that connection between you and Aurora. Yet. And I say yet because you are being watched very closely, Nicholas. There are those hoping to see you fail."

He frowned. "Yes, I suppose that is true. This viscount last night was droning on about how titles are birthright."

She rolled her eyes again, but this time he wasn't the subject of it, which helped. "That's how a great many see it. And those that do are going to fight your appointment to marquess with any piece of ammunition they can drum up. Especially an association to a woman who just created a massive scandal."

He gritted his teeth at the truth of that.

"Do you want to tell me what happened between the two of you?" Selina pressed. "You didn't come back."

He was silent, unwilling to share the very personal connection he and Aurora had forged in his bed the night before.

She tilted her head. "A row?" she insisted when he didn't respond.

"No, not a row," he said softly.

She sighed. "You fucked her?"

"Selina!" Nicholas burst out, and desperately wanted to distance himself from her again, but all this getting up and down wasn't exactly easy. Especially since he'd so beautifully taxed his body with pleasure last night. He had no choice but to stay with her, though he bent his head as some kind of buffer.

She cursed again beneath her breath and said, "You're in trouble, aren't you?"

He agreed with the assessment, the same one he'd given Fortescue a short time ago. The dog was far less judgmental than his sister. He refused to give her the satisfaction of telling her. "I'm in control, Selina. That's all I'll say."

She snorted in a most unladylike fashion and it *forced* him to look at her. Her arms were folded across her chest and one fine brow was arched in accusation.

"You liar," she said with a laugh. "The worst part is I can see you're lying to yourself as much as to me or anyone else."

He tried to speak but couldn't find words. After all, she wasn't wrong. There were a great many things he was trying not to face, trying not to focus on, and his sister was now throwing all of them up in front of him like a set of barricades in a foot race.

"I don't know what you're talking about," he mumbled.

To his surprise, for once she didn't laugh or tease him. Instead she reached out and took his hand. She looked truly concerned as she said, "You don't want to say it. I understand. I didn't want to say it either, when it became painfully clear with Derrick. I didn't want to be so vulnerable to another person. Especially one who would blow apart my world."

"Selina," he said, tugging at his hand, but she didn't release him.

"You loved Aurora," Selina said, and those words froze him in place. "Probably you loved her even longer than you knew you did. Children are like that. Friendships blur sometimes. You thought you had a future with her and she threw you over for a title instead like a fool."

Now he did pull his hand away. "Derrick?" he breathed. "Derrick told you about that?"

"No." Now she did smile. "My husband, good man that he is, is silent as the grave when it comes to your secrets. I figured it out myself. I'm clever, if you recall."

"So it seems," he said, and tugged his hand away to run it

through his hair. She let him be silent for what felt like forever, not intruding on what he was processing in his mind. Not pushing, even though that was her way.

"Fine," he said.

"Fine, I'm right?"

He nodded without looking at her. "Yes. I wanted to marry her. I…I actually thought that was the plan until she threw me over for that title. And so I went to the army."

"How could she?" He looked and was surprised at how angry Selina looked. Her blue eyes flashed fire on his behalf. "Nasty cow."

"No," he insisted, invested, somehow, in keeping Selina from hating Aurora. He didn't want that. He wanted quite the opposite. "Please don't say that. We were young. I don't know the circumstances that led to it."

"The circumstances were greed and position, obviously," Selina huffed. "Things their kind are obsessed with."

"*Their kind*, like Roseford? Or Lizzie?"

That took some of the heat from her face, and she sighed as if there were a great concession to come. "Fine. Not *all* of them. Robert is…better than I gave him credit for. And Lizzie is lovely, daughter of a duke or no. She never gave Morgan's lack of position a thought, it seems."

"No, she is truly dedicated to him," Nicholas agreed, and felt a frisson of jealousy at the difference in the outcome of their disparate positions.

"Why do you care if I hate Aurora?" Selina asked.

He shrugged. "Because *I* don't hate Aurora. I know you think I should. Maybe even *I* know I should. But I don't."

"No, you follow her from the room like her lost puppy." Selina shook her head. "You want to put a smile on her face and keep her from harm. But do you really know she's any truer now than she was before?"

He wrinkled his brow. "What do you mean?"

"You're about to have a title, Nicholas. I'm sure they'll give it to you in the end, after they make you jump through their ridiculous hoops like a circus animal. Marquess is far higher than viscount, isn't it?"

He flinched at that thought. One he hadn't allowed into his mind last night or any moment they'd been together. "You're saying Aurora might be…open to what I want because she wants something in return."

"If you married her, it would save her from her scandal. Or at least soften it. And if you had that title, it would make her more powerful than ever."

That concept stung, even though Nicholas hadn't seen any indications that Aurora was title hunting. But then his complicated feelings had always blinded him to her motives in the past. Hadn't they? He wasn't even sure what had really happened anymore.

"You don't know her," he said softly.

"Do you?"

He jerked his head up to look at Selina, but before he could retort, the door to the terrace opened and they were joined by Robert. His brother was smiling, but Nicholas saw the same concern in the duke's eyes as he saw in Selina's. Wonderful. It was going to be a long morning.

"Good day, Roseford," Nicholas said. "Was this a planned ambush between the two of you? Let Selina soften me and then you'd come out to add to the chorus. Is Morgan lined up next or Derrick?"

Robert blinked and looked genuinely confused as he glanced at Selina. "What did you do?"

Selina threw up her hands. "Just trying to be a good sister."

Robert chuckled as he met Nicholas's eyes. "Inserting herself in your business, is she?"

Selina tossed her head and got up from the table with great theatrical aplomb. "Well, I never." Her expression softened as she leaned down to kiss Nicholas's cheek. "I do adore you, you know. I just don't want to see you get hurt." She pivoted and stuck her tongue out at Robert, eliciting the same from the duke. Then she laughed as she flounced off toward the house.

"How is she so utterly frustrating and entirely enchanting all at once?" Nicholas muttered.

"She's a force of nature," Robert agreed with a laughing shake of his head. "And Huntington manages the bulk of it."

"He adores her," Nicholas said with a sigh. "And so he deserves her, and she him. It's heartwarming, really."

"It is," Robert said slowly, his brow wrinkling. "But you sound less than warmed. Are you that annoyed with her interfering in your life?"

"Yes." Nicholas bent his head. "No. I'm defensive about all this, I know."

"I think you earned that right, given what little I've gleaned about the situation," Robert said slowly.

Nicholas let his gaze roll over his brother. Robert looked so much like their late father that it was sometimes startling. And once upon his time, his reputation for being a libertine had also matched their father's thirst for pleasure. And yet, time had changed him. Love had changed him. That was evident in every way he moved and interacted. In the way he'd quietly reached out to all their half-siblings in the last few years, helping and guiding and welcoming them in one by one.

"I owe you my thanks, it seems," Nicholas said.

"For what?" Robert asked, as he flopped down in the seat Selina had abandoned. He looked truly confused. "I threw you a ball you hated so much you slipped out not even halfway through."

Nicholas arched a brow. "You're going to pretend you don't know where I went? That all of you didn't discuss it at length in the family sewing circle?"

"We are terrible gossips," Robert admitted with a laugh. "Though we have good intentions so that may excuse us."

"Aurora told me you intervened with Sweeting last night," he said.

Robert's face grew stormy, bright anger in his eyes. "I always thought the man a smug know-it-all but I never knew he was such a disgusting arse."

Nicholas clenched his fists at his sides. "He tried to…touch her."

"Yes." Robert's nostrils flared. "But he didn't. And he won't. And I think he'll find himself far less welcome in good company once he hurries along to London to whine about his treatment. I may be worthless, but my friends have a great deal of power."

"You are certainly not worthless," Nicholas said, and extended a hand to him. "And I thank you again for helping her."

Robert shook the hand offered to him, but there was a look on his face that said volumes. "I appreciate the gratitude, but I wonder why you think you are the one who must express it. Is that your place now, Nicholas?"

He pulled his hand away and stared up at the sky as he tried to calm his suddenly racing heart. "Jesus, Robert, I just did this with Selina. Can we not repeat it?"

"Of course," Robert said, almost gently. "But may I just say that your family loves you? And we are perhaps a little too protective because we almost lost you, and that realization and memory brings all of us to our knees when we allow it to take over. But you are a grown man, a very smart one. And well capable of making your own decisions. I just hope you take the time to get all the vital information before you do that."

He patted Nicholas's shoulder before he got up turned toward the house, calling back, "I know you ate, but the rest are gathering in the breakfast room if you want to make an appearance. Or take a little time to yourself. There is no pressure from me either way."

Nicholas didn't respond, but watched Robert disappear into the house. His words resonated in Nicholas's brain. *Get all the vital information.*

It was good advice. Something he'd known he needed to do from the first moment he saw Aurora step from the carriage days before. Last night he'd known it too. They had to face the past together.

And that was difficult and frightening because he knew that shared past could destroy whatever it was they were rebuilding at present.

But he had to do it. He had to face it. He had to face her and determine what the next step to take was in all this.

He got to his feet, taking his time and stretching out his leg since there was no longer an audience beyond the dog at his feet. Fortescue sat up at attention as he did it, watching him as intently as his siblings had.

"Don't you start," he muttered as he caught his cane and flicked his hand toward the house. "Go get your own breakfast."

The dog's ears perked up with that, and when they entered the house, Fortescue padded off toward the kitchen where he'd been given his meals each day. As for Nicholas, he pushed his shoulders back and walked down the hallway toward the breakfast room where he heard laughter and talk from the guests.

He turned into the room and stopped. Aurora was standing by the sideboard, a plate in hand, laughing with Morgan as she loaded eggs onto her plate. She looked so very lovely. So happy and so free. So much like the girl he had loved and lost. And so much like the woman who had bewitched him all over again.

It was true they needed to deal with the past. But in this moment, he only wanted to focus on the present. The rest would come, and he wanted to enjoy her while he had her.

# CHAPTER 13

Aurora stood at the sideboard with Nicholas's brother and sister-in-law, Morgan and Lizzie Banfield. They had been the first in the breakfast room that morning, though the others had begun to trickle in one by one, smiling and saying their good mornings.

Still, she stayed with the couple, enjoying their easy banter. Two more different people she could not have designed in her mind. Lizzie was soft and gentle, a little timid and quiet, while Morgan was boisterous and playful, the perfect depiction of a reformed rake who still knew how to turn a situation to his own advantage.

And yet, despite how different their personalities were, they matched like one piece of a puzzle to its mate. He drew Lizzie from her shell. She calmed Morgan with just a look or slight graze of her hand. They did it effortlessly, almost as if it took no thought to balance the other. Dark and light, always together, always in perfect harmony.

Aurora knew Lizzie was the sister of the Duke of Brighthollow and, of course, Morgan was one of the previous Duke of Roseford's wayward bastards. So the pair were from different worlds entirely.

Rather like her and Nicholas, in truth. That had always caused friction between them when their love was just blossoming. She'd known her father too well not to fear his reaction and wanted to run away together. Nicholas had insisted on approaching her father like a gentleman.

Only he hadn't. He'd just left.

So it seemed he had decided, without input from her, that their worlds *couldn't* mesh like Lizzie and Morgan's. Did he feel the same way now? Now that she was the one down on her luck and he about to take a title? Certainly tying his star to hers would not make it easier on him.

"Are you still with us, Lady Lovell?" Morgan asked, but his tone was playful.

She shook her head. "I am, Mr. Banfield, forgive me. I was just thinking of the past, I suppose."

Lizzie sent a brief side glance to her husband and then smiled. "You and Nicholas knew each other as children, I have heard. I wonder what he was like as a boy."

"Yes, was he so very serious and good?" Morgan asked. "Or do you have wicked tales I could hold over his head?"

Despite her tangled feelings, Aurora couldn't help but laugh. "Ah, the younger brother always wanting to find a way to best the older. That is an old tale."

"I suppose it is to most," Morgan said with a smile that was suddenly a little sad. "I often wonder what kind of relationship we would have had if we had all been raised together."

That comment pushed Aurora's troubles away. She knew the separation was something each of Roseford's illegitimate children suffered from. It was actually very warming to see them begin to develop those strong familial bonds after all these years apart. She wanted that for Nicholas.

"His father...er, the man who raised him," she began with a blush. "Bertrand Gillingham was my father's man of affairs."

"Was he?" Morgan said with a genuine look of surprise. "I didn't know that. I'm Lizzie's brother's man of affairs now. It's an interesting job."

"It is, and his father was very good at it. He had a difficult subject to manage, though. I think, more difficult than your own."

Lizzie smiled now. "Sometimes."

"Oh, your brother is only everything good and decent and you know it," Morgan said with a broad smile.

"He is that," Lizzie said.

"Well, my father was…not," Aurora admitted slowly, for this was revealing a great deal about herself. "He could be cruel. He didn't look upon anyone else as his equal, even those with similar title. He made Gillingham's job difficult. I think my mother felt sorry about it, so she offered a boon. Or a balm, perhaps, to keep the man working for my father. Nicholas was allowed to join us in the schoolroom. And he and my brother and I became fast friends."

It was funny. So often she only thought of those last few months together with Nicholas. The bubbling passion that had never been fulfilled, the desperate love, the broken heart. But talking about the early years put her to mind of far happier times.

"He must have been a good student," Morgan said. "Smart as a whip, that one."

"It runs in the family," Lizzie interjected, and was rewarded by a brief smile from her husband.

"He was an excellent student," Aurora agreed. "He bested my poor brother Thomas at all the subjects. They had a friendly rivalry, but it never exited the schoolroom. When Thomas went away to Eton, my mother convinced my father to sponsor Nicholas, as well."

"I would wager our real father might have had something to do with that, too," Morgan mused. "He did with me."

"You're probably right. Though Nicholas didn't know about the duke until much later—fifteen, I think." She remembered how devastated he'd been, how hurt and out of place. She'd so desperately wanted to comfort him.

It might have been then that she first fell in love with him without recognizing it.

Lizzie tilted her head. The younger woman almost looked like she was reading her. Seeing something Aurora hadn't meant to reveal. She smiled. "I can see that Morgan has exactly eleven hundred questions to ask about Nicholas and his childhood."

"Exactly eleven hundred, yes," Morgan teased.

"We'll be here a while then," Aurora said with a laugh.

"And many of those questions are either very boring or very wicked," Morgan continued. "I see Selina motioning to you, Elizabeth, if you wish to escape my truly terrible ways."

Lizzie laughed. "This is his way of saying he wants to talk to you alone. He's very subtle."

Aurora continued smiling, it was impossible not to in the face of their playful banter, but her heart thudded in her chest. Morgan wanted to talk to her alone. About Nicholas. Was it to warn her off? She deserved that, likely, but still didn't look forward to it.

"I'll join you in a moment," Morgan said, and leaned forward to kiss his wife's cheek gently.

Lizzie smiled at him and Aurora, then slipped away. Morgan picked up the tongs and began carefully nudging through the links of sausage on the plate before them. "It's nice to hear what Nicholas was like as a boy," he said. "Especially from someone who knew him so well."

"He was my brother's best friend and they always included me, which was kind considering I was younger."

She frowned. Thomas hadn't spoken to Nicholas since he left for the army. Even when Nicholas was injured, he hadn't reached out. Because of her. That past they hadn't yet addressed had destroyed so much.

"And was he always such a serious creature?" Morgan asked, the teasing in his tone making her smile. "Please tell me he at least played pranks or something. I need to hold some wicked moment over his head."

The word *wicked* made her flash to Nicholas perched between her legs, mouth making magic against her clitoris, and she blushed as she shoved those thoughts away.

"*Oh*, if it's moments to hold over his head you'd like, then I could probably provide a few," she said. "Give me a bit to compile a list. It will be longer than you might think."

Morgan tipped his head back and laughed, and for a moment she was put to mind of Nicholas at twenty, right before they'd been torn apart.

"Well, I look forward to that, my lady, very much," he said with a tip of his head before he slipped off to join his wife, sister and brother-in-law.

She worried her lip. She'd expected him to engage in some kind of interrogation. And perhaps he had at that. Morgan seemed capable of reading people on a different level than anyone else she'd ever met. Perhaps his questions had allowed him to see whatever it was he was looking for. She just had no idea what it was.

She sighed and turned to go to the table herself, but came to a sudden stop. There, standing in the door, watching her, was Nicholas. She hadn't seen him since she reluctantly slid out of his bed just a few hours before, but the way her heart thumped, she would have thought it was days, weeks, years all over again. He'd been much more mussed when she'd kissed him goodbye, but now he was back to his usual fully pulled-together self, not a hair out of place.

She rather liked him in both iterations, liked knowing she could make him come undone. She also looked forward to doing it all again. After all, they'd both said they wanted more of what they'd shared.

Even though she had no idea what more meant or how long it would last.

"Nicholas!" Selina called out. "Come and sit. Join us."

That shook Aurora from her slack-jawed distraction. She smiled at him, then took her seat between the Duchesses of Roseford and

Northfield. The opposite side of the table from Nicholas, but it didn't matter. The connection was there, just as it always had been. And she was realizing more and more that time and distance had never erased it. Changed it, perhaps, but not destroyed.

She wasn't certain whether to be comforted or saddened by that fact.

"—what we do today," Katherine was saying, and once again Aurora was pulled from her thoughts and back to reality.

"It's true, the fine weather does change things," Robert said. "And I hate to trap our party inside with it so sunny."

She blinked as she realized they were discussing the day's activities. The original plan had been cards, she thought, because it was supposed to rain.

"What about a picnic?" Lizzie said from the opposite end of the table.

"Oh, an excellent idea, my dear," Morgan agreed. "I have not had a chance to truly explore this estate since our arrival and steal all of Roseford's best management tools to impress your brother."

Roseford chuckled. "I have no good tools, Morgan, you should know that by now."

"I would tend to disagree," Katherine muttered with a half-smile. No one else heard her except for Aurora and the Duchess of Northfield, but the two of them giggled together. Katherine cleared her throat with a guilty look for the pair and said to the room at large, "I think Lizzie's idea is perfect! A walk through the grounds and a picnic would be lovely. I'll make the arrangements and we can leave in an hour. Does that suit everyone?"

The room murmured its agreement and then everyone went back to eating and talking in small groups, which afforded Aurora the ability to watch Nicholas once more. He smiled with his siblings, though it seemed strained. And his gaze kept sliding toward her, their eyes meeting, the tension between them humming like a constant noise under the surface.

By the time breakfast had ended and everyone had begun to

leave the room to prepare for their hike through the property, Aurora's knees were shaking with renewed desire for him. With the physical *need* to touch him.

He moved to the sideboard, fiddling around with the coffee and tea pots as his siblings and the other guests finally departed. When the last had disappeared through the door, he crossed to it and shut it.

Her heart leapt and she drew in a breath to say his name, but before she could, he crossed the room to her, cupped her cheeks and kissed her.

Nicholas's mouth was hungry on hers, his tongue seeking hers as her arms came around him, but her ardor matched his own. She dug her fingers into his jacket, clinging for purchase as the room spun out of control. He tilted her head, deepening the kiss, drinking of her like he was dying of thirst and she was all the sustenance in the world. Perhaps she was, perhaps she always had been. So he took and took and took.

He had no idea how long it went on. Not long enough. At last he parted from her, breath short, cock throbbing with an insistent rhythm that demanded he do something they had no time to finish.

"Good morning," he gasped out.

She broke out in a wide smile, and for a moment he was mesmerized. He had always loved her smile. She had always been a light, bright and joyful, but when she smiled? It lit up the world like the sun.

"Yes it is," she said, and reached out to catch his hand.

Their fingers intertwined and his entire body relaxed in a way he hadn't felt for…years. He smoothed his thumb over the back of her hand. "Are you tired?" he asked.

"I should be, with so little sleep," she said, pink entering her cheeks. "But I'm not at all. I haven't felt so invigorated in a long time."

He nodded. That was his feeling, too. Like he could take over the world. But there were still things to talk about with her before he could. "I think you should know that my family is aware we snuck away together last night."

He watched as the good feelings fled her face and she tensed up immediately. Her hand fell away from his. Nicholas couldn't help but think about what Selina said about her. That she might be using him to gain access to yet another title. But that didn't feel right. Wouldn't she be *pleased* to be caught in a compromising position if that were true?

"I see," she whispered. "I suppose I should have known they would mark that we left at the same time. That neither of us returned. And combined with the scandal I entered this house dragging behind me, they all must question my character."

Hearing that waver in her voice, the defeat and heartbreak, he couldn't help but move to her. He tugged her into his arms and held her. She softened against him, almost collapsing, and he realized what a weight she had been carrying. He wanted so much to bear some of it for her.

"I don't think anyone judges you," he said as he pressed a soft kiss to her temple. "I know them and that is not who they are. It's more that they…they worry about me."

She drew back a little. "Because of our past."

He nodded. Their eyes met and he saw she knew what had to happen as much as he did.

"We need to discuss that, I think," she whispered.

He nodded again. "But not right now. There isn't enough time before the picnic. Can we promise to talk about it later? Tonight?"

She moved against him slightly, and every nerve in his body felt like it fired at once, despite the darker topic they'd finally approached head on. "Maybe in bed?"

"I'd like that," he said, smiling.

She lifted on her tiptoes and brushed her lips across his. "Then that's what we'll do." She sighed as she stepped away. "But do you think I should go on the picnic? Will they want me there?"

He wrinkled his brow. It was so hard to see her struggling. Even with the past sitting right there, ready to be faced, ready for his questions and the difficult answers he might not want to hear.

"They want you there," he reassured her. "And I *need* you there, Aurora. These long walks are often tortuous."

Her lips parted. "Of course they are. And after all that exercise last night—"

"Which I very much enjoyed," he interrupted. "And do not regret in the slightest. They just don't think about the difficulty. It isn't out of cruelty, of course. It's just that none of them have experienced what I do."

"Could you…tell them?" she asked.

He shifted. Tell them. "If I knew them better…perhaps," he said. "But right now I don't know if they would respond with pity. I don't want that."

She nodded slowly. "I think I understand, at least as much as I can."

He forced a smile. "But if you're there, you'll be the carrot for this old rabbit."

"I'm having a hard time picturing you as anything but a wolf, but why would I be a carrot?"

"Because if you're there, at least I'll know I can enjoy the day with you."

Her expression softened and her eyes lit up with happiness that warmed him to his toes.

"How can I deny you?" she asked. "Now I should go ready myself. I'll see you later?"

He nodded as she left the room with just a backward glance. Once she was gone, he gripped the back of the closest chair. It had hit him like a shot to the chest in that moment. The thing he'd been trying to pretend away, trying to ignore, trying to label as anything else but what it was in truth.

He was still in love with Aurora. Worse yet, he'd *always* been in love with Aurora. Even when he'd tried to forget her, even when he tried to despise her, even when he'd tried to ignore that she existed in the world...he had loved her all along. And he didn't see that changing or stopping any time soon. So he had to decide what the hell to do about it.

# CHAPTER 14

Nicholas walked along the grass, up and over the rolling hills of his brother's estate. He was behind the others, but he managed to keep his own pace. It was heartening, actually. Even a few months ago, he wouldn't have been able to manage this long a walk on sometimes uneven ground, but today he was stiff but carrying on. It seemed he continued to heal. That would likely have a limit, an end…but he still felt good about the progress.

Graham Everly, the Duke of Northfield, had fallen back with him and they had been chatting together for the last half an hour. It was a good distraction from the physical, at least, for the duke was a kind and interesting companion. Still, Nicholas's attention continued to be drawn to Aurora, who was walking with Katherine and Graham's wife, Adelaide, Fortescue at her side. From time to time, she threw his stick out ahead of the group and the behemoth took off to return it to her, tongue lolling joyfully.

"I suppose you'll know soon enough about whether or not the prince will be gifting you the title," Graham said.

That pulled Nicholas back to the conversation. He let out a long sigh. "It seems so. I received a letter from my steward just before we left for our picnic. He's been informed the decision will be likely before the end of the summer. Once I return, I'm meant to take some meetings with those in power. The jockeying is…taxing, I admit."

Graham grimaced. "I can imagine. Do you mind if I ask you something?"

"Certainly," Nicholas said, and glanced at him from the corner of his eye. The man looked deep in thought.

"I've watched you since our arrival," Graham began. "Trying to determine who you are."

"I expected as much. Of course you want to have a great deal of information before you decide if you'll support me."

"What?" Graham shook his head with a laugh. "No, no. I intended to offer my endorsement to your bid from the beginning. Not only is Robert one of my best friends, but you're a damned hero and obviously a good man. You would make an excellent addition to the ranks of the titled. I think you'd fight the good fight for those who weren't raised with the privileges those of my class enjoy and sometimes don't see."

Nicholas thought of the life he'd lived, one that straddled two worlds, one that saw the good and the bad in both. "I suppose my experience would give me a different view, though I know I have blind spots of my own."

"Everyone does. Anyone who says they don't is selling something," Graham said with another brief smile toward him.

Nicholas returned it. "Well, if it isn't about you determining your support, then what is your question?"

The duke stopped on the path, and Nicholas did the same, stretching his leg gently. Graham looked off toward the party, which had finished their descent and come upon the beautiful picnic site that had been set up for them during their walk. Their increased laughter and chatter could be heard all the way up the hill.

"There were times I would have traded this title for almost any other life," Graham said. "It seems you have friends and respect, you are loved by your family…why do you *want* to be a marquess? Especially since I'm certain that title, long fallow, will come with a great deal of trial."

Nicholas had heard all the whispers since the rumors that he might be given a title had begun to spread through Society. Men like Sweeting from the night before, who thought rank was only deserved by those with a bloodline. People who thought he couldn't rise to the occasion for other reasons. Those who questioned his ability, intelligence and education.

But Northfield was the first person outside of his closest friends and family who had questioned why he might want such a title. If the position was good enough for him, not the other way around.

Nicholas sighed. "You have already said you are one of Roseford's best friends, and everything I've seen of you these past few days and heard of you over the years tells me you are a good and decent man."

"I try to be," Graham said softly.

"I will answer you honestly," Nicholas continued, meeting his eyes. "I want the control that rank will offer me."

Graham stared at him a moment, and then flashed a grin. "Control? No, that's an illusion, mate."

"Says the man who's always had it," Nicholas retorted, perhaps with a little more heat than he'd intended. "You can do as you wish, help who you wish, go where you wish and no one can stop you. No one can take away what you have."

"Ah, then what you want is *power*," Graham said. "Power and luck. Because don't think for a moment that I don't realize, in a little throb in the back of my head, that the wife I love more than anything in this world, the children back at home who make the future brighter…those things that truly matter could be taken from me in an instant."

Nicholas heard the slight waver in the man's voice, saw the seriousness in his eyes. "You've lost others."

Graham nodded slightly. "And trust me, future duke or not, there was no control in what happened. There isn't much control in the world at all, not for the things that have true meaning. You've felt that." He motioned to Nicholas's leg. "It changed your life."

"Yes," he said softly.

"*That's* why we have to appreciate those things every moment we have them. Hold on to them and not let anything foolish stand in the way. Because there lies the path of regret. Regret is all the things left unsaid and undone."

Nicholas stared down the little rise, found Aurora amongst the revelers in a heartbeat. She was sitting on a blanket, Fortescue's big, tawny head in her lap. She leaned back on her arms, bonnet discarded, face lifted to the sun. And she was so utterly glorious. So much the same as she'd ever been and so much more than he'd ever dreamed.

"Lady Lovell is a beautiful woman," Graham said.

"Mmmm." Nicholas hoped he sounded noncommittal.

"I mean, I assume it isn't my wife or Katherine who you are looking at like that. You don't seem the kind of man to covet. Are you going to fight so hard for control that you instead give up on whatever it is between you?"

Those words hit home, but Nicholas forced a wry smile. "You all have your opinions, don't you?"

That elicited a chuckle from Graham, and his intensity faded. "That's what families do."

Nicholas jerked toward him. "Family?"

"You are the brother of a man I consider my brother," Graham said with a shake of his head. "You're family."

Nicholas blinked. Family. It had been a long time since he'd had one of those. His mother had died while he was in the army. He only saw his adoptive father rarely. Perhaps because of guilt on both sides.

He bent his head. "My father…the one who raised me…he served hers, you know."

"I've heard. She speaks in glowing terms of the elder Gillingham, you know. Far more of him than her own father." Graham shook his head. "Fathers of birth don't have to be fathers. Mine was a cruel monster. I wish I'd had a man like yours to guide me."

Nicholas nodded slowly. "He is the best of men. He raised me to fight whatever nature the last Roseford's blood put in me. He raised me to be decent."

"And what does he think of the title?"

Nicholas flinched. That was part of why they saw each other so rarely. "He thinks he has served terrible men and good men over the years. Title never mattered as much to him as heart."

"But it matters to you."

"Yes." Yet as he looked down over the group below, his family of blood, half or not, his friends new and old, Aurora…he was beginning to doubt himself. Doubt everything.

"Come, we've jawed enough," Graham said, clapping a hand on Nicholas's shoulder. "They'll start calling for us if we don't join them."

They fell into step again down the hill. But as they reached the others, Nicholas turned toward him. "I—thank you, Your Grace. You gave me a great deal to ponder."

"Of course," Graham said with another of those friendly smiles. "And for God's sake, call me by my first name. Brothers only use titles in public or when they're giving each other endless shit."

With that, he moved off to the blanket, to his wife, whom he kissed without any seeming care of who was around. And then he fell into a conversation with Aurora with the same seamless, effortless kindness he had exhibited with Nicholas.

Nicholas sighed as he moved off to be closer to Selina and Derrick and settled himself slowly on the blanket, straightening his leg out with relief. As he massaged the muscle, his mind raced. He'd planned his life one way and had it torn apart, planned it another and the same had happened, this time with blood and fire. And now he was on the precipice of the third grand plan of his adult life and he questioned it all.

Questions he'd have to answer eventually. Questions he *needed to* ask before he could truly move on.

~

Aurora was laughing as she entered the house with Lizzie and the Duchess of Northfield, who kept insisting on being called Adelaide. The three of them were the last to return from the picnic that afternoon, because they had stopped to examine Roseford's garden as the rest returned to the house. Lizzie knew everything about a garden. She'd even promised to come to Aurora's little house in London and help her plant and prune the wilderness currently behind her home.

She felt so welcomed and cared for in this group. Even Selina Huntington, Nicholas's sister and the one who seemed to have the most hesitation about Aurora, had been kind all day. Aurora hadn't felt so relaxed and uninhibited since…

Well, since before her marriage, that was certain. Back when she was planning a life with her best friend and greatest love. A man who had not quite avoided her all day, but certainly hadn't made an effort to join her, despite saying how much he wanted her there with him.

She had no idea where they stood, even though the distance had allowed her to observe him. Observe the careful ways he adjusted himself for his injuries. Observe the connections he was building with his family. Observe how remarkable he was, even more now that the years had given him experience and strength.

"I should go up," Adelaide said as they stepped into the house. "We have a few hours before supper preparations will have to be made."

"Yes, I promised Morgan I would join him for a game of billiards," Lizzie said.

"Is he teaching you to play?" Aurora asked with a smile.

Lizzie's cheeks turned almost plum. "He says he's going to teach me to cheat."

"I think billiards is a euphemism," Adelaide said with a singsong teasing tone.

"Oh, go on," Lizzie said, giggling as she scurried up the stairs.

Adelaide grinned at Aurora. "You'd never know she was a wallflower not that long ago. Bad influences, these wicked husbands. Speaking of which, I'll go find mine. See you tonight."

Adelaide all but skipped up the stairs, which left Aurora to her own devices. And her devices were pointing her toward Nicholas. She'd been watching him all day as those happy couples all around her laughed and joked and teased and loved. One thing had become increasingly clear: her cowardice about facing the past had to end if she wanted to figure out the future.

And she did. So very much.

She marched down the hall, peeking in parlors and libraries and any room for him. But there was nothing. The last room she entered, she found Roseford's butler, Jenner, talking to a housemaid. When he noticed her, he gave a slight bow. "May I help you, my lady?"

"I don't know. I was looking for Mr. Gillingham," she said, hoping she sounded casual and not desperate. She felt desperate.

"Ah, I believe he went up for an afternoon constitutional," the butler said.

"I see," she said. "Well, I'll have to see him later, then. Thank you, Jenner."

She exited the room and stood in the hallway. If Nicholas was resting, he might not wish to be disturbed by her. Normally she would respect that boundary. After all, if he'd wanted her to join him, he would have likely signaled her in some way during the picnic or on the walk back.

Her nature was to respect the distance. But then again, what good had that done her? She and Nicholas were such respectful creatures that together they never confronted anything. Not the past, not the future. Not even the present. They danced around things so the other wouldn't be uncomfortable.

"It's time to be uncomfortable," she told herself as she marched up the stairs and down the same winding hall he had led her the night before. She knocked on his door, and smoothed her hair and her gown as she waited for him.

But he didn't come.

She knocked again, this time slightly louder. But still no reply. She girded her loins and turned the door handle. To her surprise, it opened, and she peeked into his chamber. Fortescue lounged across the bed, but otherwise the chamber was empty.

"Nicholas?" she whispered into the empty room, but he didn't respond, and the dog just grunted at her as she backed from the room.

Nicholas wasn't there. She frowned. If he had gone wandering the estate by himself, she would likely never find him. It was just too big.

Frustration rose in her, though it wasn't fair of her to feel it. Nicholas had agreed they should speak on the past tonight. He wasn't hiding from her—they'd had no agreement to meet. And yet she still worried. Would they *ever* be brave enough to face the past? Would everything get in their way over and over until they just let it go and moved on? She hated the idea that could happen. She feared it was the path they were on.

She trudged down the hall to her own door and entered her chamber. She locked the door behind her and was about to ring for her maid to help her when there was a rustling from behind her.

She pivoted and found Nicholas rising from a chair in the darkened corner of her room. Her heart leapt into her throat as she stared at him, jacket already gone, sleeves rolled to his elbows to reveal and expanse of toned forearm, soft brown gaze focused on her.

"Should I have come?" he asked.

She couldn't help but smile then. "I have spent the last quarter of an hour searching this house for you, including your chamber," she said. Then she crossed to him. "I'm so glad you came."

He caught her hand, his fingers smoothing across the flesh as they stared together at the place where their bodies met. His hand was so much bigger than hers, rougher, a scar slashed his knuckles. And she loved that hand. Loved every imperfection and how they made him fit against her all the better.

"I have so much to say to you," he whispered.

She nodded. "So do I."

"But first..." He trailed off as he let go of her hand and slid his fingers into her hair instead. He tilted her face toward his as her hair came down around them. His breath was harsh in the quiet air around them as he dropped his lips to hers.

She lifted to meet him, starved like they hadn't started their day this way. Like it had been nine years all over again. The kiss began as a greeting, a welcome, but it transformed in a heartbeat. His mouth grew hungrier and she lifted to meet him. His arm encircled her waist and she felt his desire in the hard press of his cock against her belly.

They had a great deal to say to each other. But it was evident they were going to say something with their bodies before they were finally bold enough to use their words.

Nicholas backed her up in a few steps and Aurora gasped as her bottom hit the door behind her. Now she was wedged between a hard door and a hard man, and she'd never felt so soft and vulnerable in her life. Nor had she ever enjoyed that little thrill of danger so much.

He kissed her, deeply at first but then he pulled away with a sigh. "I really want to hold you up against the door and take you until you shatter. But..." He stepped back, steadying her even as he leaned down to rub the muscle on his injured leg.

"It was such a long day," she finished for him. "Come, lie down on the bed. Let me help."

His brow wrinkled as he stared at her. She thought he might

refuse. Thought he might deny her that desire to help if she could. Perhaps he didn't yet trust her enough. But finally he nodded and eased his way up on her bed. She tugged off his boots and as he pulled his jacket and shirt off, she unfastened his trousers.

He was half-hard, despite the exchange at the door, and she smiled as she drew a finger along his length. It jolted to full attention as he growled above her. "That's one way to distract me."

She laughed as she tugged his trousers down, discarding them over her shoulder so he was naked once more. She could see the muscles in his leg twitching slightly and her ardor faded. "Ooch," she murmured. "It was too rough a day."

He shrugged. "It is what it is."

"I saw you rubbing the muscle," she said. "Would that help?"

"I mean, help, yes. I might grouse about it regardless. You'll have to ignore that."

She smiled and placed her hands on the muscle. She stroked gently at first, and he hissed out a sound before he eased back on the pillows and flopped a hand over his eyes. He didn't want her to see his face. His pain. That was still too private in some ways.

But she didn't do this for herself, after all. She was doing it for him. She increased the pressure of her hands and he jerked slightly. "Too much?" she asked.

"It's doing what it needs to do," he said, the tension high in his voice. "But I much prefer literally any other way you touch me."

"And that will be your reward when you get through this," she promised, and repeated the kneading motion, watching him react as she loosened a few of the knots beneath his skin. After a little while, the muscle stopped twitching and he let out a ragged sigh.

"I think that's enough for now," he said. "Not only because I'm at my limit, but also because I didn't come here to be babied."

She tapped on his forearm, still flopped over his face, and he slowly slid it away to meet her stare. His brown eyes were dilated, but not with pleasure—with lingering pain.

She cupped his chin and leaned in closer. "Taking care of you doesn't mean you're being babied," she said softly. "I like taking care of you. The way I just did or…" She lowered her hand and traced his cock again with her fingers. He went half-hard again almost instantly. "Or that way."

"I prefer the second," he grunted as he cupped her backside and pulled her closer by one staggering step. She was pressed to the edge of the mattress now and laughed as she kissed him at last.

He lifted up on one elbow while he held her firm against him with his other hand. His kiss deepened, his tongue swirling against hers, sucking her until her knees shook with growing desire.

"I can't take my time," he whispered as he trailed his hand down her body, found her breast, squeezed the fullness, stroked a thumb over her already hard nipple.

"Don't," she mumbled around his tongue. "Hurry, hurry."

He nodded against her lips. His hands found their way to the back of her silky gown and parted the buttons with a few flicks of the wrist. She giggled at the ease with which he'd done it.

"You'd think you were a libertine," she whispered.

He laughed, low and rough. "I've never been so happy to have Roseford blood rushing through my veins. Although I think what truly makes me a libertine is you, and the fact that I can't wait to touch you."

As he said it, he peeled her dress over her shoulders. She stepped away from him and tugged it off the rest of the way. It pooled at her feet, leaving her in her flimsy chemise. He cursed beneath his breath, and she smiled. "Is that a compliment?"

"Always," he groaned. "Come up here. I need you up here next to me."

She pulled the chemise off and moved to the bottom of the bed. She took a place at his good side, so that when he rolled he wouldn't have to lie on the injury. He shook his head as he drew his fingers along her bare shoulder. "You're always thinking, aren't you?"

"I'm barely functional, I assure you," she gasped as he leaned in and dragged his bristled cheek against her breast.

"God, your curves," he murmured as he licked her nipple, dragging his teeth gently against the hardening flesh. "I could write a soliloquy about these curves. A sermon. Form a whole religion about worshiping your amazing body."

"I only want one disciple," she muttered as she dug her fingers into his hair and held him there. He sucked her nipple hard. Her head lolled back. "Suck harder."

He did so, swirling his tongue around and around and around her until her whole body was hot with unquenchable fire. He switched his attention to her opposite breast, laving and sucking and tormenting all over again. She mewled out pleasure, rocking her hips to his.

"I'll go slower next time. I'll take my time and—"

She interrupted by stroking his cock gently. "Please shut up and just take me."

He laughed as she rolled so that her back faced him. His mouth came to her shoulder. He licked there, then lightly bit, and she pushed her hips back in mute demand. He met it, opening her slightly from behind, aligning his cock, and then he slid inside in one slick thrust.

They both gasped in this new joining and she ground back, turning her face so that he could kiss her. He cupped her breast as he thrust, toying with her, and the pleasure was heady and hot. "I'm going to touch myself while you take me," she whispered.

He nodded against her shoulder and she felt him adjust, looking over to watch as she drove a hand between her legs. She ground in time to his thrusts, the pleasure building and building until it overtook her. She came, jolting around him as he held her tight to his chest.

"Fucking hell," he growled. "You are like a glove."

She panted as the pleasure faded and then briefly separated their bodies to face him again. They were nose to nose, eye to eye, and she felt so connected to him that her chest actually hurt from it. "There has never been pleasure like this for me. Never like this."

His expression softened slightly, and he nodded like he understood. But then his gaze flitted down her body and he smiled, the wickedness back. "I want a taste."

He rolled on his back as he said it and slid down on the bed, motioning for her to come up to him.

Her eyes went wide. "Straddle your mouth?"

He nodded. "Oh yes."

"Er, I'm not some delicate little slender reed," she said, motioning to the same curves he'd been waxing poetic about a few moments before. "I don't want to crush you."

"You won't," he promised as he pulled her forward.

She straddled his stomach first, then inched up his chest, the hair there tickling her still-quivering sex. She moved over his face, gripping the headboard behind him, lifting herself a little as he helped guide her into position.

She was still uncertain, but all that vanished when he swiped his tongue over her the first time. Her head dropped back and she moaned his name until it echoed in the room around them.

He chuckled and the vibration shot through her. She ground down, rocking against his tongue and feeling the pleasure mount almost immediately. She was back on the edge in moments as he swirled his tongue against her, sucking as she rode his mouth. She gripped the headboard so hard she feared she might break it. She didn't want that. She also didn't want to stop what they were doing, not when she was so close to...

"Yes!" she gasped, her hips flexing out of control as wave after wave of orgasm ripped through her. He did just as he'd done the night before, too. He licked her through the crisis, drawing out the pleasure until it edged right up to pain but never tipped over the cliff. Until she was incoherent and shaking.

Only then did he push her away a fraction. She tipped onto her back, head at the foot of the bed, and he sat up, adjusting to cover her body with hers. She stared up into his face, his chin and beard slick with her juices, and her body twitched with need all over again.

"How do you do that?" she whispered as she leaned up to kiss him. She tasted herself on his tongue, drank of her own pleasure like it was heady wine.

"Practice," he said.

She shook her head, ignoring his teasing. "How do you make it so easy?"

"Because I want to make you happy," he said, staring down into her eyes, the lightness gone from his voice. "Your pleasure is the most important thing."

Tears stung her eyes. She'd never been the most important thing to anyone. Even to him in the long ago past. But here he was, declaring it without hesitation.

She opened her legs a little wider. "I want your pleasure, too."

He was already guiding himself back into her body, and she quaked as he slid through the evidence of her release, filling her completely. His mouth fused with hers and then he fucked her. He didn't make love to her, he didn't take his time, he didn't savor her. He fucked her, hard and fast until she scratched her nails across his shoulders and her over-stimulated body shuddered in another quick release.

Only then did he pull away and come between them with a harsh, heavy cry of passion.

He collapsed across her, panting, whispering her name, pressing kisses into her neck, her shoulder, his teeth abrading her collarbone. She wrapped her arms around him and held tight, losing herself in this moment.

But only for a moment at that. The bliss couldn't last. It couldn't be a shield anymore, a barrier. Now was the time to ask the question that had been on her mind for days. Years.

"Nicholas?" she said softly, still tracing her fingers in faint patters across his scarred back.

"Mmm?" he murmured, his voice sleepy and sated.

She hesitated. Did she want to ruin this moment?

He lifted his head, and there was recognition in his gaze. He realized the time had come as much as she did. "Just say it," he said. "One of us has to say it."

She nodded. "Why...why did you go to the army instead of marrying me as we planned? Why did you leave me all those years ago?"

# CHAPTER 15

Nicholas's vision actually blurred as Aurora said those words.

"What?" he snapped, probably harsher than he should have been. It was only that he was shocked by the question. This twisted version of their shared history that she was repeating. "What are you talking about, Aurora?"

She shifted and her hands dropped away from his skin. Just a little distance, but it felt like a chasm in that moment. "You and I had talked of marrying, and you said you wanted to speak to my father," she said.

"Yes," he ground out.

She turned her face. "You went to the army instead. I was so angry about it at the time. How could I not be? My father encouraged that, of course, telling me you never wanted me. I had to come to terms with it and I'm not angry anymore. I just want to understand the past so we can move forward."

He sat up now, separating their bodies even farther as he stared at her. "What the hell are you talking about?"

Now her eyes flashed and he saw the anger she claimed she didn't still feel rising up in her. A fire goddess, and he almost leaned into her. Except the subject matter didn't allow it.

"Stop looking at me like I'm daft," she insisted. "You didn't marry me, did you? You left for the army instead, didn't you? What part of that is something you don't understand?"

He shook his head. "I-I didn't join the army because I didn't want you. I joined because you were marrying Lovell and there was nothing left for me in my old life if there wasn't you." Now *she* looked confused, like he was speaking a language she didn't understand. He ignored the look and continued, "I *saw* you together in the garden the night I came to speak to your father about permission to wed. The earl said he'd arranged the marriage and that you were thrilled to get a title. You looked happy together. I saw you smile—I felt it in my soul."

Her mouth dropped open and she stared at him. "Wait. I-I don't understand."

He held her gaze as the understanding dawned on them both. The manipulation came clear. Tears filled her eyes and she lifted both shaking hands to her mouth.

"He lied," Nicholas whispered. "Your father lied to both of us."

The tears began to fall, rolling over her cheeks, her hands as she stared at him. Her voice was muffled as she said, "I don't understand. What did he do?"

"When did he tell you that I left you for the army?" Nicholas asked.

She was fighting to speak and her words were breathless and pained. "Th-the last night we saw each other, when you said you would come in a few days to speak to my father…it was the next day. He produced a letter, Nicholas, in what looked to be your hand. Written to him, telling him to let me down easily. That you'd never intended to wed me."

"I never wrote such a thing."

She shook her head, back and forth. As if that movement could erase what had been done. "Then who did?" A sob hiccupped from her throat. "He *forged* it?"

"He must have." His throat ached from gripping his jaw so tight, from the frustrated emotion that boiled up in him. "That was two days before I came to the house and saw you with Lovell. I'd written you during that time."

"I never got another letter," she whispered.

"I thought it odd you didn't write me back, but I knew I'd see you when I made the offer for your hand. What else did the earl say about my leaving? How did he know I was intending to go to the army?"

"He said something about your father helping to arrange it."

"My father…" he repeated, needing clarity. "You mean, Gillingham?"

But he already knew the answer. He knew it before she shook her head. He knew it before she spoke.

"No. The last Duke of Roseford," she whispered.

That hung in the air like a cloud. A question. Was the late Roseford indeed involved in the events of that horrible night? Had he inserted himself? And why? Except Nicholas had his suspicions.

He shook his head. Aurora would have none of those answers, but he wanted different ones from her at present. "How did Lovell come into the picture?"

"My father gave me all of two days after he ripped my heart to shreds to invite Lovell to the house. It was evident he wanted me to marry the viscount. That the match was in his favor politically and, after seeing the mess he left for my brother since his death a few years ago, I would assume financially."

"So the night I saw you…"

"Was the first night I met Lovell," she whispered. "And if I seemed to be smiling, Nicholas, I was grimacing. Trying not to cry every moment. Lovell was…he could be cold, and he embarrassed me regularly during our marriage, but he could also be kind when it suited him. He was kind that night, and I knew my father would force my hand. What did it matter? If I couldn't have you, I might as well not fight him. I didn't have the strength anymore."

She pulled her knees up to her chest and rested her head there, the sobs shaking her now as what had happened in the past washed over them both. She wept while he sat, numb and empty.

At last she lifted her head. "My father was so many things, but I cannot wrap my head around the idea that he would be so cruel as to part us in that way."

He stared at her, hating himself as much as he hated the late earl. "I-I believed him. I believed him, Aurora."

Her tears slowed and she wiped them away. "That—that's it, isn't it? We were both so young. Too young to believe in ourselves or in each other. So I, like you, believed that you would leave me. That… that you couldn't truly want me or the difficulties we'd face together."

He pushed from the bed and walked to the fire. It warmed his bare skin, but inside he still felt cold. "And I believed that you didn't really want me. That you would choose a title over a less exalted life with me." He gripped his hands at his sides. "We failed each other. He played a hand you and I dealt him in our uncertainty and our youth."

To his surprise, she pulled a pillow up and screamed into it. He pivoted toward her, but she held up a hand as she lifted her face to him. Her cheeks were red, expression lit with anger and pain and heartbreak that hit him in the stomach like a punch to the gut.

"All that misery, all that pain, your injuries, my empty marriage…it was all for nothing!" she cried out.

"No!" He lunged for her and caught her arms, dragging her against his chest and holding her there. He felt her shake, he knew she felt his heart pound. "It wasn't for nothing, Aurora."

"But it wouldn't have happened without his lies," she sobbed.

He smoothed her hair. "No, it wouldn't have. But we don't know what our future would have looked like if he hadn't. I learned in the past two years, as I fought through enormous physical pain, that I cannot think about what might have been or even what should have been. I can only live in what is. What I went through losing you, during my years in service and after I was injured…it's made me the person I am today. The same is true for you. You wouldn't be the Aurora here today if it weren't for the struggle. And the Aurora of today is magnificent. Truly magnificent."

She looked up at him, cheeks shining with tears, but also lit with what he recognized was love for him. He hadn't trusted that emotion, not fully, all those years ago. But the man he was today saw it and felt it and knew it to be true. He also knew it might not matter, it might not change anything, it might not mean a happy ending for them.

"We can't change what happened," she whispered.

"No."

She bent her head. "I-I suppose you're right. But I'm still sorry it happened. You have to let me be sorry that any of it happened."

He kissed her cheek, tasting the salt of her tears. "You can be sorry for as long as you need to be."

She wrapped her arms around him, and for a moment they just held each other. She took deep breaths and he found himself matching them until he felt calmer. More at peace despite the horrifying truth they'd just uncovered.

"They'll be meeting downstairs soon," she whispered. "I should get ready."

He nodded as he pressed a kiss to her hair. "I should, too. Can we talk about this more later, Aurora?"

"Of course," she said, but her tone was flat. Her faith had been shaken, perhaps more than his, because it was her father who had ripped her life away. She hadn't thought him capable, even if Nicholas had.

But that didn't mean he didn't have questions that needed answers.

He tilted her chin up and kissed her. She clung to his arms, desperation in her kiss. And when they parted, she didn't look satisfied. He stepped away and slowly dressed in the quiet of the room.

No longer a comfortable or companionable quiet. A quiet of heartbreak and regret.

"I'll see you tonight," he said at last.

"Yes," she murmured as she pulled the covers up around herself like a shield. "Tonight."

He left her even though he felt uneasy about it. But he didn't go to his room to ready himself. No, he had another destination in mind. One person who might have the answers he needed... assuming that person hadn't been keeping them secret all these years.

"Did you know?" Nicholas said as he stepped into Robert's office and slammed the door behind himself.

Robert had been going over some papers, Derrick standing behind him, looking over his shoulder, and both men glanced up. "What?"

"Did you fucking know about Aurora?" He hated that his voice was shaking. "About what our...*your* father did?"

"Calm yourself," Robert said as he got to his feet and exchanged a side glance with Derrick, who shrugged. "What are you so upset about?"

"Nine years ago I believed Aurora had chosen a title over me," he panted, the weight of it hitting him all over again. "And today I found out that wasn't true. Her father lied to us both. He manipulated the situation and made her think I chose the army over her, made me believe she wanted a title more. And it sounds as though the last Duke of Roseford might have been party to the deception. *Did you know?*"

The color bled from Robert's face and he looked truly stricken, though Nicholas didn't know if it was horror over what had been done or that he'd been caught in the thick of it.

"My God, it sounds like something our father would have done," Robert whispered.

"You must have had his diaries, his records. I *know* he kept notes about his bastards." Nicholas could hardly breathe, and he leaned on his cane as he glared at his brother.

Derrick placed a hand on Robert's shoulder and squeezed lightly before he came around the desk and motioned Nicholas to one of the chairs there. "Sit," he ordered, and Nicholas barely had a choice because he was shaking so hard, his mind racing so, that his body couldn't keep up.

For all his words to Aurora about how the past couldn't be changed, he was overwhelmed at the moment by the pain, the loss, the regret. He sank into the seat, hands trembling.

"You don't really think that Robert was involved in something so dastardly?" Derrick said softly, almost gently, as if he were soothing a child. Perhaps Nicholas wasn't far off, emotionally. "You *know* he was a victim of Roseford too."

Nicholas looked across the desk at his brother and saw how affected Robert was by this accusation. Some of his emotions softened. "I...no. I can't imagine you would have been directly involved in such cruelty. But did you know about it afterward? Did you keep it from me to reduce my pain?"

"No," Robert said firmly. "I wouldn't have kept such a secret from you. Especially once you arrived here and reconnected with Aurora. I would have told you if I'd known, I swear that to you on my life."

"Then I'm sorry. You've been nothing but good to me since my arrival. You didn't deserve my accusations," Nicholas said, bending his head.

"I'm your brother. I will always be on your side," Robert said softly. "I know you don't think much of me—"

"That isn't true," Nicholas said, jerking his face back up. "I've gotten to know you, really know you, in the past few weeks. And I was a fool to avoid what we could have had all along. You are a good man."

Robert twisted his face. "No need to insult me, now."

That elicited a smile from Nicholas, but he could do nothing more than that weak expression. "I think I'm just in shock finding out what her father did. What *our* father might have done."

"Well, first let us find out if this is true," Robert said, and got up. He crossed to the bookshelves on the opposite side of the room and skimmed along the neat lines. "These are our father's journals," he explained. "I keep them out so I can see them and always know what he was. What I never want to become, despite my nature. What year was it again that he did this?"

"Summer of 1807," Nicholas choked out. "July 23, if you want to be specific. It was a warm night. It rained at midnight and I wanted it to flood the world."

Robert slid his finger along the line and stopped abruptly to pull out one of the journals. He flipped it open. "Near the end of his life," he muttered as he skimmed the pages. "Ah, here is the general timeline."

He read for a few moments, his lips pursed in disgust, and then his eyes went wide. He looked at Nicholas. "Roseford came to you that summer?"

Nicholas nodded. "Yes, a few weeks before. He wanted a relationship of some kind. I told him I already had a father and wanted nothing to do with him."

Robert flinched. "Well, it seems he decided to exact a cost for that." He moved to Nicholas and handed over the journal.

It was written in the late duke's scrawl, which was as undisciplined as the man had been. Nicholas had to squint to understand the words when they blended together. But the meaning was crystal clear. He read it out loud:

*"Took care of that little problem with Gillingham. If he doesn't want my support, then he shall understand the pain of its absence. Off to the army he goes, where he'll find his precious independence isn't as exciting as*

*he believes. Earl of Bramwell pleased as he didn't want a bastard, even my bastard, clouding his treasured line."*

Nicholas let the book droop. "And then he just goes on about some woman he was fucking behind her husband's back."

"I'm sorry," Derrick whispered. "I'm so desperately sorry for you both and for Selina and Morgan that this man was your so-called father."

Nicholas pushed from his seat and crossed to the sideboard. He poured himself a tall glass of whisky and downed the entire thing in one slug, then slammed the glass down with enough force that it screeched.

"I would kill them for what they did, but they're already both dead men." He threw up his hands in frustration. "There is no revenge for this. No way to balance the damned scales. They conspired together to destroy my life and hers and there is *nothing* I can do about it."

"That's not true," Robert said softly.

Nicholas pivoted and glared at his brother. "What do you suggest? Dig them both up and have my row?"

To his surprise, a flicker of a smile passed over Robert's face. He glared harder at the appearance of it. "Is this funny to you, brother? Does my pain cause you amusement?"

Robert shook his head. "Never. I'm just not accustomed to this passionate streak coming out in you. I see the rest of us in you in this moment. The part of you that you hate."

His lips parted. "I-I don't hate the blood I share with you. Though I do hate our father right now."

"I hate our father every day," Robert said with such calm even though the truth of it rippled through his expression for a moment, dark and terrible. "I hate him so much I hardly even notice that the feeling is there anymore. I lived with him. He focused his attention, when he could tear it away from whoring around England, on me. I will tell you he was a horrific person who destroyed many lives on a whim."

"My mother," Nicholas whispered.

The other two men stiffened when he did so. His mother had been dead a long time, fifteen years now. He rarely spoke of her because it still stung that she was gone. She'd been a servant in Roseford's home. He'd taken advantage of her, against her will, and thrown her into the street. It was only Aurora's mother who had saved her as she swelled with child, giving her a position despite her lack of reference.

And Bertrand Gillingham, man of affairs, who had settled her and claimed her son as his own. Loved Nicholas as his own. Nicholas had been lucky in that. Selina and Morgan had suffered far more in their families of upbringing.

"Your mother was the worst of what that fiend did in his wretched life," Robert choked out, and for a moment that rage he seemed to be accustomed to containing flared higher. "Still, it doesn't shock me that he turned on you when you didn't give him what he wanted. That doesn't mean you're helpless in this."

"I agree," Derrick said. "As angry as you may be at the past, you aren't out of control *now*. As you said a moment ago, the duke is dead, the earl is dead. And the barriers of belief that kept you from Aurora are gone too. You *know* she didn't leave you for a better prospect, as you believed all these years. She was manipulated."

"You have a rare gift," Robert said. "A second chance. I know a little about that."

Nicholas stared at him, his brow wrinkling. "With Katherine?" He heard the incredulity in his tone.

"Oh yes," Robert said softly. "I hurt her once. Unlike you, it wasn't manipulated by others. *I* did it because I was dangerously close to walking the exact same path as our demon of a father. But when the opportunity arose, I knew I couldn't lose her again. And I was lucky enough to earn the opportunity to love her for the rest of her life."

Nicholas swallowed. "You two are so happy. I never would have thought…"

Robert shrugged. "Happiness isn't a gift, my friend. It looks like it. It feels like it sometimes, but when it comes to love, it is a decision one makes every day. I wake up with the clear thought that I'm going to do whatever I need to do to make Katherine's life better. That I'm going to act in a way that never makes her regret surrendering her heart. Love is a choice and a vocation."

Derrick nodded. "It is."

Robert smiled at him briefly before he turned his attention back to Nicholas. "I've watched you with Aurora since the party began. I've seen her connect with our friends. I've seen what a light she could be to our lives, to yours. I've seen her connect with *you*."

"I've seen the same," Derrick agreed. "Even Selina, who is protective of you to a fault and wants so desperately to hate Aurora for the crimes it's evident she didn't actually commit...likes her. She likes what *you* are when you two are together. And so do I. I've watched you suffer firsthand, my friend. When I see you happy, it's something I hope you're brave enough to grab on to and never let go."

"I suppose that is the ultimate question, and it's one only you can answer: what do you want?" Robert asked.

Nicholas flinched because the only answer that came zinging clear and loud through his mind was…

"Her," he said so softly it almost didn't carry even though it was a scream echoing in his mind. "It's always been her."

The other two men smiled at him, as if they'd already known. Certainly they approved, given the discussion they'd just shared. Derrick's smile wavered just a fraction, though. When Nicholas tilted his head in expectation, Derrick shrugged. "You know you might not be given the title if you pursue her. Some are looking for an excuse to fight against it, and her scandal could offer that."

Nicholas pursed his lips. The concept of becoming marquess had been driving him for nearly two years. Since his injury, since it had been held out before him like some kind of carrot. So those were his two futures: one with her and one where she would have to wait until he had been judged worthy.

Could he give her a good future without the title? Did he even know what he would do without it?

"I must think, I suppose."

"Well, at least you have friends while you do it." Robert smiled and slung an arm around him. In that moment, Nicholas felt a swell of love for his brother that he'd never allowed before.

And a future that suddenly felt brighter than it ever had before.

# CHAPTER 16

Aurora tightened her robe around her waist and tried to appear calm as her maid entered the chamber. Jeanette's gaze flitted over her, and Aurora was certain she could see the flush of pleasure all over her face. Not to mention the dress still crumpled on the floor. One she would not have been able to remove without assistance.

"I took a nap," she blurted out. "But I need to ready myself for supper."

Jeanette nodded. "Yes, my lady. Of course. And you also received a letter that Jenner gave to me when you rang."

She handed over the folded sheets before she moved to Aurora's wardrobe and began to choose a few selections for supper. As she did so, Aurora broke the seal and gasped.

"It's from Imogen," she murmured, heart suddenly throbbing faster as she skimmed the words from her missing friend. The more she read, the more nervous she became. "It doesn't matter which dress," she said. "We must hurry, I need to speak to the others."

"Of course, my lady," Jeanette said, and swiftly chose a dress. Aurora hardly noticed which one as she grabbed for hair pins that were scattered on the floor. She began stabbing them through her hair, forming it into a loose, messy bun as her maid buttoned her.

"Oh, my lady, couldn't I just—" Jeanette said, reaching for Aurora's bed-mussed hair.

"I'll come back and you can fix it later!" Aurora called as she hurried for the door. "I'm sorry!"

She clutched the letter in her hand as she all but ran through the halls and down the stairs. A footman was at the bottom. "Do you know where Mr. Huntington or the duke are?" she asked. She didn't ask after Nicholas. She didn't want to involve him and threaten his goals.

"I believe they're together the duke's study," the young man said with a quick glance at Aurora's hair.

"Thank you," she said, and hustled that way. The door was closed and she began to open it when she realized Nicholas was speaking inside. Softly, so she could only hear a few words.

"...always been..."

She peeked into the room to find Nicholas standing facing the door, though his view of it was likely blocked by Derrick Huntington and the Duke of Roseford, who each had their backs to her.

Huntington spoke, his deep voice laced with emotion. "You know you might not be given the title if you pursue her. Some are looking for an excuse to fight against it, and her scandal could offer that."

She froze, the letter in her hand forgotten for a flash of a moment. They were talking about...*her*. That was obvious from the words. Obvious from Nicholas's expression. He looked torn as he pursed his lips.

She stepped away from the door, leaning against the wall beside it to catch her breath. There it was. The truth at the heart of the matter. She and Nicholas might want each other. They might still love each other. He might even want a future with her. But if he pursued any of it right now, he might and probably *would* lose the title of marquess. And it would be entirely her fault. *She* would be the excuse men like Sweeting or Roddenbury whispered in the Prince's ear that Nicholas wasn't worth the reward. Even though he was worth a dozen of them, a hundred, a thousand.

It wouldn't matter. Merit rarely came into play in the ranks he aspired to. They would crush him as quickly as they would embrace him.

But she could change that. She could give him the future he wanted to make up for the past her father had destroyed. The past their own hesitations and uncertainty had crushed. She would do it. Even if it hurt her.

She forced a smile to her face, smoothed her skirts and turned back to the door.

"Your Grace," she called out so that the men would know she was entering the room and stop talking about her. "Jenner said you and Mr. Huntington were in—" She cut herself off and feigned surprise. "Oh, and Nicholas."

"Aurora," Nicholas said softly as his gaze flitted over her. All of them stared, truth be told. She was certain they all marked her mussed hair, her flushed cheeks. Would they guess what had made her so undone?

Did it matter?

"I didn't expect to see you…right now. Are you well?" he asked, his brow wrinkling as he crossed to her a few long steps.

She nodded. "I am, but I received a message from Imogen and I hoped the duke and Mr. Huntington might be able to help me." She stepped past him and handed out the note to Derrick.

"I'll let you read it, of course, but the summary is that Imogen has been in hiding the past few weeks," she said with a shiver. "Apparently she saw something in one of those brothels that put her in danger. But she is alive and unharmed thus far."

"She wants to meet with you," Derrick said, his eyes darting up from the letter.

"Yes, I think she must have sensed the desperation in my messages once she received them," Aurora said. "So I must return to

London. I hoped perhaps His Grace could help me connect with his friend in the War Department."

"Of course," Robert said, coming around the desk. "I'll write to Willowby right away with instructions he meet us at my home in a few days."

"The Duke of Willowby?" she and Nicholas said together.

Robert's brow lowered. "Both the duke and his duchess are master spies. I believe she's in line to take over the running of that entire part of the War Department."

"I appreciate your offer to introduce us," Aurora said. "But you all still have a few days planned for your party. I would need to leave tomorrow at the latest."

"We'll all go," Robert said. "A young woman is in danger, we're not all going to stay here and kick up our heels while you hurtle yourself into an investigation. At any rate, I think I shall lose half my party if you depart. Obviously Nicholas would follow, and I think Huntington and Selina would also want to depart with you."

Derrick nodded. "The moment I understood what was happening, I wrote to my partner, Barber. He has been working alongside Willowby. I'm going and Selina will want to help too."

She shook her head. For such a long time she'd felt so alone. Her mother and brother loved her, but they didn't understand her life because she'd been careful to shelter them from her problems. After all, they had too little funds themselves to assist, thanks to her father's wretchedly bad management. She couldn't add her own issues to the fires burning at their feet.

But here in this house she had been embraced by Nicholas's family and their friends. Even if they discouraged him from the match, they still welcomed her and folded her into their circle.

"Your help means…" She choked back tears. "It means the world to me."

Nicholas's lips parted and he moved to her, seemingly not caring that the others saw him. He took her hand, lacing his fingers through hers, and just held it as he stared down into her eyes. All his support was there, all his goodness, his heart. Because of who he was, he would sacrifice anything to save her. To help her. Maybe even to love her.

She should tug away, but she didn't.

"I think we're *all* happy to help," Robert said. "Now I'll go speak to Katherine and we can spread the word amongst our guests that we must return to London for a family emergency."

"I'll send word to Barber and speak to Selina," Derrick said. The two men exchanged a quick look with Nicholas, and then they left him and Aurora alone.

"They're too kind," she whispered. "No one should…should sacrifice so much for me."

She hoped he understood the double meaning of those words. He didn't break eye contact with her, though. He traced his thumb along her cheek gently, then across her lip, and her breath caught. God, what he could do so easily. Make her want physically and even more deeply than that.

She blinked and pulled away a fraction.

"What can I do?" he asked.

She shrugged. "You are doing it. Your family has been kind enough to help me thanks to you."

"I want to do more," he said, and moved toward her. His hand found hers again, he lifted it to his lips.

She shook her head even though it was nearly impossible. "You'll risk yourself if you do any more, Nicholas." His brow wrinkled with confusion and she pulled away a second time. "I should go fix the hair you ruined so sweetly earlier."

That brought a smile to his face, and she returned it. "Then I'll see you at supper?" he asked.

She nodded and cast him one last look as she exited the room. She had to do what was right, both for Imogen by helping her and for Nicholas. Even if that meant pushing him away to protect him. They'd survived nine years parted. Surely they could survive a little longer.

Nicholas had no idea why Aurora was pushing him away, but he felt it as keenly as if she'd stood with both hands on his chest, shoving with all her might. She sat at the opposite end of the table, hardly touching her supper and never looking at him.

The dismissal, for that was what it felt like, stung like she'd slapped him. And it brought back those same feelings of abandonment and pain he'd felt nine years before.

"—don't you think, Aurora?" the Duchess of Northfield was saying.

Aurora blinked and jerked her head up. "I-I'm sorry. I'm distracted and I'm being very rude."

Nicholas watched Adelaide's face softened a fraction. She was very kind. All of them were so very kind. "You aren't. I think, though, that since we are amongst just friends, perhaps it would do us all some good to confront the topic we're all dancing around out of politeness. I've learned that being direct often helps." She reached out and touched Aurora's hand. "My dear, how can we help you in London?"

Aurora blushed, her embarrassment plain. But then she sighed. "All I want to do is find my friend. And I know I have a great deal of help. Just knowing you are on my side is enough."

Adelaide smiled. "I think I can do a bit more. Mr. Huntington, it might interest you to know that I have a few contacts in the underground, myself. I'll reach out to them if that would be of help."

Nicholas nearly choked on the wine he'd just sipped and as he dapped the dribbles from his chin, he said, "*You* have connections in the underground, Your Grace?"

Graham chuckled as he met his wife's blue eyes. "My wife contains multitudes, my friends. You never know what she might do and I think it's wonderful."

Adelaide giggled at the cryptic compliment, but her expression grew more serious as she looked again at Aurora. "Truly. We will fix this. As a group. As a family. It's what we do."

The last of the plates were cleared away then and the table rose as a group. Normally they would be entering the parlor for after supper drinks and entertainment, but because the party was leaving for London early the next morning and it had been such a last-minute decision, tonight they were retiring early to prepare.

So farewells were said and the couples walked away together. Finally it was just Nicholas and Aurora in the dining room. He thought that might have been the design of their friends.

"Aurora," he said softly.

She flitted her gaze to him. "I think you'll remember that I'm nothing but trouble after today."

He wrinkled his brow. "That isn't true. Is that why you've been acting so strangely since this afternoon?"

"I'm not acting strangely," she said, but she turned her face so he no longer was able to look her in the eye.

"Yes you are," he insisted. "We made love—"

"Nicholas!" she said, a harsh whisper. "The walls have ears."

"Then they certainly heard you keening my name," he said, frustration rising to the surface. He moved a bit closer and lowered his voice. "When we made love and afterward when the truth came out, I thought we were starting something...new. Turning a corner. But after you came to my brother's study with your letter, I feel the change in the air between us."

She worried her lip and he could see her fighting herself. Fighting whatever she wanted to say.

"Please," he said, coming around the table and catching her hand. "Didn't we let enough misunderstanding come between us in the past? Can't we be honest with each other now?"

She let out her breath in a long sigh. "I think it's hard for me to see the future right now, Nicholas. I realized when I saw Imogen's letter, when I read it and felt the fear in her, that I had been pretending my life was normal while I was here. But it isn't and it won't be until I know she is safe."

He drew back a fraction. "I see."

"I just think that perhaps I shouldn't lose myself too much," she said, pulling her hand away. "In a…a fantasy world."

He pursed his lips. She cared for him. He knew that to be true now. He loved her and that was absolute fact. But somehow it wasn't enough. Had it ever been?

"You want a little space to deal with this problem with your friend," he said softly.

She nodded. "Yes. I think that's it."

He gave a slight bow. "Then I'll do whatever you need. I-I'll see you in the morning, then."

She caught her breath like she wanted to say something. Like she wanted to do something more than let him walk away. But in the end that was just what she did. His world had been flipped on its head and he had no idea what to do to right it.

Or to move forward with the woman who had held his heart for over a decade. The one who still hadn't decided to fight for what they could have.

# CHAPTER 17

If Aurora had thought the trip out to Roseford was long, returning home felt interminable. They had caravanned as a group and it should have been very jolly. After all, the women of their group traded off, sharing carriages so they could read and talk and sew together. She'd even had the company of Fortescue at times. The big dog rode in her carriage, his great, dear head on her lap as she read.

Still, all Aurora could do was watch Nicholas. He'd granted her the space she'd lied about needing. He didn't ride with her. He was polite but distant when they talked at suppers at the inns where they stopped at night.

He hadn't touched her or kissed her since that magical afternoon back at Roseford when they last made love in her bed. She sensed the pulsing drive of need in him, but he was so disciplined that he never wavered.

Perhaps he was trying to show her how empty her life would be without him. But oh, she already knew that. It had been weighing on her mind since she overheard Derrick say that Nicholas might not get his title if he chose a life with her right now.

She blinked as the carriage rounded a corner. They had entered

London nearly an hour ago and were coming closer and closer to the Duke of Roseford's city estate, where Huntington's partner and Willowby would meet them to discuss their plans to find Imogen. That was what Aurora had to focus on now. That was what was important.

The manor house rose up large and impressive in the distance, and she leaned against the glass to look at it more closely. There were two men and a lady standing on the drive waiting for them, and her heart leapt. These had to be the investigators.

Her carriage stopped, and to her surprise it was Roseford himself who opened the door and helped her out. Katherine was already on the step chatting with the other three strangers, her arm around the lady.

"Lady Lovell," Robert said, taking her arm and guiding her up the stairs. "May I introduce you to the Duke and Duchess of Willowby and Mr. Barber? They've all been working on finding your friend."

She stepped toward them, holding out her hand in greeting. "I cannot thank you all enough. I'm sure you were taken from very important things."

The Duke of Willowby, an exceedingly handsome man with short-cropped hair and a clean-shaven, hard-angled face, shook her hand first. "Not at all."

His wife, a petite and curvaceous woman with dark auburn hair, nodded. "We've actually been doing some work on a case of an underground group that takes women and forces them into trading their bodies for money. We think your friend narrowly dodged that fate thanks to some help. This will only aid in our larger case."

Aurora moved to the other man. He had warm brown skin and friendly eyes. "It's really a blessing you connected us, as I've been working on a similar matter for a private party. Now we've exchanged information and you and your friend might help bring this to a conclusion."

Suddenly she felt a warm hand on her back and jumped. While

she'd been so engrossed in the terror of what Imogen might have involved herself in, Nicholas, Selina and Derrick had arrived. And while her anxiety had begun to ratchet up as Barber and the Willowbys talked, now she felt calm seep into her. Nicholas's touch did that. That safe and warm feeling that no one could ever hurt her because he would always be there.

She found herself leaning into the strength of his palm, seeking the support she perhaps hadn't earned, didn't deserve. But she needed it.

There were introductions all around and the others repeated what they'd already told her about Imogen and the monsters who had been pursuing her.

When they were finished, Aurora sighed. "Imogen's letter said that she was coming back to Town from wherever she's been sequestering herself by Friday. She'll tell me then where to meet with her. So we have a day or two to prepare."

"Excellent," Willowby said with a glance for his wife. "That gives us a few more days to finalize preparations. Mr. and Mrs. Huntington and Mr. Barber will make good partners in that."

Aurora bent her head as the facts of this horrible thing hit her all at once. As if he sensed that, Nicholas caught her elbow, shoring her up before she collapsed under the weight.

"I think if you don't need Lady Lovell anymore, I shall escort her back to her home since her maid was sent ahead," he said.

"Of course," Katherine said, shooting a look to the others before anyone could argue. She moved toward Aurora and bussed her cheek, whispering, "You're exhausted. You can trust these people to work for your friend. Go rest."

Aurora nodded, because it was all she *could* do in that moment. "Please contact me with anything I can do to help."

"We'll reach out to you tomorrow with more details of the plan," Huntington said.

Nicholas said his goodbyes and then helped her back into her carriage. They turned onto the street and began the trip back to her little home. She flinched at the idea that he would see it and how far she'd fallen.

"You don't have to see me home," she said. "I'm sure you have a great deal to do now that you're back in London. You have meetings to take, I think, regarding the matter of the title."

"This takes precedence." His voice was low and rough.

She turned her face away. So he *would* sacrifice his dream for her. Exactly what she didn't want.

"Aurora," he said softly. "It's been three days of this. Please, won't you tell me what changed? Why you've been pulling away, putting up the walls that kept us apart for so long? Haven't I earned that trust after everything?"

She glanced at him, her lips parting. "It isn't about a lack of trust," she promised him.

He arched a brow and just *looked* at her. Waiting, patient and expectant, for her to do the one thing he'd asked of her and she'd avoided.

She cleared her throat and glanced out the window. They had at least a quarter of an hour before they'd reach her home. Perhaps this was best. She could tell him the truth, he'd understand, then he could just drop her off at her home and go on his way.

"You asked me for honesty a few days ago," she said. "And I suppose I have been avoiding it because it might cause us both heartache."

"I'd rather have the truth and suffer the consequences than live a lie," he said. "I've learned that."

She nodded. "Yes. I just hate to be the one that causes the anguish."

He straightened his shoulders and his expression went blank and hard, like he was steeling himself for something horrible. "Out with it then. I can take pain."

"I…overheard what Derrick said to you in his office a few days ago," she admitted. When Nicholas's brow wrinkled, she continued, "When he said that if you chose me, you might not be given the title.

That my…scandal…might preclude you from the future you've wanted since your injuries."

His lips parted. "Aurora. Bloody hell. I had no idea you heard that, I'm sorry."

She held up a hand. "He wasn't being unkind, I know that. I like him a great deal, I know he likes me."

"He does," Nicholas agreed.

"But he also wasn't…wrong," she whispered. "That was what stung me so harshly. Whether or not the rumors that have circulated about me are correct or not doesn't matter. Society will view me a certain way now, and probably for the rest of my life. And if you link yourself to me in any official way, whether through courtship or anything else, you will be tainted with the same poison. That could swing the tide of support in the wrong direction."

He shook his head. "But Aurora—"

"I know you'll make all these lovely arguments because you are such a good man. But in the end, they don't matter. You've had so much taken away from you because of my father's lies, because I didn't have enough faith in you. I refuse to be the reason you lose something else."

"But the something else I may lose is…you," he said, and leaned over to take her hands. He smoothed his thumbs over her knuckles and she shivered with a need that had gone unfulfilled for what felt like a lifetime even though it was only a few days.

"If you…want me…" she said carefully, because they had made no promises and she didn't want to leap to some conclusion. "You will have me, I promise that. I'll wait for when it's right for you. We could even meet in secret if we wanted to do that. Anything not to endanger you and your future."

The carriage slowly came to a stop in front of her home, and she sighed. "Think about it, will you? Perhaps we can talk about it after this situation with Imogen is resolved."

He stared at her. "Do you think I'm leaving?"

She nodded. "I...you escorted me home. I'm home. I didn't expect for you to—"

He laughed. "I haven't touched you in days, Aurora. I have no intention of leaving...unless you don't want me here."

She looked into his face, that face she loved so desperately, and smiled. It seemed he would accept her terms, that he would allow them to hold off on decisions about the future until his hopes and dreams were secured at last.

"I want you here," she whispered. She leaned in and wrapped her arms around his neck. His mouth came down on hers, soft at first, then harder, more insistent as he nearly brought her into his lap. They were both panting when they broke the kiss.

"Come in," she gasped. "Please."

Nicholas followed Aurora into her bedroom and looked around. Like the rest of her small home, it was an austere chamber, devoid of almost all decoration. It didn't fit her vibrant spirit or her bright personality. But it had a bed big enough for two and right now that was all that mattered.

She glanced at him over her shoulder, her pupils dilated with a need that echoed his own. With shaking hands, she locked the door. Her breath was short and harsh, her hands shook as she flattened one palm against the barrier.

He edged up behind her, wrapping his arms around her and pulling her back against him so she was flush from shoulder to hip. Their bodies molded naturally, beautifully, just as they had from the beginning. Made to be together. She made a soft sound of pleasure, one that ricocheted through his body like lightning through his bloodstream.

"I missed you," he whispered against her ear before he traced the shell with the tip of his tongue. He felt her body react, felt the heat of her rise.

She nodded. "I-I did too."

He tried not to think about the fact that they'd been parted these past few days out of her attempt to protect him. That she couldn't see a future that didn't involve secrecy or distance. He could think of those things later. Right now…

He slid the buttons along her spine open and pushed her dress down. She tugged it away as he leaned in, pushing the loose bun at the base of her nape to the side and kissing there. She tasted like summer.

She shivered, made an incoherent sound of pleasure. Her hips bumped back against his and the sensation shot up his cock.

He pivoted, drawing her with him, and now they faced that bed he'd noticed earlier. He edged her forward, kissing her neck the whole time, and bent her down, placing her hands against the edge of it. She clung to the coverlet with both hands, spreading her legs a little wider, as if she knew his plans exactly.

He pushed her chemise up with one hand, reveling in every inch of soft flesh he revealed. She was a goddess and he wanted to worship at her shrine until he forgot everything else in the world. With a shaking hand, he loosened the placard on his trousers. His cock bounced free and he took himself in hand even as he pressed a hand against her lower back, flattening her further against the bed. Her pink, wet sex taunted him, and he groaned as he stroked the head of his cock back and forth against her. She was hot and ready and he ached, he burned, he was lost.

"I had so much in mind in terms of pleasuring you," he gasped. "But…"

"Just do it," she pleaded. "I need you."

He didn't have to be asked twice. With one long thrust he slid to the hilt inside of her tight, wet heat. She pulsed around him and he was nearly unmanned at the otherworldly sensation of their joined bodies. He drew back, almost all the way out of her clenching sex and then glided forward again. She let out a wail that she buried in her coverlet, then snaked her hand between her legs. He felt her fingers stroking her clitoris, the tips slick against the root of his cock when he fully seated himself.

That she pleasured herself while he pleasured her was too much. He gripped the soft flesh of her hips to balance himself and took her. Hard and fast until he was nearly undone, then slower, slower, circling against her as she moaned and flexed, her fingers stroking wildly.

When she came, she pulsed around him, gripping him hard as she called out his name. He jerked against her in time to the rhythm of her orgasm, letting her milk him with her pleasure until he could take no more. With a grunt, he pulled out of her just in time and let his seed splash over her bottom and lower back before he collapsed over her, their sweat mingling, their breath matched.

He had no idea how long they leaned against the edge of her bed, but at some point she crawled out from under him, up onto her pillows. She reached back for his hand and he followed her, cradling her into his side and reveling in the remarkable feel of her.

He could have this forever. He wanted *her* forever.

And yet…he couldn't help thinking of what she'd said before they made love. She wanted to protect him, give him what he'd wanted for years. Her answer to that was to make herself some kind of dirty little secret. What would he do? Come here to her home three times a week and tup her? Put her up in some finer house like she was his mistress? They could be careful as they liked, but people would find out. His friends would know.

*He* would know that he was treating her as a shame to be pulled beneath the covers so no one would know about her.

"Oh, don't go doing that," Aurora whispered.

He jerked from his thoughts. "Doing what?"

"Thinking," she said with a husky laugh. "I can practically *hear* you thinking, and right now I don't want to think. I want to just…feel."

She didn't say anything more. Instead, she trailed her mouth along his chest, unbuttoning his shirt as she went, reawakening him so quickly he was taken off guard. And so he pushed away the troubles in his mind and simply sank into the pleasure of her lips as she closed them around his length and brought him back to the ready.

But his unease remained. As did the knowledge that if he made a mistake, it might just ruin the rest of his life.

# CHAPTER 18

Nicholas didn't know what to think as he stood in the parlor of the Earl of Bramwell. He'd come home the day before to find a missive from the new earl—his old friend, Aurora's brother. As well as one from Nicholas' father, who still served that household as man of affairs. Considering that he hadn't spoken to the earl in nine years and normally met with his father at his own home, he had no idea what either man would wish to say to him.

The door to the parlor opened and Thomas stepped inside. The dowager countess followed at his heels and Nicholas straightened up a fraction. Both had broad smiles. They seemed welcoming. And they both had so much of Aurora in their faces that he almost stepped back. Thomas shared her dark eyes, Lady Bramwell the shape of her face, the graceful glide of her movements.

"My lord, my lady," Nicholas said with a slight bow.

"Oh, don't do that," Bramwell said as he crossed the room and offered a hand. "We were friends too long for that."

Nicholas shifted as he smiled at his old friend. "Thomas, then," he said. "Great God, it's good to see you."

"You too," Thomas said.

"And my lady." Nicholas bowed his head again. "You are radiant, as always."

The countess blushed and smiled at him. "You do look handsome as ever, young man. I wish we'd reconnected earlier. I was forever asking your father after you when you were injured. Are you well?"

Nicholas flinched slightly. "I am. Thank you for your thoughts. Is my father joining us?"

"In a moment," Thomas said, giving his mother a quick side look.

The countess inclined her head. "I hope you'll join us for supper, Nicholas. And now I'll leave you to my son. Good afternoon."

She slipped from the room and shut the door softly. Once she was gone, Thomas looked him up and down a little closer. "Aurora isn't here."

Nicholas arched a brow. "Did I ask about her?"

Thomas shrugged one shoulder as he came around the desk and sat down. "No. But you had your wondering about Aurora look on your face. So I thought I'd answer the question before you got up the gumption to ask it."

Nicholas swallowed. "You know we were at Roseford's together."

"She wrote and mentioned you," Thomas said. "All that...*longing* was still in every word. The thing I never realized existed when I was a boy and couldn't see it."

"We tried to hide it," Nicholas said, and couldn't help but think about his last encounter with Aurora the day before, when she'd suggested they should do the same now. "Because your father didn't approve."

"No, he did not," Thomas said. "Are you going to ask me if I do?"

"Do you?" Nicholas asked, sitting down in the seat across from him.

"I approve of anything that would make my sister happy," Thomas said softly. "Do you know what my father did?"

Nicholas's eyes went wide as he stared in shock at the implication. "Are you talking about what he did all those years ago? The lies he told to part Aurora from me?"

Thomas nodded. "Yes. That's what I'm talking about."

"*You knew?*" Nicholas asked in horror.

"I found out when I took the title a few years ago," Thomas admitted. "He left such detailed accountings of all the ways he left destruction in his wake."

"Why didn't you tell me?" Nicholas asked. "You could have written me. After I was injured you could have come to call. You could have told your sister, for God's sake—it was as much a shock to her when we figured it out as it was to me."

Thomas tilted his head. "Are you finished? Because if you need to shout some more, get it out of your system."

Nicholas pursed his lips. "Bloody fuck, Thomas."

His friend sat for a moment and then he drew in a long breath. "You walked away from my sister and her heart was broken. She changed, she folded into herself. I hated you for that. And for the fact that you wrote me off with the same brush that you used to write her off."

Nicholas clenched his jaw. He and this man had been best friends their entire lives, and then it had just...ended. Because he couldn't bear to talk to Thomas and know that he couldn't ever be near Aurora again.

"That was a bad mistake on my part." He bent his head. "On both accounts."

Thomas gave a ghost of a smile. "I appreciate that. At any rate, by the time I realized how you'd both been manipulated, she was long married. What good would it have done to tell either of you the truth? Would you have come riding home from war to break up whatever life she had made for herself?"

"I don't know," Nicholas admitted. "I can't even picture what I would have done if I discovered the truth and she wasn't...free. Perhaps created more of a scandal than she's dealing with now."

"Yes." Thomas's face was lined with troubles. "Her scandal. If I had any bloody money at all, I could fix some of that. But if my father destroyed your lives in one day, he decided to decimate mine in tiny strokes. I've been digging out of his messes for years. And I'm…helpless."

"I'm sorry," Nicholas said, and meant it.

Thomas shrugged. "Nothing you can do. I must work it out myself. But I am left with a question because I saw my sister yesterday, and when she said your name I saw what I was blind to all those years ago. You spending time together at Roseford's reconnected you. I can see how she shines the moment you come up as a topic. So what are you planning to do?"

"I could protect her better if I were marquess."

He expected this man who had been groomed and readied for a title all his life to immediately agree to that notion. But instead Thomas's face fell a fraction. "Hmmm," he murmured, noncommittal.

"What does *hmmm* mean?" Nicholas asked.

But before his friend could answer, the door to the study opened and Bertrand Gillingham entered. Nicholas pushed to his feet and faced him. His father still had a straight-as-a-ramrod posture and a serious countenance. But his eyes were kind when they flitted over Nicholas and for a moment reflected joy at seeing his boy.

"Am I interrupting?" his father asked.

Thomas shot Nicholas a side glance. "Not at all, Gillingham. I think your son and I were at an impasse. And I know you are anxious to see each other. I'll step out for a moment and let you speak. But my mother's invitation stands, Nicholas—we'd love to have you join us for supper. It will *almost* be like old times."

He clapped a hand on Nicholas's arm and smiled at Gillingham before he left the two alone together. His father's hand fluttered at his side, like he wanted to touch him but didn't. Then he moved forward and began fiddling with the items on the earl's desk, organizing them. Of course he would. He was still Thomas's man of affairs. Old habits died hard, it seemed.

At last he glanced up. "You look well, better than I've seen you since—"

His father cut off. He never spoke to Nicholas about the injuries that had nearly killed him. Not even when he came to his bedside over and over as Nicholas fought to live, Gillingham had only read to him then and spoke to him of old stories from his childhood. Of his mother, of Thomas, even of Aurora. Never that horrible day of fire and pain.

"Thank you," Nicholas said. "The country air, perhaps."

"Perhaps," Gillingham said, his gaze coming up from the papers on the desktop briefly. "How were things with your brothers and your sister?"

Now Nicholas shifted, discomfort flooding him. This man had raised him, sacrificed for him, with never a whisper that Nicholas didn't belong to him. Any time Nicholas spoke of his other family, it felt like a betrayal.

"They are well," he said. "All happily married in the last few years. It has changed them, I think, and for the better."

"Love will do that," Gillingham said with a slight smile. "And now you are back in Town. I hear word you'll be taking some very important meetings in the next few weeks. About the marquess matter."

Nicholas nodded. "Yes…that's the plan. Little steps closer all the time, though who knows when they'll make their final decision. A month, a year…it could be anything."

Now his father stopped fiddling with the desk entirely and came around closer to Nicholas. He tilted his head, his gaze taking Nicholas in from head to toe. "You're troubled by that."

"I suppose I am," he admitted, thinking of Aurora. "More now than before."

"But you've always known this process would be drawn out. That you'd have to jump through a dozen hoops and impress a dozen silly men. And yet it bothers you now."

Nicholas was pulled back to when he was eight years old, twelve years old, sixteen years old and his father had offered calm counsel. That had been one of the greatest comforts of his life, knowing if he turned toward this man, he would always be welcomed with open arms and a kind ear. He didn't always like the advice, he hadn't always followed it…but it was there, a forever beacon that helped him to the shore.

"Nicholas, my boy, you still want to be marquess, don't you?"

There was the question. Simply asked. The answer was becoming far less simple.

He sighed. "I-I'm not sure anymore, Father."

Gillingham motioned to the two chairs before Thomas's roaring fire. They took them together, and his father draped his elbows over his knees, completely engaged with Nicholas in that moment. "Tell me."

"I've lived my life on the outer edges of two worlds," Nicholas said. "It's always been true, but I've never felt it more than recently."

"Roseford and his friends made you feel on the outside?" his father asked, and sounded surprised at the idea. "The new duke seems to be making such an effort lately."

"No," Nicholas said with a quick shake of his head. "Roseford is nothing like our…*his* father. He wasn't unwelcoming, I assure you. Oh, how do I explain it?"

"Take your time," Gillingham said gently.

Nicholas leaned back in his chair a moment, staring up at the ceiling as he tried to gather the swirling thoughts that had been tormenting him since the moment he saw Aurora step from her carriage and onto his brother's drive. That moment had changed everything, even if he hadn't wanted to see it.

"Men like Robert, like his friend Northfield, men like Thomas… they've always known their destiny. It was pressed into their flesh from birth what they would be. They were practically trained from the cradle. You know, you've served men like that your whole life."

His father nodded. "Yes. That is a blessing and a curse, you know. To always know your path, to never be able to choose it."

"Of course. I've seen the damage it does," Nicholas agreed. "But being with these men who have always known their path, I also came to realize that I won't ever be fully on the inside. I'll always be what I always was, Father. Half-blood, half accepted, half in one world, half in the other."

"You fear you won't belong?" Gillingham said.

"I *won't* belong as marquess," Nicholas said. "But when I was at Roseford with my brothers and my sisters, their spouses and their friends and…and Aurora…I did feel like I belonged. For the first time I was just me and that was enough." He shook his head. "I'm so sorry, Father."

His father leaned even closer and his gaze locked with Nicholas's. "Sorry? Why are you sorry, my boy?"

"Because it's a betrayal of you. It's a betrayal of the fact that you raised me, that you treated me like your son when you never had to do that."

Gillingham's face softened, and he reached out and squeezed Nicholas's hand. It was a surprising gesture, as his father had never been overly physically affectionate. His love was always shown in other ways. But now it was like all his strength poured into Nicholas.

"You must never be sorry about who you are," his father said softly. "I treated you like a son because you *are* my son. In every way that has ever mattered, you are mine. But you are also their brother. The fact that you've all found each other in the last few years warms my heart. Those two worlds never had to be separate. It was *never* a betrayal of me to want to connect to them."

Nicholas stared at him, this man who had raised him, nurtured him, loved him. "You're saying I don't have to be one world or another."

"No," his father said. "If they are intelligent enough to accept you as you are, then you have always belonged in both. Always. Title or no title."

A strange weight lifted from Nicholas's shoulders at those words. "Perhaps," he said softly.

His father let go of his hand and smiled. "And as for Lady Lovell…Aurora…"

Nicholas held his breath. Gillingham had disapproved of their connection when he was younger. He had feared the very reprisal that had ultimately come.

But now he smiled. "I have always liked her. And I am far too old and you have lived through far too much for me to tell you what to do with your heart. Except to be happy."

Nicholas reached out, touching that face that looked nothing like his own, but was still so very beloved. His father in every way that had ever and would ever matter.

"Thank you, Papa," he said softly.

Gillingham gave a half smile at the endearment Nicholas hadn't used since he was fifteen. The old man's eyes were sparkling with tears. The same ones stinging Nicholas's eyes as he dropped his hand away.

"Enough of this nonsense," Gillingham said with a choked chuckle. "Are you joining us for supper, then? I've heard on good authority that Mrs. Bright is making lamb."

Nicholas grinned as his father offered him an arm for support as he stood. "There is nothing quite so good as her lamb."

He followed his father from the room, his mind more at peace, but with no further answers than he'd had when he entered. In fact, he only questioned everything all the more.

# CHAPTER 19

Aurora paced the floor in her small parlor, the latest letter from Imogen dangling from her fingertips. She had already reached out to everyone involved to meet with her and give them the final information, and now she tried to remain calm as she did so.

There was a light knock on her door and Jeanette poked her head in. "The carriages are arriving, my lady."

Aurora's heart leapt and she moved to the window. Indeed, there were a handful of vehicles turning in, her one poor footman rushing out to help people out. "Good," she said. "Send them in right away."

She moved to the sideboard where tea was already waiting and began to arrange cups in case her guests wanted refreshment. They began to enter the room. Mr. Barber, Selina and Derrick Huntington all came in together. The Duke and Duchess of Willowby were on their heels. Greetings were exchanged and then Aurora smoothed her hands along her skirts.

"Thank you for coming. I really do appreciate your help in this terrible matter. Let me tell you what Imogen's latest letter said and the final details for our meeting later today."

Selina stepped forward with a shake of her head. "Shouldn't we wait until we're all here? Nicholas didn't come with any of us."

Aurora's breath caught. She'd known someone in their group might be so direct. She might have guessed it would be Selina. She met the other woman's bright blue eyes and said, "I didn't send word to Nicholas," she said softly. "I know he would help me. I know he *wants* to…but…"

"But?" Huntington encouraged her as he rested a hand on his wife's back. Selina's shoulders relaxed just a fraction with the action.

The heat that filled Aurora's cheeks was instant and burning hot. Here were her sins and her secrets, all laid out for the world to see. Perhaps that was the penance for them. She glanced at the Willowbys and Mr. Barber apologetically, though they didn't look vexed by this veering off topic.

"Nicholas *deserves* to receive his title," she said at last, though her breath felt so short as she said the words. "I refuse to destroy his chances by involving him in this any more than he already has been. So I didn't contact him."

Selina's expression softened. "I see."

It was such a noncommittal tone to those two words. Aurora had no idea if his sister approved or disapproved those actions. She smoothed her skirts. "Perhaps we should get back to the matter at hand, at any rate. Imogen's letter says that she wishes to meet with me at Fitzhugh's Club."

At that, Selina took a long step back. "F-Fitzhugh's?" she repeated.

Aurora nodded. "Yes. It seems the man who has been sheltering her is the owner of the club and he has offered to close his club for a few hours so we can meet. Why? Why are you so pale at the mention of that that name?"

Selina shook her head and she looked at Derrick for…what seemed to be support. That response only made Aurora's heart race faster.

"Selina," Derrick said softly. "What makes you act this way at the mention of Oscar Fitzhugh?"

"He's…he's another of the Bastards," Selina whispered. "Another half-brother. He *never* interacts with any of us. He's rebuffed all connection."

Aurora's mouth dropped open. "Great God. But…do you know what kind of man he is?"

"A rogue. But in a different way than the rest of us," Selina said.

"Oh no!" Aurora gasped. "My poor Imogen."

"No, no," Selina said. "I don't mean he's bad. I've heard he's… decent. Too decent for the likes of Roseford's children."

Derrick put a gentle arm around her and glanced at Aurora. "I've never heard a cross word about the man. I would not assume Imogen is in danger from him, at any rate."

That news relaxed Aurora a fraction, though the coincidence of this man's relationship to Nicholas and his family made her head spin. "How many children did the last Roseford sire?"

At that Selina gave a pained chuckle. "That is an answer I could only give over a great deal of whisky, my dear."

Aurora forced herself to refocus on Imogen. "She only wanted to see me, and I suppose I'm not being much of a friend by bringing you all along. But I fear so desperately for her."

The Duke of Willowby stepped forward. "You're doing the right thing, I promise you. What time are we to meet them?"

"Three this afternoon," she said, and glanced at the clock on her mantel. "Almost exactly three hours from now."

Selina nodded. "Then Derrick and I will come for you at two," she said. "That will give us time to prepare and get there."

Aurora let out her breath. "It would comfort me not to be alone on the journey. I'm so nervous to see her, so afraid I won't be able to help her."

To her surprise, Selina crossed to her and tugged her into a tight hug. "We will resolve this. And she is very lucky to have such a good friend as you, Aurora."

Aurora found herself drooping against the other woman for a moment as all the strain of the past weeks hit her all at once. Selina bore her up for a moment, whispering gentle words of encouragement until Aurora straightened.

"Thank you," she whispered.

Selina patted her hand and went back to her husband. "We all have much to do. I say we go do it."

Willowby exchanged a grin with his wife and then saluted Selina. "Yes, ma'am. We'll see you later this afternoon, Lady Lovell."

They all departed then, talking as a group, making whatever secondary plans they had. And for the first time since Imogen had disappeared, Aurora didn't feel helpless. When it came to Nicholas it was different, but at least with Imogen, she might finally resolve this and help the woman she loved as a sister.

If she could do that, perhaps she would ultimately feel that the future could be positive. That everything could work out. Perhaps she could finally see how she could be with Nicholas in the end, even if it meant waiting a little longer.

Nicholas was at his desk in his study looking at his schedule for the next week. Several missives had arrived that afternoon, invitations for meetings with influential people and men connected to the Prince. The next step in moving toward becoming a marquess.

Even as he tried to manage all the correspondence, all he could think about was the conversation the previous day with his father. All he could think about were the questions in his mind when it came to taking this path that had once seemed so clear.

"Bloody hell," he muttered, pushing the lot of them aside just as there was a knock on his door. "Enter."

The door opened to reveal his butler, Evans. The two had served in the war together and the man was not a typical butler. His shock of red hair, the patch over one eye and the scar that crisscrossed his face made him look more pirate than proper.

At the moment he looked vexed, but as he drew a breath to speak, Selina elbowed her way past him into the room. "Might as well not even give him the option to pretend he isn't in residence," she said.

Nicholas laughed and shook his head as he rose. "It's all right, Evans. She is an unstoppable force."

Evans gave her a look. "Hate to see what will happen if she comes upon an immovable object." With that, he backed from the room and shut the door behind himself.

Selina laughed. "I always like his impertinence," she said. "And of course the answer is that I married the immovable object." She moved forward and pressed a kiss to Nicholas's cheek. "You look tired."

"Thank you?" Nicholas said. "I assume you don't want tea, but something stronger."

"It's one in the afternoon," she said. "But yes, a little stronger. But not much, I need my head. And so will you very shortly."

He wrinkled his brow as he poured her a drink. "Why is that? And where is Derrick?"

"Normally he *would* accompany me when I called on you," Selina admitted as she slugged back half her drink without so much as a cough. "But he doesn't know I came. You know him. He would tell me not to meddle and what fun would that be?"

The good humor Nicholas had felt when she entered bled away in an instant. "Not to meddle. What exactly are you not meddling in?"

"Do you know that Aurora called us all to her house an hour or so ago?" she asked, arching one of those fine brows.

He stared at her. "All of *who*?"

"Derrick, me, Barber, the Willowbys. Everyone involved in this investigation into her friend…except you. And I suppose Robert and Katherine, though I think they were really only involved insofar as the introductions." Selina quickly explained everything that had happened at the meeting, including the revelation that their half-brother Oscar Fitzhugh was the man who had been sheltering Imogen.

"God, I haven't heard that name in a long time," Nicholas mused. "Years."

Selina flinched. "Yes, he has always made it patently clear he wants nothing to do with any of us. I suppose he won't be able to avoid it now because we're coming."

Pushing his complicated feelings about his distant brother away, Nicholas paced away from Selina. There was a more pressing question eating at him now. His tone wavered as he voiced it. "Why wouldn't Aurora involve me?"

"She's cutting you out, dearest," she said. "Normally I would scratch her pretty eyes right out of her gorgeous face for it. But she's doing it for a very good reason, you see. She wants to protect you. And she's willing to sacrifice herself to do it."

"Protect me?" he repeated.

"Don't act like you don't know why," Selina said with a purse of her lips. "You *know*."

"The marquess matter," he said softly.

Selina nodded. "Nicholas, she recognizes that her presence in your life could bring you to your knees. If you are seen involving yourself in her troubles, that could do the same. She's cutting you out because…" She smiled sadly. "She loves you, Nicholas. I doubted her from the moment I met her. Protective instinct, you know, because you almost died and I couldn't bear to think of you ever being hurt again. But she cares enough that she would bring herself pain rather than taking even a fraction of what you want away from you."

Nicholas bent his head. His fingers clenched at his sides. "She said the same to me the last time we were—" He cut himself off. "I know she wants to protect me. She apparently thinks she knows how."

"Is she wrong?" Selina asked. "After all, what she is doing truly is the best thing for you if your ultimate goal in life is to be Marquess of Shithouse."

"Songstrum," Nicholas corrected with a smile. "And I think you know that."

"All the same to me," Selina said with a shrug.

"Wait," Nicholas said. "You were angry at Aurora because she didn't protect me and now you're thwarting her plans by coming to me when she is?"

Selina shook her head. "I was angry because I thought she didn't deserve you. But I was wrong. She does. And *you* deserve to be happy, love. I hope you'll steer your life with that goal in mind and nothing else."

"That seems to be the advice all the wisest people in my life keep giving," he mused.

"All the wisest people and your very silly and patently unwise sister," Selina said with a giggle.

"No, my silly sister may be the wisest of them all. I know your road with Derrick wasn't easy. You had to have faith in him and him in you when there wasn't much room for it. It paid off. I envy that. Just as I envy watching Morgan soften and warm under Lizzie's light. Or Robert tame just enough for Katherine's delight and pleasure. All of you are beacons of what love could be."

"You could have the same," Selina said. "I even have a plan for you."

He laughed. "Of course you do. Well, what is it then?"

"When I snuck out of my house today, I took Derrick's second carriage. Now your Aurora is expecting us to pick her up in our carriage in an hour. But I'll go home in your carriage instead and you take mine. You'll pick up Aurora and take her to the designated meeting place. I would go home and convince Derrick that he isn't all that angry at me for interfering."

"I'm sure that won't take much," Nicholas said with a laugh.

She winked. "I know all his pressure points. He knows mine too, but I am very wicked and convincing."

Nicholas hesitated a moment. Selina's plan would mean he was making a choice. And the choice wasn't the title. It was the woman. When she opened the carriage door and saw him there, there would be no going back. He couldn't allow there to be. The future he'd counted on for over two years would fade and the one he'd wanted since he was a young man would rise up instead. Golden and so very different. With so many other challenges.

"You must choose," Selina said, as if she understood the underlying issue as much as he did. "So what do you want to do, Nicholas? What are you going to do?"

# CHAPTER 20

The carriage pulled up on the drive at exactly two o'clock, just as Selina had promised it would earlier in the day. Aurora forced a smile for her servants so they wouldn't see her fear.

"I do not know when I'll return, so please don't worry about supper," she said.

"Yes, my lady," Jeanette said.

A footman stepped off of the carriage back and bowed slightly toward her. Then he opened the door and held out a hand to assist her. She hated that her fingers trembled as she took the help. Hated to show that weakness or to feel it when it was so important today to remain strong and calm.

As she stepped into the rig and the door closed behind her, she turned her head to say good afternoon to Derrick and Selina, but to her shock it wasn't them who waited to greet her in the seat opposite hers.

It was Nicholas. He sat ramrod straight, his dark eyes focused intensely on her as the blood drained from her cheeks.

"No!" she gasped, and reached behind her for the door handle.

He snaked a hand out and caught her wrist, his fingers folding around her firmly but not cruelly. With hardly any effort, he gently tugged her into his lap just as the carriage began to move.

"Please, no!" she repeated, squirming against him. "If you are seen on this errand, Nicholas, it could destroy everything you've worked for!"

He didn't answer her with words. His hand slipped to the nape of her neck and he tilted her head up toward his. Close enough that his warm breath stirred over her lips. She hated herself for forgetting all her very good arguments as she sighed in the pleasure only being with this man could bring to her.

He kissed her. Gently, sweetly and she melted against him. She opened the fist she'd placed between them to push him away and rested it against his heart. She felt it throbbing, just like her own.

He deepened the kiss ever so slightly, tasting her, teasing her, setting her on edge because he could do that with even the slightest touch. Perhaps he used it against her, perhaps it was just as natural as breathing to them both. It didn't matter. It was happening and she was helpless to him.

But at last he pulled away. He brushed his lips across her cheek instead, his fingers clenching against her nape as he whispered, "I'm not letting you do this alone, Aurora."

She blinked at the tears that stung her eyes and shook her head, but she no longer fought him for escape. It was impossible anyway with the carriage bobbing along at a frisky pace toward their destination across Town.

She still needed to say the words, though, to try to convince him not to be foolhardy. He didn't have to exit the vehicle when they arrived, after all. She could still convince him if she just said the right thing, did the right thing. There had to be a way.

"I-I *won't* be alone, though," she began, her voice trembling just as her body trembled in his warm arms. "The Willowbys, Derrick, Selina and Mr. Barber are all coming with me. They're vastly qualified to handle any situation."

"But they aren't *me*," he said. "You think I would be happy to stay behind while you go into a situation that might be dangerous? The very idea is outrageous. When I heard that you cut me out of your plans, I couldn't let that stand. *Please* don't argue with me."

It seemed there was no room to do so. She heard the firmness in his tone. The complete faith and peace in his decision to come to get her, to insert himself in this day, whatever the consequences.

"How did you find out?" she asked as she shifted off his lap and slid onto the seat next to him.

He arched a brow and a flicker of humor entered his dark eyes. "Selina."

She huffed out her breath. "Selina?" she repeated in shock. "And after she made such a show of hugging me and telling me I could travel with them so I wouldn't be alone. Did she come running straight to you after our meeting earlier today? She must have, for there was no time for this plan of yours otherwise."

There was something lighter in the way Nicholas laughed. Something so much more like that boy he'd once been before heartbreak and war and injury. How that sound pulled her back in time and softened some of her upset that she had been tricked.

"Selina behaved like a very good sister," he said. "I'm terribly pleased with her."

"Well, I'm—I'm very angry with *you*." She folded her arms and wished with all her heart that her voice sounded stronger when she said those words. "You *tricked* me by coming to fetch me in the Huntington's carriage. You didn't even ask for my leave, you just forced my hand."

He smiled again, seemingly untroubled by her supposed anger, which they could both see wasn't particularly hot or serious. "I did. But only because you forced mine."

She tried to think of some kind of retort to that accusation. Of course she couldn't. He wasn't entirely wrong, damn him. It would be easier if he were. But they were in a similar position: he wanting to protect her, she desperate to do the same for him.

"But Nicholas—" she began.

He held up a hand with a little sigh. "Aurora, I'm not going to talk around and around in circles about who did what. This is happening now. We can use how angry you are with me later."

Her brow wrinkled. "How?" He tilted his head and his pupils dilated with what she knew was desire. She gasped. "Are you talking about bedding me? At a time like this?"

He shrugged one shoulder. "It's making you less nervous, isn't it? Picturing how you might vent all that anger on me in much more amusing ways than merely arguing?"

She pursed her lips because he was right. She'd been obsessively running over in her mind what would happen when they met with Imogen. What would be said, how she could protect her friend, how she could cope with whatever Imogen had gone through while they were parted.

But now she felt calmer. More at ease. Because *he* was here.

The carriage had begun to slow, and she reached out and caught his hand. He held tight to her, pulling back the curtain so they could see the club their carriage had just stopped in front of. A huge building, finely designed down to the last detail.

"He's certainly done well for himself," Nicholas said softly.

She cast a quick glance at him. "Your...your brother. Oscar Fitzhugh."

"Yes, yet another in a line of my father's by-blows. The first, actually." He shook his head, and the sadness in his stare was painful. "Though he wants nothing to do with the family. It will be interesting to see how thrilled he is to see us all parade into his club. The one I believe he's banned the lot of us from."

She squeezed his hand, sending back the same comfort that was offered to her. "Then I suppose we'll be there for each other."

He glanced down at their intertwined fingers, then lifted them to his lips. He brushed her knuckles with his mouth and smiled. "I wouldn't want anyone else at my side."

She shivered and bent her head. "And I admit that, though I fought to keep you away, I'm glad you're here."

There was no lie to the statement. It felt so right to have him at her side. More peaceful, safer. She saw the other carriages arriving as she and Nicholas were helped out by the footman who had assisted them earlier. Nicholas drew a deep breath, and they headed up the short marble staircase to the door. A servant in fine livery was already holding it open and they entered a vestibule.

"Mr. Fitzhugh and Mrs. Huxley are awaiting you in the main parlor," the butler said. "Through there."

He motioned toward a door. Nicholas glanced back over his shoulder and nodded toward the others who were gathering behind them, then guided Aurora to the door. She was holding her breath. It was all she could do, for she couldn't pull in a full one as they stepped into the room.

It was a large parlor, obviously meant for bigger gatherings of the gentlemen who attended Fitzhugh's club. A pretty room with intricate moldings and a wall of windows that led the light flood in and gave a good view of the street below that even Beau Brummell himself would envy in his tiny window at White's.

There was a man standing at a sideboard. From behind she wasn't certain if he was Fitzhugh himself, but he was broad-shouldered, with dark hair streaked with a few lines of silver.

But it wasn't he who she wanted to see. She turned her attention to the mantel and let out a gasp. There Imogen was, just turning toward the door. She looked tired, but well and whole, and Aurora couldn't hold back her response.

"Imogen!" she cried out as she released Nicholas and rushed across the room to launch herself at her friend.

To say that Aurora's voice was filled with joy and relief would be an understatement. Nicholas couldn't help but smile as she raced to the lady standing at the mantel across the room. Her friend was a very pretty woman, slender with an angular face and bright, friendly eyes. Her dark hair was worn in a loose bun at the nape of her neck and she was wearing a fine gown.

As the friends embraced, Imogen promptly burst into tears. "I'm sorry, I'm so sorry I frightened you," she murmured against Aurora's shoulder.

"What the fuck are all of *you* doing here?"

Nicholas pivoted to face his half-brother. He'd noticed him at the sideboard, of course, when they first entered, but had been too focused on Aurora's needs to prepare for whatever would come.

Oscar Fitzhugh was a tall man, broad-shouldered and built like he knew how to fight. The oldest of their collection of half-blood, older than Robert even. The first of the Roseford brood to have entered the world. He had some silver in his hair and it speckled his beard. His brow was low, furrowed with frustration and his dark gaze flitted over Selina and Nicholas with unmasked disgust.

"Imogen, this was *not* our arrangement," he snapped.

Imogen stepped away from Aurora and toward his brother, and Nicholas caught his breath. He could see the connection there between them, as hot and hard and heavy as his own with Aurora. It seemed his brother had offered more than shelter to this woman, and Nicholas had no idea how *that* fact would play out now that there was a roomful of spies and investigators set to sweep her away for her protection.

"I didn't know," Imogen said softly.

Fitzhugh's cheek twitched ever so slightly, as if he didn't fully believe that statement. The two held stares for a long moment, a challenge, a battle that no one else in the room could truly understand.

"She *didn't* know," Aurora said as she crossed to stand beside Imogen and held out a hand to Fitzhugh. "Mr. Fitzhugh, you have no idea how much I owe you for helping my friend. I could never repay you."

Fitzhugh stared at her outstretched hand a moment and then

took it, shaking it gently. "There is no repayment necessary. It was my pleasure," he said softly.

Aurora's gaze flitted toward Imogen, and Nicholas wondered if she were just recognizing the connection between the two as he had. She cleared her throat and said, "But I swear to you that Imogen had no idea I was bringing this small army with me. I thought you might not see us if I told you I was bringing help. But that is what this group is. Everyone here wishes to assist with this investigation. Help Imogen."

Fitzhugh's jaw tightened and then he nodded. "I suppose I understand that." He faced the gathered crowd. "I think most of us need no introduction."

"Yes, you wrote us off long ago, didn't you?" Selina said, folding her arms. "So why waste time on pleasantries now."

"Selina," Derrick said softly, his hand coming to the small of her back. Then he nodded toward Fitzhugh and introduced himself. The others followed.

"And now that we've participated in Mrs. Huntington's required *pleasantries*," Fitzhugh said with a quick glance for Selina. "Perhaps we can get down to what we're all here for."

"Imogen, where have you been? What happened?" Aurora said, grasping her friend's hands and drawing her to a settee in the middle of the room. The rest took places around them.

Imogen's cheeks darkened. "I didn't expect to be telling this story for an audience," she whispered.

Fitzhugh snorted out a soft sound at the sideboard and poured a splash of madeira into a glass. He moved to the settee and handed it over to Imogen. She lifted her gaze to him and again their eyes held. A thousand unspoken words flowed between them.

"You have nothing to be ashamed of," Fitzhugh said at last. "And you owe them nothing. None of them were invited, so they can all get the fuck out of my club."

Imogen swallowed as she looked to the others. "Can you truly help me?"

The Duke of Willowby stepped forward. "I think we can, Mrs. Huxley. *If* we understand what is going on. But if you don't wish to tell the story to an audience, we can step out. Only my wife would stay to record your statement if that would make you more comfortable."

"But she'll repeat it to you all anyway," Imogen said with a small sigh. "She would have to in order for you to understand."

Willowby inclined his head slightly, acquiescing that it would be the truth. Aurora held her tighter, a silent support as Imogen tried to decide what to do. She glanced up at Fitzhugh again. "It will be worth the humiliation."

His jaw set and his hand fluttered at his side as if he wanted to touch her. But he didn't. He just watched as Imogen took a gulp of wine before she handed the glass back to Fitzhugh. Then her gaze dropped down.

"I...I was in dire straights after my husband's death. My prospects weren't very good and I thought perhaps becoming a man's mistress would be the best way to survive." Dark color filled her cheeks, but Nicholas was impressed with the strength with which she continued on. No wonder she was Aurora's friend. They both had that steel in their spines, hidden beneath beauty and charm. "I made a bad choice and ended up at the wrong place...a brothel called the Cat's Companion. The woman who runs it is a monster. And I saw...I saw something I wasn't meant to see."

Imogen cleared her throat, and to Nicholas's surprise Oscar reached down and pressed a hand to her shoulder. His dark expression softened a fraction as his fingers curled there, holding her steady. She sat up a little straighter at the touch.

"A-A murder," she whispered. "Or the aftereffects. There was a body. I tried to get away, but they saw me. And they made chase. I stumbled into Oscar—Mr. Fitzhugh—and he has been hiding me ever since, trying to help me prove what I know. What I saw. *Who* I saw." She lifted her gaze to him. "He saved my life."

Fitzhugh's nostrils flared a fraction and he released her. "I didn't do much. But this situation goes deep. Much deeper than one murder."

Willowby nodded and exchanged a glance with his wife. "The War Department suspects as much. Between what we've gleaned and what help we've had from Mr. Barber and Mr. Huntington's sources, I think we're close to uncovering the mastermind behind this…ring of blackguards."

Imogen's lips parted and she glanced up at Fitzhugh again. She slowly rose, as did Aurora. "If I could help I would—"

Before she could finish the sentence, there was an explosion of glass from the huge window behind them. Nicholas cried out, diving toward Aurora, pulling her to the ground beneath him as bullets and glass fell around them in a hellish rain. All he could do was hold her beneath him and hope that what they were rebuilding, what he wished to be for their future, wouldn't be destroyed in a few moments of noise and fury.

# CHAPTER 21

Aurora trembled beneath the heavy weight of Nicholas's body covering her, sheltering her. The bullets had stopped at last, but no one in the room had yet moved. She didn't know if that was out of caution or injury, but there was only one thought in her mind at present.

"Nicholas," she murmured, pushing against him. "Are you hurt?"

He rolled away from her and she followed, running her hands down his body, brushing glass away from his coat as she searched him for wounds. He caught her chin and tilted her face up so their eyes met. "I'm unharmed," he said, but his voice trembled. "Are you? Are you injured?"

"You protected me," she assured him as she cupped his face with both hands. "My God, Nicholas."

"Is anyone harmed?" Barber called out from across the room.

That dragged Aurora and Nicholas back to the room and she looked around. The couples were slowly beginning to move, checking on each other with as much intensity as she and Nicholas had.

"We're fine," the Willowbys called out first. They were

exchanging a look that said this was not the first time they'd been shot at, nor did they think it would be the last. But the duke caught the duchess's cheeks nonetheless and kissed her before they got up and began to edge around the room, easing toward the window with their own guns drawn.

"Derrick and I are unhurt," Selina said, brushing glass from herself as Derrick joined the Willowbys. "Barber?"

"I'm fine," he said from behind a chair.

"Imogen?" Aurora called out, looking frantically for her friend. They'd been standing near each other when the shooting began, but as Nicholas dove for her, Fitzhugh had come lunging over the back of the settee and grabbed Imogen. Now they slowly rose from behind the couch.

"He's cut," she said, her voice shaking as she clung to Fitzhugh's arm with both her own. His jacket had a hole in it and there was blood seeping from the wound.

"That's not a cut," Derrick said, moving forward and unwinding his cravat as he went. "You've been shot."

Nicholas's heart leapt as he watched his brother glance at the wound with an impassive glance. "It seems I have."

"Oscar!" Imogen gasped, but she stepped aside as Derrick waved him to remove the jacket and examined the wound quickly.

"It went through," Fitzhugh said with a shrug that made him flinch slightly. "Wrap it if you will and I'll have it looked at later."

Derrick's brows came up and he cast a quick look at Nicholas and Selina, but did as he'd been ordered. While he did so, Fitzhugh's jaw set as he looked around the once-fine room that was now riddled with bullet holes and broken glass and furniture.

"Bloody hell," he muttered.

"I'm sorry," Imogen whispered.

He looked down at her, brow wrinkling. "Don't."

"I don't see anyone below," Willowby called out. "There must have been more than one assailant for all this carnage. Diana,

Barber, we should go down and question witnesses on the street. Huntington, does that wound need more attention?"

Derrick tied off the cravat with a shake of his head. "It's fine for now, though he'll need a doctor later. I'll join you, you'll need as many boots on the ground as possible."

Willowby's lips thinned. "I'll send for more men."

Diana glanced at Selina, who was staring at Fitzhugh. Nicholas could see her concern, despite her earlier dismissal of their brother. "Selina, will you check on the welfare of the servants and anyone else in the building?"

Selina jerked to attention. "Yes. Yes, of course. How many are there, Fitzhugh?"

He pursed his lips in what seemed like annoyance. "It's a small staff because I closed the club for the afternoon. No more than five. My assumption is they were in the back, but I *would* appreciate you checking on them and telling them that I'll take care of this mess and that Will White will be here shortly. He's my partner and I'll send for him. Right now, though, I need to take Imogen away."

Aurora pulled from Nicholas's arms. "No, wait! Is that for the best?"

Willowby gave his wife a look, and she nodded. As Willowby, Barber and Huntington left the room, Diana approached Fitzhugh with an almost delicate air. Like she was about to tame some wild beast.

Aurora couldn't disagree with that assessment. Despite how calm his voice was, Fitzhugh's eyes were lit with emotion. This man was a caldron, ready to overflow. And judging from Imogen's concerned expression, she knew it too. But she didn't seem to fear him. Just fear for him.

Aurora glanced at Nicholas. She knew the feeling.

"Mr. Fitzhugh, obviously this event has been upsetting," Diana began.

"Upsetting, Your Grace?" Fitzhugh grunted. "You think this is *upsetting?*"

"Oscar." Imogen took his hand. He turned his head, and Imogen looked at the duchess. "Your Grace, he has protected me well in the last few weeks. Perhaps it would be better for me to go with him. I've endangered enough people as it is."

"Imogen," Aurora whispered.

Her friend turned toward her. "You could have died because of me. Please, just let me protect you."

Aurora flinched. Imogen was repeating words she'd said to Nicholas today, though certainly under much less dire circumstances. But hearing them, she revolted against them. The idea that she would turn her back on someone she loved like a sister was abhorrent.

"We are all under a great deal of strain," Diana said softly, looking between them all with a gentle expression that couldn't do anything but calm and soothe. "But the duke and I are part of the War Department, Mr. Fitzhugh."

"Yes, I know. I've heard of you before, though not by name. I heard a rumor the government was involved in investigating in some way. We clearly have a great deal to discuss."

Diana nodded. "We do. Another reason not to hide yourselves where we cannot find you. We have the weight of the entire government to bring to bear onto this case. I do think Imogen needs to be hidden, I agree with you. The fact that someone shot at all of us the moment she was brought out of hiding means *someone* is desperate to silence her."

"We know who. At least some of who," Imogen said, her voice breaking. "Oscar, please, they can help us. Stop fighting it."

"Let *us* provide the safe hiding place," Diana said. "Protected by armed guards, hidden from plain sight. Someplace where no one will find her, but where we will have access to what she knows about the people trying to hurt her."

Fitzhugh shook away from Imogen and paced off, lifting a hand to the place where Huntington had bandaged his wound. "Bloody fucking hell," he snapped. "Fine. But I'm going with her."

Imogen rushed forward. "Oscar, no! You protected me so well, but I can't ask you to—"

"I'm going with you," he said. "That's final. Let me just make some arrangements."

He said nothing else but stomped from the room. Diana smiled at Imogen and then stepped away as Aurora moved toward her. Nicholas stepped aside to speak to the duchess, and so the two friends were alone for a moment.

"Imogen," Aurora whispered, wrapping her arms around her. "How could this happen?"

"I was just in the wrong place at the wrong time," Imogen said and then glanced past her to the others. "Can I trust your friends?"

"Yes," Aurora said, and didn't hesitate.

Imogen lifted her head and looked over her shoulder toward Nicholas. "That's the one you were in love with as a child, isn't it? The one who left you for the army?"

"Turns out it's more complicated than that, but yes," Aurora said with a sigh.

Imogen stared at him. "He seems to love you."

Aurora sucked in her breath. She knew it was true, after all. She knew he loved her without him ever saying it. And she loved him so desperately in return. Enough to sacrifice everything if it meant protecting him, helping him, giving him what he wanted.

"Yes," she whispered.

"Then hold on to that," Imogen said, grasping her hands, suddenly desperate. "Hold onto it and to each other. Because others are not so lucky."

"Imogen," she whispered. "Are you talking about Mr. Fitzhugh? Because there is no denying your connection."

Her friend shrugged a shoulder. "Connection is one thing. Protection is another. But he has made it clear that he *cannot* love me. So...I just would like one of us to be happy. When this is all over, I just want you to be happy."

Fitzhugh re-entered the room, his stern face more serious than ever. "Arrangements have been made. An unmarked carriage is around the back, ready to ferry us away to whatever location you see fit, Your Grace."

"Good," Diana said. "Then I'll accompany you. Mr. Gillingham, will you tell the duke of my plans? I'll meet with him back at home. And I would suggest you and Lady Lovell also take your leave. There is nothing else you can do here. The professionals will handle this and keep your friend safe."

Aurora could tell Nicholas wanted to argue that point, as did she, but in the end they both just nodded. She turned back to Imogen, tears blurring her eyes. "I wanted to…to save you today," she murmured as they embraced. "To bring you home."

"I'm so much closer to home now," Imogen reassured her. She pulled back and kissed her cheek. "I adore you." Then she looked past her toward Nicholas. "Mr. Gillingham, I wish I had more time to get to the know the man who has held my friend's heart for her entire life."

He drew back and then nodded. "And I wish I had more time to get to know the friend she loves as a sister. But we will have that time in the future."

"Yes," Imogen said with a shaky smile. "I know we will."

She left then, moving toward Fitzhugh, taking his uninjured arm. Aurora frowned as they left together, with Diana trailing behind them. When they were gone, she felt Nicholas's arms come around her, holding her steady as she bent her head and let the tears slide down her cheeks.

Finally, she wiped them away and turned into him. "It feels odd to just…leave after all this. Anticlimactic."

"I think being shot at is climax enough," he grunted. "Come, let me take you away."

She looked around the room, now littered with glass and shattered furniture, and sighed. With Imogen gone, lost again to her, there was nothing else she could truly do. She nodded and he wrapped his arm around her to draw her from the room. They entered the drive, which was a cacophony of activity as the duke, Derrick, and Barber rushed around, now joined by a growing cadre of help. A crowd had formed in the park across from the scene, and she flinched.

People would recognize Nicholas. Word would surely spread like wildfire of his involvement in what would be an infamous afternoon much talked about the papers and in clubs and in ballrooms.

Everything she had feared would pass was now coming true. She bent her head as he helped her into the carriage they had arrived in.

"Let me tell Willowby about his wife's departure," he said, squeezing her knee from the door. "I'll be right back."

She nodded wordlessly and waited him to deliver his message. He joined her in the carriage, sitting beside her rather than across from her, and in a moment they were moving.

"Nicholas," she began softly, lifting her face to his.

He silenced her by cupping her cheeks and kissing her. In that moment, she forgot everything else. Today they had nearly died. She'd had a moment when his weight pushed her into the floor where she hadn't known if he was hurt or not. And now that his mouth was on her, hungry and seeking, she was not going to deny him, or herself, a moment to reconnect.

She wrapped her arms around his neck, lifting up into him. He groaned against her lips as he pulled her into his lap just as he'd done what felt like a lifetime ago on the journey to the club. Only this time she felt the hard press of him against her backside. Felt the desperate longing in his kiss that she answered in her own.

"You want me?" she whispered between kisses.

"Only you," he said, finding the buttons along the back of her dress. "Always you. Forever you."

She blinked at the sting of tears in her eyes at those sweet, wonderful words and found his mouth again. Branding her love on his lips because she couldn't yet say it out loud. He took it, drinking her in, shifting her against him. She straddled him, shoving her gown up, feeling the pulse of his hot and ready body against the apex of her thighs, even through all the pesky layers of fabric.

She reached between them as they continued to kiss, and loosened the flap on his trousers. He pulled her gown down, sucking the side of her neck, over her collarbone. As she freed his cock and stroked him, he hissed a hot breath over her nipple. She arched into him, crying out as he licked the sensitive peak and stroking him hard and fast.

He cupped her backside with both hands, lifting her. She positioned herself over him, pushing the slit in her draws open wide, rubbing him against her sex before she thrust down and took him deep into her body. They sat like that for a moment, foreheads pressed together, eyes locked, breath hard in the quiet carriage.

She flexed around him and he swore, lifting into her, hitting her so perfectly that she dropped her head back with a long sigh of pleasure.

That broke the peace, the quiet. That ended the gentleness. They began to rock together, hard and fast, their mouths smashing together, his hands digging into the soft folds of her flesh, marking her as his. She ground down, demanding her pleasure, and he met her every stroke with a promise to provide. The first orgasm hit her hard, and she buried her face into his shoulder as she screamed and jolted against him in out-of-control pleasure.

He caught her hips harder, forcing her to continue to ride him, drawing out her release even as he drove her toward a second. She let him, giving in to his demands, pushing herself beyond the limit, toward the horizon. He scraped his teeth against her nipple and the flash of pleasure-pain sent her over the edge again. She circled her hips wildly, saying words that had no meaning, crying out his name because it was all that mattered, all she wanted, all she needed.

She felt his pace quicken. He drove into her from below, his neck straining as the carriage grew hot and thick with the scent of sex.

"Aurora," he whispered, and she heard how close he was. "I want to come inside of you. Please. Please."

She hesitated. If he did this, it was a future. Because it was a possibility of a child that he was asking her to allow. And oh, how she wanted that, how she'd always wanted that with him.

She nodded even though it went against every best instinct she had. He let out a cry of relief and pleasure, and claimed her mouth again as he pumped hard and hot inside of her.

They stayed like that for some time, Nicholas couldn't have said how long. She was still straddling him, his softening cock inside of her, their kisses gentling and deepening in the glow of what they'd shared. He couldn't stop touching her, fingers smoothing along the soft lines of the flesh he'd revealed when he tugged her skirt up.

At last, though, she sighed and buried her face into his neck. Her voice was muffled as she said, "We're going to arrive soon. We should probably tidy up."

He didn't answer, but pulled the bodice of her dress back up. He kissed her neck as he buttoned her. Only then did she shift off of him and take a place across from him as she smoothed her wrinkled skirts.

He watched her as he put himself back in place, buttoning up so that he no longer looked like a hungry lover, but a proper gentleman. She was so beautiful flushed from his touch and his kiss and her pleasure. But then, she was beautiful always. And she had been in his dreams for so long that he'd never believed reality could hold up if he found it again.

But it was better. Being with her, it was all so much better.

The carriage was slowing now, pulling into the drive back at her home. He reached across the expanse between them and caught her hands. He met her stare and held there, lost in that warm brown that could soothe and inflame in equal measure.

"Aurora," he said softly, peaceful at last with the decision he had made. Unable to keep it from her for even a moment longer. "I'm giving up the title."

Aurora careened into her parlor with Nicholas hard on her heels. She pivoted in the middle of the room and glared at him, watching as he closed the door behind them and gave them a little privacy.

"No," she said, finally answering the terrible statement he'd made in the carriage a few moments before.

He arched a brow. "That's it? Just no. You think that is the end of the discussion, my lady?"

She folded her arms. "No, there is a great deal to discuss. Including just how in the world did you come to such a ridiculous decision?"

"It isn't ridiculous, Aurora," he said, but there was no frustration to his voice. Just infuriating calm and decisiveness. "I will not be marquess."

She moved toward him then in a few long steps. "You have wanted this for years," she said. "*Years*, Nicholas. I know that it's what you've desired more than anything. It's been clear by every action you've taken since you returned home from the war. I cannot let you give up on that because…because of *me*."

He tilted his head and his smile was almost indulgent. "Aurora, do you know *why* I so desperately wanted the title when the option of it came up?"

She blinked. That was a question she'd never considered. Her life had been led alongside men of title who inherited their roles. No one doubted that it was what would happen, so she'd never really thought about it.

"I…no," she admitted.

He reached for her, taking both her hands in his. The electric shock of his touch stunned her, just as it always did. How could she always feel so connected and desired by him? No matter how many times he made love to her, when he touched her it was always the first time.

"You were taken from me all those years ago, Aurora. I didn't know how much of it was a manipulation at the time, all I knew was that you were gone and I was *powerless*." He shook his head. "I wanted to make sure that nothing like that could ever happen to me again. I built my life around it. Somehow I foolishly conflated the idea of power with the idea of control or safety. But I don't feel that way now."

"Nicholas—"

"Willowby has a title, a high title, and today I saw his face when the shooting stopped. I saw how afraid he was for Diana. Just like I was holding you and praying that I had protected you well enough and fast enough and long enough. A title can't stop a bullet, my love. You could have been snatched from me in an instant, or I from you. And there is no protection from that. Not truly."

She nodded, her arguments lost in the very real discussion of how close they'd come to losing each other that day. "I was so afraid when you stood up that your blood would be on me. That you'd be torn away from me again when we'd only just found each other."

"And yet you are so willing to *push* me away so I can have…what? A new name and a false power that can't fight the worst outcomes?" he asked.

"Only for a while," she reasoned. "We'd hide our connection for a while and then it will be over and we can be free."

"A while," he repeated. "A day, a week, a month, a year, five years —we have no idea how long this will go on before decisions are made. Those in power don't give it away lightly, love, or swiftly. I don't want to lose even one more moment with you. We've already lost too much, Aurora."

"And you'll lose more if you walk away from what you could have," she said, gripping his hands all the tighter. "In the heat of the moment, tied up in the dramatic incident we endured today, you say you don't mind losing this. But when the fear we both feel right now fades, you might come to regret it down the line. Resent *me* for taking it from you."

He shook her hands away and instead cupped her face. "Let me be very clear with you: I would surrender everything I have or ever had or *could* ever have if it means loving you, being with you."

Aurora's heart was throbbing, it hurt in her chest it pumped so hard. She backed away a step because when he touched her she couldn't think. Her mind screamed yes over and over. She needed space to still be able to say no if it was best for him.

"But so much has changed, Nicholas," she whispered.

"Never my heart," he said. "It is yours, Aurora, and it always has been. You have been the first thought in my mind when I wake, the last thought at night for nearly all my life. I said *your* name during the explosion all those years ago because you were the one I thought of when that breath could be my last. When I worked to rebuild my body, it was you I was always reaching for in the fog of pain. I kept trying because of you."

"Nicholas," she breathed, swept away by those beautiful words. And by the thought that somehow, no matter how the world had conspired to keep them apart, they had still been together. He in her heart, she in his.

"I love you," he said, and there was no hesitation to his voice. "I have *always* loved you. I *will* always love you. And that is the only thing that matters. Isn't it?"

She felt the tears streaming down her face as she stared at him. He closed the distance she had created and wiped one of those tears away.

"Isn't it?" he repeated softly.

She nodded slowly. Because there was nothing else to do. He was right, and her heart sang as she finally let go of all her drive to protect him and embrace the pulsing, powerful decree to love him. For now and forever. Through whatever would come and whatever would be gained or lost. The love would always be there, just as it had always been there.

And it would be enough.

"I love you," she said, and then she laughed as she shouted it louder. "I love you, I love you, I love you, I love you!"

He cut her off with a kiss, and they clung to each other, this time not in desperation but in surrender. And it was the most beautiful feeling she'd ever felt. She was his, he was hers. There was nothing else but that now.

He broke away from her at last, and his smile was so wide and bright that it could have lit up her parlor on its own. She couldn't help but return that smile and laugh with pure joy.

A laugh that was cut off when he said, "I did not plan to do this in your parlor after we were nearly killed," he said. "But in the spirit of not letting another day go by..."

He tensed his body, and she saw the flicker of pain on his face as he put all his weight against his cane and dropped to one knee. She covered her mouth with both hands as she realized what he was about to say.

"Nicholas, you'll hurt yourself," she whispered.

"You are worth the pain," he said. "You are *all* the pleasure. And one must be on one's knee when one asks the woman he adores to marry him. Aurora...marry me."

It was a request and an order all at once. And she nodded

without hesitation before she followed him to her knees and kissed him with all the love she felt, all the joy she now allowed and all the hope she could finally let in after everything they'd gone through. And as he pulled her closer, she knew that would be the rest of her days. No matter what came.

The ring, when Nicholas later produced it, was the most beautiful thing Aurora had ever seen. She couldn't help but keep looking at it as they gathered with their friends in Robert and Katherine's parlor. It was a joyful party, for not only were they celebrating the engagement, but that the case involving Imogen was solved.

"She'll be free to return to her life within a few days," Willowby said. "I know she is anxious to see you."

"And I her," Aurora said, finally able to look away from that sparkling ring. "Thank you for all your help when it came to her."

"It was our distinct pleasure," Diana said. "And congratulations on your engagement."

The couple smiled and then peeled away to join Robert and Katherine, who stood with Aurora's brother, her beaming mother and Bertrand Gillingham. While Nicholas's father didn't look entirely comfortable being included as a guest at this gathering, she could tell he was as pleased as any of the rest for his son's joy.

"They look happy for us," Nicholas said when they were alone and she realized his gaze had followed hers.

"They are," she said. "My father may have been a cruel arse, but my mother and my brother approve of us." Her smile faltered. "Even though the scandal I created and the one furthered by what happened at Fitzhugh's club has made their own situation all the harder."

"I'll help them," Nicholas said. "I promise."

She glanced at him. "I know you will."

"I'm probably the only Roseford bastard who actually invested their settlement," Nicholas said with a laugh. "And I am happy to share it with your family."

"*Our* family." She smiled up at him and found him watching her as he always watched her, with deep and abiding love. With protection and respect. With everything she had ever dreamed of, and more than she ever could have hoped for.

"Only a few more weeks until the wedding." he said.

She nodded. "It's been a very long time coming."

He smiled, that bright smile that took years and pain from his countenance. The smile she wished to keep on his face every day for the rest of their days. "It was," he agreed. "But our future starts today. And the next and the next."

"I can't wait," she said, and then leaned up to kiss him.

# THE DUKE'S BY-BLOWS

ENJOY AND EXCERPT OF BOOK 4, THE
REDEMPTION OF A ROGUE

"Wait here," Oscar said.

"Yes, Mr. Fitzhugh," Bentley said softly, his gaze darting away with something suspiciously like pity.

Oscar's stomach clenched at the sight. No one fucking pitied him. Even when he was pitiable. He stepped forward, ready to sneak through the unlocked back door to the place. He'd been banned from official entrance months ago. But this entrance allowed him to sneak in and blend in. Another faceless man in a sea of faceless men there to take their pleasure. Take advantage.

But before he could open the door, it flew out toward him. He stepped back, just barely missing being cracked in the face and opened his arms to regain his balance. Which allowed the woman who had thrown the door wide and now raced from the darkened, smoky hall to collide directly into his chest.

Oscar closed his arms around her, a natural reaction to keep them both from depositing themselves on the dirty ground. The moment he did so, she began to thrash, tugging to escape him.

He was about to release her when she cried out, "No, please! Don't! They'll kill me! Don't!!"

He froze at those words. How many months had he come here,

searching for some proof that nefarious things were happening within these walls? Dark and desperate things like murder.

And now this slender reed of a woman all but shouted that proof in his face. The extremely beautiful and terrified face that now turned up toward his. His heart stuttered at the abject terror reflected in a remarkable pair of amber eyes. Almost like a cat or a bird, they were so lovely.

"What is going on, miss?" he snapped out, perhaps more harshly than he intended thanks to the shock of her crash into his chest, her pointed words and her lovely eyes.

"Please," she wailed, her voice catching now. "They're coming. They're right behind me. You must release me or I'll never get away."

He heard voice from behind the door, shouts within the walls of the building and it kicked him from his shock. He grasped her arm and yanked her toward the carriage. She scrambled to escape as he hauled her up and slammed the door shut.

"Stop kicking me," he growled, tugging her even closer and speaking low against her ear. "I am trying to help you."

As he said the words, the door to the club opened and two large men burst out. Oscar leaned closer to the window, but didn't recognize either of them. Two of Maggie's ruffians, it seemed.

The woman froze in his arms, trembling as they shouted up to his driver, "Did you see a whore come out here?"

"Went that way," Bentley said from above and the men took off toward the docks.

Oscar smiled. He only hired the best. And Bentley would get a nice bonus in his wages this week for that lie.

"Please let me go," the lady said softly and Oscar realized she was still in his arms, pressed with her back to his chest, her breath coming short and heavy.

He loosened his grip on her arms as he said, "Don't run." She ignored him and lunged for the door. He sighed heavily and caught her wrist to pull her away from the door as gently as he could.

"Please don't run," he repeated. "I've no intention of hurting you. As I said, I want to help."

Her struggle ceased though from the way her body slumped he felt it was more out of exhaustion than any kind of trust. She slid to the carriage seat across from his and he released her. She stared at him, wary like a bird being stalked by a cat, and rubbed her wrist. He didn't think he'd hurt her, he'd been trying very hard not to do so, but he wondered it she were trying to sooth herself with that touch.

"Why were those men chasing you?" he asked.

She didn't respond, but folded her arms and looked longingly toward the door he was blocking.

He arched a brow. "Did you steal something?"

"No!" she cried out, indignant as she glared at him. "No, sir!"

"Then why were you running?" he repeated, more slowly, more firmly.

She shook her head. "Won't you please let me out?" she asked. "The men are gone, at least for the moment. It will give me time to get a hack and go home."

"That isn't happening," he said softly. "They could return at any moment. You're clearly in danger, miss and I am your best hope. Tell me what is going on."

She bent her head and her breath came sharp and hard in the quiet of the carriage. Oscar could see she was fighting tears. Winning that fight, though he wasn't certain that would last long. Every graceful line of her body spoke of her deep fear. It wasn't an act, it wasn't a trick. In his line of work, he had long ago learned to spot those.

No, this was real.

"Please," he said softly.

Her gaze lifted to his and for a moment their eyes locked. He could see her reading him, analyzing if he could relieve her trauma, or if he was just another part of it. Then her eyes darted back to her lap and she whispered, "They...they killed a woman. I-I saw her body."

His gut clenched and for a flash of a moment he wasn't certain he wouldn't cast up his accounts all over the carriage floor. But he drew a deep breath, calmed himself as he'd learned to do over the years and opened the carriage door.

"Bentley, home." He ordered before he closed them in again.

She jerked forward to the edge of her seat. "No! Sir, please. You cannot take me. You must let me out. Please!"

He leaned forward, hating that his presence was as much a fear to this distressed woman as anything else she'd been through that night. But he also knew he couldn't let her go. Not under these conditions.

"Miss, you are in real trouble and if I let you out of this carriage, you'll be in even worse. Let me take you somewhere safe and we can work this out."

"Work it out on my back, you mean?" she snapped and through the fear he saw a spitfire nature that almost made him smile but for the horrific circumstances. "You were here for a purpose, weren't you? And now you act like some hero come to save me? You are just as dangerous as those men after me for all I know. You're nothing but a stranger who forced me into a carriage."

He blinked. She had a point at that. He leaned forward and extended a hand. "Mr. Oscar Fitzhugh at your service, miss. I'm the owner of Fitzhugh's club. And while I agree that you have no reason yet to trust me, I do vow to you now that I won't hurt you. But I will try to save your life if you let me."

The Undercover Duke

The Duke of Hearts

The Duke Who Lied

The Duke of Desire

The Last Duke

**Seasons**

An Affair in Winter

A Spring Deception

One Summer of Surrender

Adored in Autumn

**The Wicked Woodleys**

Forbidden

Deceived

Tempted

Ruined

Seduced

Fascinated

**The Notorious Flynns**

The Other Duke

The Scoundrel's Lover

The Widow Wager

No Gentleman for Georgina

A Marquis for Mary

To see a complete listing of Jess Michaels' titles, please visit:

http://www.authorjessmichaels.com/books

ABOUT THE AUTHOR

USA Today Bestselling author Jess Michaels likes geeky stuff, Vanilla Coke Zero, anything coconut, cheese, fluffy cats, smooth cats, any cats, many dogs and people who care about the welfare of their fellow humans. She is lucky enough to be married to her favorite person in the world and lives in the heart of Dallas, TX where she's trying to eat all the amazing food in the city.

When she's not obsessively checking her steps on Fitbit or trying out new flavors of Greek yogurt, she writes historical romances with smoking hot alpha males and sassy ladies who do anything but wait to get what they want. She has written for numerous publishers and is now fully indie and loving every moment of it (well, almost every moment).

Jess loves to hear from fans! So please feel free to contact her in any of the following ways (or carrier pigeon):

www.AuthorJessMichaels.com
Email: Jess@AuthorJessMichaels.com

*Jess Michaels raffles a gift certificate EVERY month to members of her newsletter, so sign up on her website:*
http://www.AuthorJessMichaels.com/

facebook.com/JessMichaelsBks
twitter.com/JessMichaelsBks
instagram.com/JessMichaelsBks
bookbub.com/authors/jess-michaels